"Are you going to kiss me?" she whispered.

"Do you want me to?"

"Well…"

"If you're not sure, I won't kiss you." Connor's hand stilled on the back of her neck.

"Wait." Elizabeth caught his arm. "Do you want to kiss me?"

A big smile spread over his lips. "I've wanted to kiss you since the day I laid eyes on you outside the bank."

"But I punched you in the stomach."

"I know," Connor said. "I figured any woman with that much spirit was a woman I just had to kiss."

Her stomach quivered. "Really?"

Connor looped his arm around her waist. "How about just a little kiss? I'll stop when you tell me to."

"How can I tell you to stop if you're kissing me?"

"Just punch me in the gut again. I'll get the message…!"

Judith Stacy

THE LAST BRIDE IN TEXAS

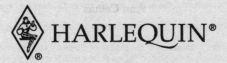 HARLEQUIN®

TORONTO • NEW YORK • LONDON
AMSTERDAM • PARIS • SYDNEY • HAMBURG
STOCKHOLM • ATHENS • TOKYO • MILAN • MADRID
PRAGUE • WARSAW • BUDAPEST • AUCKLAND

ISBN 0-373-29141-8

THE LAST BRIDE IN TEXAS

This edition published by arrangement with Harlequin Books S.A.

® and TM are trademarks of the publisher. Trademarks indicated with ® are registered in the United States Patent and Trademark Office, the Canadian Trade Marks Office and in other countries.

Visit us at www.eHarlequin.com

Printed in U.S.A.

Available from Harlequin Historicals and
JUDITH STACY

Harlequin Historicals

Outlaw Love #360
The Marriage Mishap #382
The Heart of a Hero #444
The Dreammaker #486
Written in the Heart #500
The Blushing Bride #521
One Christmas Wish #531
   "Christmas Wishes"
The Last Bride in Texas #541

Please address questions and book requests to:
Harlequin Reader Service
U.S.: 3010 Walden Ave., P.O. Box 1325, Buffalo, NY 14269
Canadian: P.O. Box 609, Fort Erie, Ont. L2A 5X3

To Judy and Stacy—my two little angels on earth

To David—my first and last love

Chapter One

Texas, 1882

Of all the times for the bank to get robbed.

Connor Wade shook his head in disgust as he gazed out the window of the Cattleman's Café. He'd just ridden into this town, just sat down to his first hot meal in weeks, and this had to happen.

Across the street in front of the bank, one would-be robber hunkered down behind a water trough while another took cover inside the bank doorway, both with pistols blazing.

Connor scraped the last bite of potatoes from his plate and leaned closer to the window. To his right, just down the street, the sheriff returned fire from behind a freight wagon.

"Damn fools..." Connor muttered, pushing the plate aside and biting into his apple pie.

These robbers must have been green as new-mowed hay. Noon was the worst time to hit a bank.

They'd left their horses too far away. And they'd picked a bank within sight of the sheriff's office.

Connor mumbled another curse. Without a doubt, the worst planned robbery he'd ever seen. And he'd seen his share of robberies.

More than his share, really.

Connor brought his coffee cup to his lips, then stared into it. Empty.

"Excuse me?" he called.

The woman who, judging from the size of her waist, owned the café huddled with four other diners around the front door, watching the commotion through the glass window. Connor looked around. He was the only one still eating.

And the only one who wanted more coffee, it seemed.

"Ma'am?" he called, raising his cup. "Could I get more coffee over here?"

Noses pressed against the glass window, whispering and pointing, they ignored him.

"Ma'am? Excuse me?" he called again.

No response.

"Dammit…"

All he wanted was a cup of coffee to finish off his pie. Was that asking too much?

Connor frowned at the crowd gawking out the window. Apparently, it was.

Connor dropped his cup on the table with a thud, dragged the napkin across his mouth and pushed to his feet.

"Stand aside," he called, crossing the café.

The two men and three women gathered at the door looked back at him. One of the men had gone white, and two of the women looked like they might faint.

Connor leaned down and peered out the window. The two robbers, their attention focused on the sheriff, weren't likely to notice him from this angle. Connor doubted they were smart enough to keep watch.

Around the corner in the alley, out of the sheriff's line of sight, Connor saw their horses. Three of them. That meant another robber was still inside the bank. One more robber the sheriff probably didn't know about.

Connor pulled his black Stetson hat lower on his forehead and opened the door.

"You can't go out there, mister!" one of the men exclaimed. "There's a shoot-out a-going on!"

Connor looked back over his shoulder. "Fill up my coffee cup while I'm gone, will you?"

He stepped onto the boardwalk. Behind him, the door slammed shut.

The midday sunlight reflected off the glass storefronts lining both sides of the dusty street. Shots rang out. Horses tethered to the hitching posts tossed their heads and pawed the ground. The smell of gunpowder hung in the air.

Connor held his position outside the café. The bank was across the street, two doors off to his right. The sheriff, behind the freight wagon, was farther down the street. Their attention fixed on the sheriff, the robbers didn't see Connor.

He drew his Colt .45, took aim and squeezed off a shot. The bullet drilled the hand of the robber leaning out the bank's doorway. The gun flew from his hand. Connor put another shot into his shoulder, sending him sprawling across the boardwalk.

Connor fired again. This shot buried into the thigh of the robber hiding behind the water trough. He yelped, dropped his gun, grabbed his leg and fell sideways.

Echoes of the gunshots bounced off the wooden buildings along Main Street. A numb silence fell over the town.

Connor didn't move. Both men were down, but it wasn't over yet. He stood his ground, arm extended, pistol trained on the entrance of the bank. Waiting.

From the corner of his eye, Connor saw the sheriff lower his rifle and move out from behind the freight wagon.

A mistake.

The third robber burst out of the bank. Connor adjusted his aim, ready to squeeze off another shot.

Instead, he froze. The robber had a hostage.

''Damn...'' Connor muttered.

A woman. Young. Dark skirt, white blouse, pink shawl around her shoulders, a little hat set in her brown hair. The robber wrapped his left arm across her shoulders, holding her in front of him, pressing her back against his chest. The barrel of his pistol prodded her temple.

This bandit looked like the other two Connor had already shot. Not much more than a kid, dressed in dusty clothes and a battered hat. Young and stupid, but dangerous.

The robber focused his attention on the sheriff, unaware that it was Connor who'd shot the other two members of the gang.

"I'll kill her!" he screamed.

The man inched backward down the boardwalk toward the horses waiting in the alley. To Connor's surprise, the woman stayed calm. No crying or sniveling. She didn't even tremble.

Raising his pistol, Connor took careful aim and squeezed off another shot. The bullet blew by the robber's head. Just where he wanted it.

The robber jumped. He turned. He saw Connor.

The woman turned, too. Her gaze met his. Connor hadn't meant to look at her, hadn't wanted to break his concentration. But it was too late.

Big blue eyes bored into him. Now he saw her fear, the terror etched in the tight line of her mouth and in the furrow of her brow. It arrowed through him, overwhelmed him, held him captive for a few seconds.

A few seconds too many.

The barrel of the robber's gun swung toward Connor, aiming square at his chest. The hammer clicked back.

Connor fired first.

The bullet impacted the robber's shoulder. Blood jetted out, splashing the woman's cheek, her neck, her shawl. The robber fell backward. His gun fired into the air as he hit the boardwalk with a thud.

The woman spun away into the street, staring down at the robber, who was writhing in pain. The sheriff ran forward. A man came out of the bank and kicked the robber's pistol away.

Behind Connor, the folks inside the café rushed out, craning their necks. Shop doors all along the street opened. The sheriff shouted orders.

Slowly, Connor holstered his Colt, only vaguely aware of the crush of people around him slapping his back, asking questions. He watched the woman. The pretty young woman who'd had a gun to her head and not flinched once.

Blood oozed down her fine porcelain cheek, spotted the collar of her white blouse and spread in dark streaks over her pink shawl. Townsfolk gathered around her, talking in low voices, touching her arm, her shoulder. She stood straight and tall, not needing their sympathy, it seemed.

But they hadn't seen into her eyes, as Connor had. They didn't know what she felt, as he knew.

Connor took a step toward her. He needed to get closer. Needed to make sure she was all right. Needed to—

She whirled, wrestling away from the well-intentioned townsfolk, and yanked the shawl from her shoulders. Horrified, she stared at it, then searched the crowd until she spotted Connor.

He stopped cold in his tracks.

The crowd parted as the woman batted her way toward him.

"You!" She stopped in front of Connor and waved her shawl. "Look what you've done!"

Stunned, Connor just stared, conscious of the people crowding around them both.

"You've ruined it! You've ruined my shawl! You horrid, thoughtless man!"

Connor shrugged. "Look, lady, I—"

"Oh!" She drew back her fist and drove it into his stomach.

A little *woof* slipped through his lips as he leaned forward slightly, pressing his palm to his belly.

He drew himself up straight, glared down at her and lifted one eyebrow. *"You're welcome."*

She burst into tears.

They weren't little tears. They were the kind of tears men hated. Big, gut-wrenching sobs. The ones nothing could be done about. The kind that just had to run their course. And in the meantime, all a man could do was stand there feeling stupid and useless.

Connor hated it when women cried.

Usually.

His gut tightened and started aching.

"Lady, I didn't mean to…"

Words failed him. Connor pulled on his neck. What could he say, anyway? He didn't even know what the devil was wrong with her.

Three women with big hats and bigger hips bumped him aside and surrounded the woman, sheltering her, clucking sympathetically. He should have been glad, but somehow it bothered him.

A path opened in the crowd and Sheriff Parker waded through. Tall and thin, he wore a mustache and a sour face.

"You do this, mister?" he asked Connor, squinting and nodding toward the bank.

Over the heads of the crowd Connor saw a half-dozen men helping the wounded robbers to their feet, herding them down the street.

"Sure did," one of the men from the Cattleman Café said. He slapped Connor's back. "Finest shooting I've seen in these here parts, that's for dang sure."

"Took care of the whole gang," another man said. "Single-handed."

"The man's a hero," the café owner declared, her voice shrilling above the others.

Heads nodded and praise echoed through the crowd.

"You've got this all wrong," Connor said, and waved his hands. "I'm no—"

"Sure you are!" She gave Connor a solid whack on the arm. "You come on back to the Cattleman anytime and have yourself any meal you want. On the house."

The sheriff eyed Connor for a long moment, apparently not happy with what had gone on in the streets of his town.

A man stepped forward and the crowd went silent. Tall and muscular, with a square jaw and big shoulders, he was probably around thirty years old, Connor guessed. A man who worked hard for a living.

"My name's Heath Wheeler," he said, and extended his hand to Connor. "Thanks for what you did. If I'd had my gun on me, I'd have helped you out."

Connor shook Heath's hand. "Could have used the help."

"Didn't look like it to me," Heath said. He turned to the sheriff. "I saw the whole thing. This man came out of the café, saw what was happening and took care of those robbers. You ought to be thanking him for what he did."

Sheriff Parker eyed Connor for another moment, then pulled on his bushy mustache. "Guess that's the end of it."

"The end of it?" a voice called out. "This calls for a celebration!"

Connor shook his head. "No. I told you—"

"Don't be so modest." A short, thin man in a rumpled suit caught Connor's hand and pumped it hard. "Name's Ike Canter, and I'm proud to know you. Come on over to the saloon. I want to buy you a drink."

"We all do!" another man shouted.

A cheer went up as the crowd headed down the street, sweeping Connor along with them. He stole a glance over his shoulder at the women huddled on the boardwalk.

"Is that woman all right?" he asked.

"Oh, don't pay her no mind," Ike said. "She's fine. She's always fine."

Connor moved along with the men, but couldn't help glancing over his shoulder once more.

A dozen men flanked Connor as he walked through the bat-wing doors of the Foxtail Saloon. Like the other saloons he'd been in, this one had gaming tables, and a bar with a mirror and shelves of glasses behind it.

The bartender offered a round on the house, and Ike Canter proposed a toast to Connor. More men filtered inside and raised their glasses. Ike told the story of the shoot-out.

Connor leaned on his elbow at the bar as Heath Wheeler ambled over.

"You sure livened up this place," Heath said. "You're a hero, just for that."

Connor grinned and sipped his beer.

"Staying or passing through?" Heath asked.

"Staying," Connor said.

"Is that your sorrel outside the café?" Heath asked. When Connor nodded, he said, "I'll take care of him for you. I run the livery stable."

"Much obliged," Connor said.

"I'll drop your gear off at the hotel," Heath said. He drained his glass and shouldered his way out of the saloon.

A few minutes later Sheriff Parker walked in. He ordered a whiskey and stood off to the side. Connor felt the lawman's gaze on him.

Typical. Connor took a long swallow of beer.
He'd gotten that reaction more than once.

After another hour the crowd was still going
strong, the story of the shoot-out started to stretch,
and Connor had had enough.

As he eased his way toward the swinging doors,
several men slapped his back and called out words
of praise for his bravery. Ike Canter started the story
again and nobody seemed to mind.

The streets of Sterling looked pretty ordinary
when Connor stepped onto the boardwalk. Nobody
shot at anybody. Carriages and wagons rumbled
down the street, women carried baskets and pulled
children along, while men and ranch hands went
about their business.

Connor spotted the Sterling Hotel down the block.
As he headed toward it, most everyone he passed
nodded pleasantly, some introduced themselves, and
several more made a point of thanking him for what
he'd done to stop the shoot-out and the bank robbery.

Finally, Connor ducked inside the hotel. The
lobby held a gold velvet circular sofa and two
chairs; gold framed pictures hung on the walls. The
place looked a little worn, but clean and respectable.

"I need a room," Connor said, and leaned his
elbow on the registration desk.

The young man behind the counter swiped his
thick dark bangs off his face. His eyes widened and
his mouth sagged open. "You're that Mr. Wade,

aren't you? The man who stopped the bank robbery?"

Connor nodded, a little surprised that his name
had been spread all over town so quickly.

"Golly..." The clerk's smile broadened. "My
name's Johnny Davenport, sir. Proud to meet you,
Mr. Wade, real proud. I heard about what you did
over at the bank. How you shot all of them no-
account robbers, and how you saved Miss Elizabeth."

Connor looked up sharply. "Elizabeth?"

"Miss Elizabeth Hill," Johnny said. "Yes siree,
that was some fancy shooting, no two ways about
it."

Connor took a step back as the young man
launched into the bank robbery story, looking up at
him with awestruck eyes. But Connor didn't hear a
word Johnny said.

The woman at the shoot-out was Elizabeth Hill?
Elizabeth Hill. The woman he'd traveled weeks to
find. He'd stumbled on her and hadn't realized it.

A little smile tugged at Connor's mouth. Elizabeth Hill. The woman who would change his life.

Whether she wanted to or not.

Chapter Two

Darn that Mr. Wade. Could he have found a better way to humiliate her?

Elizabeth Hill kicked up a little dust cloud as she left her house and headed toward town. The morning sun shone at her back, warm and reassuring in the gentle breeze.

A lovely morning. Except that she had to go see *that man*.

Shifting her market basket to the other hand, Elizabeth marched determinedly onward, telling herself this had to be done. She'd have to endure it. Put on a brave face and get it over with.

Her footsteps faltered. It wouldn't be easy, though. She'd been made a spectacle before the whole town.

Again.

Become the object of gossip.

Again.

Just when the last round of talk had died, *this* had

to happen. And all because of that awful Mr. Connor Wade.

Elizabeth stepped up onto the boardwalk at the edge of town. Her home lay only a short walk away, and this morning, fueled by her simmering anger, she'd gotten to town more quickly than usual. She gazed down Main Street. The early hour had brought few shoppers to town. Only a couple of horses were tied to the hitching rails and one solitary freight wagon waited outside the mercantile.

Good. Less people to witness this further humiliation.

Drawing in a deep breath, Elizabeth reminded herself this was the Christian thing to do. The man—that horrible Mr. Wade—had, according to everyone in town, saved her life.

She wasn't so sure about that. But the dozens of people who'd come by her house last night had told her that's what he'd done. Rescued her. Saved her life. He was a hero, they'd said. The bravest man who'd ever hit Sterling, they claimed.

And for his trouble, she'd punched him in the stomach, then burst out crying. Right there on Main Street. In front of the entire town.

How unseemly. How unladylike.

How humiliating.

Elizabeth cringed. She'd really made a spectacle of herself this time. Small consolation that neither her mother—called to heaven twenty years ago—nor her father, the distinguished town doctor gone to his reward just last year, were here to witness her latest debacle.

But a debacle it was. And now she had to go *thank* that man.

Elizabeth pondered the thought for a moment, then decided she didn't *have* to advertise to the whole town what she was up to this morning. She didn't have to parade herself down Main Street and make a spectacle of herself at the hotel, turn herself into grist for the town's rumor mill—yet again. Another, more discreet way to handle this situation was possible.

Elizabeth slipped down the alley between Gunther's General Store and Mrs. Merrick's Millinery Shop, cut behind the businesses that faced Main Street, then circled the block and darted into the lobby of the Sterling Hotel.

No one was there, thank goodness. But to her dismay she realized Johnny Davenport wasn't at his station behind the registration desk. She wanted to give him her basket with instructions to pass it on to Mr. Wade, then leave, her Christian duty done and her reputation—what was left of it, anyway—intact.

Elizabeth looked around, listened at the door that led to the back of the hotel, but she heard nothing. Johnny always wandered away from his post. He could be anywhere. And the longer she stood in the middle of the lobby, the greater the chance that someone would come in and see her. Question her. Start talking about her.

Again.

Elizabeth pinched the bridge of her nose and cringed inwardly. She'd been gossiped about enough in the past year to last a lifetime.

Turning the guest registration book around, Elizabeth scanned the names scrawled on the page. Only three rooms were rented. That horrid Mr. Wade had room number four.

Taking one final look around and seeing no one, Elizabeth fortified herself with a deep breath, then hurried up the steps.

The boards in the upstairs hallway squeaked as Elizabeth searched for Mr. Wade's room. The wall lanterns had been extinguished already this morning, leaving nothing to brighten the faded blue wall paper.

Standing in front of room number four, Elizabeth shook out the skirt of her dark green dress and brushed a speck of lint from her sleeve. She straightened her hat and knocked.

No one answered. Elizabeth tapped her foot impatiently against the hardwood floor. She knocked again. Still no answer.

Nervously, she glanced up and down the hallway. The last thing she wanted was to be caught lurking in the upstairs hall of the hotel.

Elizabeth raised her hand to knock again when the door jerked open. She gasped and fell back a step. Connor Wade towered over her, scowling.

She'd awakened him. He'd pulled on black trousers, but hadn't fastened the top button. His black shirt hung open. Rough whiskers covered his jaw. His dark hair stuck out on one side.

And he was handsome. That realization took Elizabeth by surprise. He had thick black hair and the prettiest gray eyes she'd ever seen on a man. His nose was crooked, as if it had been broken, more than once.

Connor Wade was tall, too. Elizabeth herself was tall, but her nose didn't even come to his chin. His shoulders were wide, his legs and arms long and sturdy.

Yes, Connor Wade was handsome. But Elizabeth remembered nothing of that from the confrontation outside the bank yesterday. It surprised her. Startled her.

"Yeah?" he growled.

Elizabeth gulped. Her heart banged harder, thudded into her throat and hung there.

Connor swiped the backs of his hands across his eyes, as if rubbing away the sleep.

"What do you want?" he asked.

What did she want? Elizabeth stood rooted to the floor. What did she want? What *did* she want?

Then it came to her: she wanted to run her fingers through the hair on his chest.

Elizabeth's cheeks flamed. She couldn't believe she'd actually had such a thought.

How horrifying. How low. How common.

How—intriguing.

She'd seen a man's chest before, lots of times. Her brother, her father, her father's patients when they'd come to his surgery in the back of their house. But none of those men had looked like *this*.

A wide chest, hard with washboard muscles, covered with crinkly dark hair. Her fingers tingled at the thought of touching him.

Elizabeth suddenly came to her senses. Good gracious, what was she doing? Ogling a man's chest. Having unladylike thoughts. She knew her cheeks were red. Heat consumed her. Could he feel it wafting from her?

She cleared her throat and forced her gaze upward, straightening her shoulders and struggling for a little dignity.

"Mr. Wade?" she asked. "I'm Miss Elizabeth Hill."

He rubbed his eyes again and looked harder at her. "Oh—yeah—" That seemed to chase the sleep from his brain. Connor pulled his shirt closed and threaded his fingers through his hair, slicking it in place. "From yesterday."

"Yes. From yesterday." Elizabeth felt her cheeks flush again. "Well, anyway, I've come to thank you for your assistance."

He just looked at her.

"So…thank you." She shoved the basket at him, then lit out down the hallway.

A fire roared inside her. Her skin tingled. Strange sensations throbbed within her. Elizabeth hurried toward the staircase. She had to get out of this hallway. She needed air. She must—

"Is this all you think you're worth?"

Elizabeth halted dead in her tracks at the sound of Connor Wade's voice booming after her. She turned and saw him holding up her market basket with the red-checkered cloth pulled back.

"Is this it?" he asked, lifting the basket higher. "A pie?"

The strange heat that enveloped her boiled down to a hard knot that congealed in the center of her belly. Elizabeth marched back down the hallway and stopped in front of him.

"That happens to be my award winning apple pie," she informed him. "I've gotten blue ribbons for it the last two years at our Founders' Day festival. Last year a bidding war broke out for it."

Connor's gaze narrowed. "I saved your life. You came to thank me. And this is what you think you're worth? An apple pie?"

"Well…"

He edged a little closer. "Well?"

"Well…" Elizabeth's temper shot up again. "Well, I think you are a very ungrateful man, Mr. Wade. I came here to do the decent thing—to thank you—and this is how you act?"

Elizabeth folded her arms across her middle, drawing in a cleansing breath in an attempt to calm herself. "So, fine, Mr. Wade. Have it your way. If you don't want the pie, what do you want?"

A lazy smile pulled at the corner of his mouth. "I think this apple pie doesn't even begin to scratch the surface. I think you've got a whole lot more to offer, Miss Hill."

His gaze dropped to her shoes, then climbed slowly, deliberately, over the skirt of her dress, her waist, her bosom, her face, to the top of her head, then back to her face again. His gaze locked with hers.

The silence in the hotel hallway roared in Elizabeth's ears. Had he just made an indecent proposal?

The realization of her situation knifed through her. No one else was around. Mr. Wade's room door stood open, and inside, only steps away, she saw the rumpled sheets on his bed. He was only half-dressed.

Elizabeth's stomach quivered. Her skin heated. She should confront him, demand an apology. But at the moment she didn't seem to have enough air in her lungs to get a word out.

Elizabeth turned her head away, breaking eye contact, snapping the spell between them. She cleared her throat and tried to will away some of the red in her cheeks.

"I have something else in mind," Connor said, his voice low.

Refusing to admit that he'd gotten the upper hand, Elizabeth turned to face him again.

"And what might that be?" she asked, and pushed her chin outward in a challenge.

He gave her one more lazy look.

"I'll tell you what I want from you, Miss Hill," he said. "When I'm ready for it."

Connor Wade sauntered inside his room and started to close the door.

"Wait!" Elizabeth pushed her hand against it. "What about my apple pie?"

He looked down at the basket and grinned. "I never said I didn't want your pie."

The door closed in Elizabeth's face.

"Oh!" She put her nose in the air and stomped away.

By the time Elizabeth's feet touched down in the lobby of the hotel, she'd thought of a hundred things she *should* have said to that awful Connor Wade.

She stood there for a moment, hand on the newel post, staring up the stairs, sorely tempted to march right back up to his room and tell that man exactly what she thought of him.

Her temper boiled. How dare he suggest that she *owed* him something—other than the pie she'd already given him. How dare he say that he'd inform her what that something was—*when* it suited him.

Just because he fancied that he'd saved her life.

Elizabeth tossed her head. That Mr. Wade was arrogant. Pushy. Presumptuous.

And he had, probably, saved her life.

Some of the anger drained out of Elizabeth as she headed for the front door of the Sterling Hotel. She did owe him. He'd been right—her apple pie wasn't enough.

But what was an appropriate thank-you? What else could he want?

Surely he didn't mean...

A warm shudder passed through Elizabeth, and

the image of Connor Wade's big bare chest flashed in her mind. His bed. The rumpled sheets. The plumped pillows. The cool morning breeze flirting with the white eyelet priscillas. The two of them—

Elizabeth stopped at the entrance of the hotel, clutching the door frame for support. Good gracious! Such thoughts! What had come over her?

True, at twenty-seven years of age she was plenty old enough to know about men and such. More than old enough, really.

But that chance had passed her by many years ago. And spinning yarns about rolling around in bed with a man she hardly knew and didn't especially like—except for his chest—would do her no good.

Somehow, her well-intentioned, Christian thank-you had blown up in her face. Now she was on the hook for another sort of thank-you. Something that Mr. Wade would inform her of—when he was ready for it.

Elizabeth shuddered. Once again, here she was in the middle of an awkward situation. How did this keep happening to her?

Elizabeth headed down the boardwalk toward home. A few more people were on the streets of Sterling now as the business of the day got under-way. Wagons and buggies rumbled along. Passing Gunther's General Store, Elizabeth glimpsed her friend, Gena Blake, through the window. She stopped and waved.

Gena smiled and came outside. Her parents, the Gunthers, owned the store; Gena worked there. She was slender, blond and pretty, and she and Elizabeth had been friends most of their lives. She was about the same age as Elizabeth, but Gena had done more living.

She'd married her childhood sweetheart and shared several years with him until he'd died after being thrown from his horse nearly two years ago.

Elizabeth had always been a tad envious of Gena, even though she'd lost her husband and had no children. Gena and Phillip had been desperately in love. Elizabeth had caught them kissing once, their bodies pulled full against each other, lost in their private moment. Elizabeth had ached at the sight. Oh, to be loved like that.

"Good morning," Gena said, as she closed the front door of the store behind her. "I wasn't expecting to see you in town this morning."

Elizabeth huffed irritably and leaned a little closer to Gena. "I had to go to the hotel," she said in a low voice. She glanced around. "I had to thank that Mr. Wade for his assistance yesterday."

Gena shook her head ruefully. "You managed to do it again, Elizabeth. The whole town is talking about what happened at the shoot-out."

Elizabeth rolled her eyes. "I'll just be glad when the whole thing dies down."

"That's not likely to happen soon."

A knot of dread jerked in Elizabeth's stomach.

"Why not?"

"I overheard the mayor's wife talking to Mama this morning," Gena said. "She and the other ladies are going all out. They've planned a special ceremony after church tomorrow.''

''What sort of ceremony?''

''In recognition of what happened at the bank robbery yesterday,'' Gena said. ''The town is honoring Connor Wade for his heroics.''

''But—''

''You have to be there, too,'' Gena said. ''You're presenting him with the award.''

Chapter Three

Connor woke with a start and sat straight up in bed. His breath came in heaves; a fine sweat covered him.

He blinked, rubbed his eyes and stared at the furnishing around him. A marble washstand. A small mahogany bureau with a mirror. A rocker in the corner.

Seconds dragged past and finally, he remembered where he was.

Or, more importantly, where he *wasn't*.

Connor fell back on the pillows and kicked off the covers. He also remembered the dream that had just awakened him.

The breeze wafting through the open window cooled his heated body, bringing the morning sunlight with it. Scenes from the nightmare sped through his mind again. He pushed them away determinedly.

Then another image floated into his thoughts, this one more pleasant. Much more pleasant.

Miss Elizabeth Hill.

He'd come to Sterling in search of her, but never expected to find her so easily. And certainly never expected that she'd show up outside his hotel room earlier that morning.

Connor flopped over and buried his face in the pillows. The last thing he'd expected of Miss Elizabeth Hill was that she'd be so pretty.

A little smile pulled at his mouth as he remembered her flushed cheeks and her flashing eyes as she'd stared up at him in the hallway an hour ago. After she left, Connor had fallen briefly back to sleep, but the vision of Elizabeth Hill hadn't gone away. She'd been the only sweet moment in the nightmare he'd just had.

Connor lay in bed a few minutes longer, then pushed himself to his feet. He yawned, stretched and ruffled his hands through his hair.

How good it felt to sleep in a bed again, a real bed with a soft feather mattress. To wake without his bones aching. How good it felt to have a roof over his head after being on the trail for so long.

As Connor pulled on his long johns and socks, the market basket on the bureau caught his eye. He smiled, remembering Elizabeth again, and peeked under the red-checkered cloth.

Inside sat the apple pie she'd been so proud of. Connor chuckled when he saw what else she'd packed in the basket: a knife, a fork, a napkin and a plate.

The laughter died on his lips. Miss Elizabeth Hill

was a lady. She assumed him a gentleman requiring all these amenities just to eat a slice of pie.

Connor's chest tightened. If only she knew...

Carefully, Connor lifted the items from the basket and placed them on the bureau, feeling the weight of each, turning them over in his hand.

The knife and fork were heavy silver pieces, not the tin utensils he always ate with. The napkin felt like fine linen. The plate was thin, delicate, with pink roses and white doves on it.

The tableware of a genteel woman. A woman who accepted the finer things in life as commonplace.

The scent of Elizabeth caught his attention. Connor shut his eyes, savoring it more appreciatively than the aroma of the apple pie.

He'd suspected Elizabeth Hill would be like this, a fine lady. But still...

Connor served himself a slice of pie and ate it, then had another while he finished dressing. He caught his reflection in the mirror over the bureau and studied himself for a moment, turned his head from side to side and rubbed his hand across his jaw.

If he could eat apple pie off a china plate with a silver fork, he could avail himself of a bath, shave and haircut. Connor pulled on his hat and left the room.

Out on the street, he squinted in the bright morning sunlight, then headed down the boardwalk. People he didn't know gave him a pleasant nod or a friendly greeting. One man stopped just to shake his hand. Mystified, Connor stared after him as he walked away.

"Everybody appreciates what you did."

Connor turned and saw Heath Wheeler standing in the doorway behind him. He was glad to see a friendly face, the face of the man who'd vouched for him with the sheriff yesterday.

"The bank robbery," Heath said, and walked over. "Everybody's still talking about it."

"Thought that would've blown over by now."

Heath grinned. "Not in Sterling."

The two men fell in step together.

"Where you from?" Heath asked.

As a newcomer in town, he'd be a subject of curiosity, Connor knew. It was only natural. But he'd meant to ease into the town of Sterling quietly and not draw attention to himself.

The shoot-out at the bank had changed all that.

"Missouri," Connor said. "Moved around a lot, since."

"What line of work are you in?"

"I've done a little of everything. Ranching, mining, logging," Connor said. "What about you?"

"Lived here in Sterling most of my life," Heath said. "Guess I always will."

"Seems like a nice enough place," Connor said, glancing around at the shops, the pedestrians, traffic on the street. "In fact, if—"

Across the street, Elizabeth Hill stood on the boardwalk in front of the general store, talking with another woman. Connor's footsteps dragged to a halt. A few minutes passed before he realized he was blatantly staring at her. Uncomfortable, he glanced at Heath. He was staring, too. But not at Elizabeth.

Heath's cheeks turned a light shade of pink. "That's Mrs. Blake. Gena…"

Connor dragged his gaze from Elizabeth long enough to give the other woman a cursory look. Pretty. Yes, she was pretty, all right. But not quite as pretty as Elizabeth, not nearly as curvaceous as Elizabeth, as Connor liked.

Heath drew in a long breath, held it for a few seconds, then let it out slowly, never taking his eyes off Gena Blake.

"Gena's husband died a couple years back," he said. "She's not over it yet."

Heath didn't say anything else and Connor didn't expect him to. They both stood on the boardwalk staring across the street, watching the women. Finally, the men came to their senses at the same moment, looked uncomfortably at each other and moved along.

Elizabeth kept herself busy all afternoon at home. The house her father had built, the biggest in Sterling, was a handful to maintain. Two stories, a double parlor, a kitchen, a dining room, more bedrooms than the family needed, and the surgery, of course.

It was furnished with family treasures her mother had carefully packed and brought west when she'd moved here with Theodore Hill so many years ago. Now it was all Elizabeth had left of her family.

Elizabeth had no one to help with the upkeep of the big house. And no one but herself to live in it.

She glanced at the clock on the parlor mantel and swung the broom faster. Nearly three o'clock. The mayor's wife would arrive any minute with her grandson for his piano lesson.

For a fleeting second, Elizabeth toyed with the idea of canceling the lesson. After what had happened at the bank yesterday she might get away with claiming she wasn't up to giving little Timmy his lesson today.

But, in fact, the only thing Elizabeth wasn't up to was facing Abigail Rogers. The mayor's wife ran the town, as much as Mayor Rogers did. The woman would have plenty to say to Elizabeth, no doubt.

Including how the town planned to honor Connor Wade after church tomorrow. And how Elizabeth was expected to participate in the ceremony.

With a heavy sigh, she finished her sweeping and went to the kitchen. If the town wanted to honor Mr. Wade, she had no objections. Really, he deserved the honor.

But Elizabeth didn't want to be part of it. She didn't want to stand in front of everyone and have them stare at her. She didn't want the town to be reminded of what had happened in the not so distant past.

"Oh, Raymond…" Elizabeth let her brother's name tumble from her lips. She squeezed her eyes shut and grasped the back of the kitchen chair for support. "How could you have done such a thing?" she whispered.

Shame washed over Elizabeth, strong and painful. The town hadn't forgotten what her brother had done. They hadn't let her forget that she was his sister. What he'd done had spilled over onto her.

The burden hadn't been so hard to bear when her father was alive. Theodore Hill was the town doctor, well respected and well liked, despite what Raymond had done. But after her father died last year, Elizabeth was left alone to shoulder the family shame.

Dr. Hill's death had brought even more unwelcome attention to Elizabeth. He was the only doctor Sterling had. Now there was no one trained to attend the sick and injured. No new doctor had been found, though the town council had searched far and wide for a replacement.

Elizabeth felt the responsibility for that, too.

A forceful knock sounded at the front door, jarring her from her thoughts. She pulled off her apron, checked her hair in the mirror beside the stove and hurried to the front of the house and opened the door.

"Good afternoon," Abigail Rogers declared, and walked inside. The mayor's wife was a big woman with gray streaking her dark hair.

"Hi, Miss Elizabeth."

Elizabeth smiled down at six-year-old Timmy, a

handsome little boy with brown hair and big dark eyes.

She ruffled his hair. "Go ahead and get started. I'll be right there."

Timmy scooted into the parlor.

Abigail Rogers made no move to leave. She folded her arms in front of her and looked down her long nose at Elizabeth.

"You're feeling much better, I see," Abigail said. "As one would expect, of course."

No one in Sterling suffered from the misconception that Elizabeth had fallen to pieces after being held hostage by the bank robber yesterday. The town had no illusion that Elizabeth was faint of heart, although that impression might have worked in her favor at the moment.

"We're holding a ceremony after services tomorrow honoring Mr. Wade," Abigail said. "You'll be there, of course."

The temptation to beg off nearly overcame Elizabeth. Anything to keep the town from staring at her, talking about her again. Remembering…

But she liked going to church. She enjoyed the service, and especially the fellowship. Living by herself in the big house was lonely sometimes.

"Yes, Mrs. Rogers, I'll be there," Elizabeth said.

"Excellent. I'll tell the mayor."

Abigail Rogers left before Elizabeth had a chance to say anything else. She closed the door and went into the parlor.

Timmy Rogers sat on the piano bench, diligently

practicing the scales. Elizabeth smiled at his little frown and his tongue clamped between his teeth.

Of all her students, Elizabeth favored Timmy. He enjoyed the lessons, unlike some of the children who came to her for instruction, forced there by well-intentioned mothers.

Elizabeth taught everyone who came to her door, whether they wanted to be there or not. The death of her father had left her with no source of income except what she could generate on her own. She had no trade and not nearly enough money to start a business.

So Elizabeth gave music lessons and tutored children who needed extra help with their studies. She put her award-winning apple pie recipe to good use, baking and selling pies to the restaurants in town. It wasn't much, but enough to keep her fed, clothed, and to buy herself a few extras occasionally.

"You're doing much better," Elizabeth declared, at the conclusion of Timmy's lesson.

"Really?" he asked, looking up at her.

"Really."

Elizabeth presented him with a peppermint stick and sent him on his way.

She put away the simple sheet music Timmy had practiced today, and for a moment, Elizabeth considered sitting down and playing a tune herself. Instead, she closed the lid on the piano and sank onto the bench.

Connor Wade drifted into her mind. Elizabeth pinched the bridge of her nose, annoyed with herself. Why did that man keep interrupting her thoughts?

Visions of him sprang into her mind at the most inopportune times. How tall he was. How rumpled his appearance. How his chest—

Elizabeth bolted from the piano bench and busied herself straightening the parlor, although she'd done it once today already. She simply would not allow another thought of Connor Wade inside her head.

The ticking of the clock on the mantel broke the silence in the parlor, making Elizabeth achingly aware of her solitude.

And not just because she'd been thinking of Connor Wade again.

At one time, not so very long ago, the house had bustled with people. Her brother, her father, his patients, visitors. Dr. Theodore Hill's home had been a vital part of Sterling.

Slowly, Elizabeth walked toward the kitchen, past the staircase that led upstairs. Her father had dreamed of filling up the bedrooms in his house with his children, his daughter-in-law and son-in-law, and all the grandchildren who would follow. Now it seemed the rooms would be empty forever.

A quick knock at the front door brought Elizabeth out of her thoughts. She peeked out the window and saw Gena Blake on her front porch.

Elizabeth opened the door, smiling. "Aren't you supposed to be working?"

Gena waved away her question as she walked into the house. "I told Mama I had an errand," she said.

"But I was concerned about you, after we talked this morning."

Elizabeth pressed her lips together. "I couldn't believe it. There we were, standing outside your store talking about the awful Mr. Wade, and the whole time he was standing across the street staring at us."

Gena smiled. "Staring at *you*, I'd say."

"Me?" Elizabeth's cheeks flushed. She shook her head. "You should talk. Heath Wheeler was watching you like a lovesick moose, if ever I've seen one."

Gena gasped and touched her hand to her mouth.

"Oh, Gena, I'm so sorry," Elizabeth said. "That was a thoughtless remark. I shouldn't have said it. That darn Mr. Wade gets me all befuddled. I know how much you loved Phillip."

"Phillip was a wonderful husband," Gena said, and smiled gently. "I know he's gone to a better place, and I've accepted that. But another man? I'd never considered such a thing."

"Maybe you should," Elizabeth said. "Especially after the way Heath looked at you."

They walked to the kitchen, a big and airy room furnished with a cookstove, a worktable, cupboards and shelves, and red-checkered curtains on the windows. A small table and chairs sat in the corner.

"Are you sure you're feeling all right?" Gena asked. "That was quite an ordeal you went through at the bank yesterday."

Elizabeth paused as she took cups and saucers

from the cupboard. Another reminder of Connor Wade.

"I was scared," she admitted. "But, honestly, it happened so fast. And I wouldn't have been half so upset if it weren't for my shawl getting ruined."

"Good thing Mr. Wade was there," Gena said, fetching the warm coffeepot from the cookstove.

"Oh, yes. Wonderful," Elizabeth muttered.

"You don't appreciate what Mr. Wade did?" Gena asked, sitting down.

Elizabeth took the chair across from her friend. It wasn't that she didn't appreciate what the man had done. Yes, he'd risked his life to save hers. But what she didn't like were the results.

Elizabeth shifted in the chair, wondering what Connor Wade would decide she owed him. And when he'd want it.

"He's quite the talk of the town," Gena said. "Everyone who's come into the store this morning has mentioned him. Where is he from? Why is he here? How handsome he is. Connor Wade is quite the mystery man in Sterling."

Elizabeth jerked her chin. "People should mind their own business."

"Well, he is handsome. You can't disagree with that," Gena said. "Every unmarried woman in town will be setting her cap for him."

Elizabeth looked up from her coffee cup. "Do you think so?"

"Of course." Gena grinned. "Does that bother you?"

"Certainly not. I've got much more pressing problems than that terrible Mr. Wade."

"Like what?" Gena challenged.

"Well…" Elizabeth sat up straighter. "Such as…"

"What?"

Elizabeth drummed her fingers on the table. "Such as this house."

"What's wrong with the house?" Gena asked, glancing around.

"It needs fixing up since Papa died and Raymond…well, you know. And I've been thinking about doing something special with it." Elizabeth studied her coffee cup for a moment, then looked up at her friend. "I've been thinking of converting it to a boardinghouse."

Gena's mouth dropped open. "Elizabeth, are you serious?"

"Well, yes."

Until this moment, it had been only a vague idea that had bounced around in Elizabeth's mind for the last few months. She hadn't had the nerve to say it aloud, hadn't dared hope she could actually do it until just now.

"I think it's a wonderful idea," Gena said. "You have all those bedrooms. And Sterling has only one other boardinghouse, which no decent person would stay in. It's a perfect idea."

Elizabeth toyed with her spoon. "People would talk."

Gena nodded. "Yes, that's true."

"A single woman alone with a house full of strangers. Tongues would wag," Elizabeth said. "And it would require money for repairs and renovations. More money than I have right now."

"Sounds a little as if you're trying to talk yourself out of it."

Elizabeth drew in a deep breath. "I have the room. I could certainly use the income from the boarders. And, well, I get lonely here sometimes."

"It is a big house," Gena said, nodding. "Big houses feel lonely when they're empty."

"Then you think I should do it?"

Gena leaned forward and patted Elizabeth's hand. "Yes, you should definitely do it. And who cares what everybody in town will say?"

Who cared? Elizabeth cared.

Gena rose from the table. "I'd better get back to work before Mama has a hissy fit. Jane is covering the store for me."

"That sister of yours doesn't have much on her mind these days but wedding, wedding, wedding."

"She's excited," Gena said. Her smile faded. "I wish I liked Boyd Sherman better."

"You're just being an overly protective big sister," Elizabeth stated.

"Maybe so," Gena said. "Well, I'll see you tomorrow morning at church."

Elizabeth paused as she lifted their coffee cups from the table. Her heart thumped in her chest, and a strange warmth spread through her.

Tomorrow morning at church she'd come face-to-face with Connor Wade again.

Chapter Four

Reverend Brady stood in his usual position at the foot of the church steps when Elizabeth arrived on Sunday morning. Tall, thin, garbed in black, the minister greeted each member of the congregation by name. His wife stood dutifully at his side.

In the yard under the shade trees, children played, dodging the adults gathered in small knots, talking.

Elizabeth's heart lightened as she hesitated at the edge of the churchyard. She always felt at peace when she arrived for services, and stronger when she left.

Today she intended to pray for guidance about her boardinghouse idea; Elizabeth thought the Lord could hear her better from inside the church. Last night, after Gena left, she'd made a list of the repairs and renovations required to convert her home into a boardinghouse. The list was long. It was costly.

Elizabeth drew in a big breath. A lot of prayers would be needed to accomplish this task. A little divine intervention wouldn't hurt anything, either.

The boardinghouse idea flew from Elizabeth's head as she started across the churchyard. She stopped still as her gaze homed in on the newcomer in Sterling.

Connor Wade.

He stood under a shade tree a few yards away, talking with a group of men. Connor looked at ease, comfortable, as if he'd lived here all his life.

Immediately, Elizabeth was annoyed with herself for spotting him so quickly. But, really, how could she not? He was taller than most of the men. And he'd cleaned up considerably since she'd last seen him.

Visions of Connor Wade in the hallway of the hotel zoomed through Elizabeth's mind. His shirt open. His chest bare. His trousers unfastened.

She shuddered, then chastised herself. Gracious, such thoughts on the Lord's day.

Connor wore a white shirt and a string tie, dark trousers and vest. He'd polished his boots. Gone was the unruly hair curling at his collar and the stubble of whiskers on his jaw. Connor looked respectable. He looked neat, clean. Handsome.

No, not handsome. Elizabeth huffed, doubly annoyed with herself now. Connor Wade absolutely did not look handsome.

He glanced up from his conversation with the other men. His gaze collided with hers.

Oh, so handsome...

Breath left Elizabeth's lungs. Her cheeks flushed.

A crooked smile pulled at Connor's lips. He'd caught her staring at him.

Elizabeth's cheeks flushed bright red. He'd caught her staring and it pleased him. What an annoying man!

She turned away sharply and nearly ran right over sweet old Miss Pitney. Elizabeth stepped around her just in time and didn't stop until she heard Gena Blake calling her.

"Good morning," Elizabeth said, grateful for the distraction.

Gena took one of the two baskets she carried, and grinned. "You wore your lavender dress. Hoping to catch Mr. Wade's eye today at the ceremony?"

The lavender dress was her favorite, but Elizabeth seldom wore it, thinking the color too showy.

"Of course not," Elizabeth insisted, but glanced over her shoulder at him despite herself.

"Then you'll be the only unmarried woman here today who isn't."

For some reason, that notion bothered Elizabeth. She pushed it aside and walked with Gena into the fellowship hall.

The wing had been added on to the church last summer. Inside was a kitchen and the large room with tables and benches where most of Sterling's social functions were held.

A dozen women were already inside. Abigail Rogers directed the morning's activities. Two of the long trestle tables held food donations for today's social: desserts, breads, fruits, cold meats.

"Items requiring cooking should be taken directly to the kitchen," Abigail announced to the women. "Elizabeth? Elizabeth?"

"Good morning, Mrs. Rogers," Elizabeth said, and walked over.

"Good, you're here," she said, and consulted the notepad in her hand. "We'll need you to fry the chicken today."

"Of course," Elizabeth said. She always fried the chicken.

Elizabeth placed the apple pies she'd baked on the table with the other desserts, then went back outside with Gena.

The congregation was moving toward the church. Services were about to start.

Freddie and Betsy Brewster passed in front of them. The young couple owned a small farm just outside of town. Their first child—destined to have Freddie's bright red hair—was due soon, and Betsy looked it. Freddie was at her elbow, steadying her.

"Now, just take it easy, darlin'," he said. "You're doing fine, now."

Betsy glared at him. "I know I'm doing fine, Freddie," she told him.

"'Course you are, sweetie."

Elizabeth and Gena fell in step behind them.

"How have you been feeling, Betsy?" Elizabeth asked.

"Fine, just fine," Freddie said.

"I can talk for myself, Freddie Brewster," Betsy said.

''Sure thing, honey bunch.''

Betsy turned to Elizabeth. ''I'm feeling fine, just fine.''

Freddie licked his lips nervously. ''You're going to be around when the time comes, aren't you, Miss Elizabeth?''

Alongside her father, Elizabeth had attended almost every birth in Sterling. Since his death, the women still came to her to deliver their babies.

Elizabeth smiled. She'd never known such a nervous papa-to-be, or a happier expectant mother. Freddie and Betsy had been in love since they were little more than children.

''Don't worry, Freddie,'' Elizabeth said. ''I'll be here.''

''Good, that's good,'' Freddie said, and heaved a sigh. He turned back to his wife. ''Now, just watch yourself on the steps, sugar, just watch yourself.''

Betsy jerked away from him. ''I'm watching, Freddie.''

Freddie dragged his hand over his forehead. ''I know you are, dumplin'. I know you are.''

''I'm not sure who's more excited about this baby,'' Gena whispered to Elizabeth. ''Freddie or Betsy.''

Elizabeth smiled, touched by the way Freddie fussed over his wife.

''Good morning, Miss Elizabeth.''

Garrett Whitmore appeared beside Elizabeth. He pulled off his hat and nodded pleasantly at Gena.

The smile faded from Elizabeth's face. "Good morning, Garrett," she said.

Garrett took Elizabeth's elbow and assisted her up the steps. Inside the church, she eased away from him.

The congregation of Sterling was a generous one. The inside of the church was painted white. A stained glass window depicting Jesus with a lamb at his feet was at the front of the sanctuary.

Elizabeth took her seat at the piano behind the altar. The ten-person choir was already in place. She flipped her sheet music to the hymn they'd practiced on Thursday night, "Onward Christian Soldiers."

Generally, Elizabeth used these few moments before the service started for quiet thought and prayer. But this morning the congregation filing into the church held her attention. She watched the doors as the people she'd known most of her life entered the sanctuary.

She saw Gena's parents, the Gunthers, and her younger sister, Jane. Boyd Sherman, the man Jane was so excited about marrying, held her elbow possessively, and as usual, didn't allow her to sit with her family but rather with him, a few rows away.

Heath Wheeler dragged off his hat as he came into the church, and Elizabeth was almost sure she saw him searching the gathering for Gena.

Then Connor Wade stepped inside.

Elizabeth glanced away. Determinedly she kept her eyes trained on the choir, but after a moment her gaze drifted back to Connor.

She wasn't the only one paying attention to him. Looking out over the congregation, Elizabeth saw heads swivel, then bend to whisper. A little knot jerked in her stomach as she realized that Gena had been right about all the commotion the man had stirred up in Sterling.

Connor found a seat near the rear of the church beside Heath. Between the two of them they took up most of the pew. Both were big men. Both were handsome, but in different ways. Both were—

"Elizabeth?"

She jumped. Reverend Brady and the choir were staring at her, and apparently had been for some time.

"Please begin," Reverend Brady said, for what Elizabeth feared wasn't the first time.

Flustered, she adjusted her music and began to play. Goodness, what the Lord must think of her ogling two men at Sunday service.

After the opening hymn, Reverend Brady made the announcements, asked for prayers for the sick and introduced their visitor.

Connor Wade didn't hear the minister at first, it seemed, because it took Heath's elbow in his ribs to get him to stand. Towering over the congregation, Connor gave a quick nod and took his seat again.

Elizabeth's gaze met his for a fraction of a second. What had he been thinking? she wondered.

After Reverend Brady's sermon, the offering plate was passed, the choir sang another hymn, the minister gave one final prayer and the congregation streamed outside.

At the back of the church Connor waited as long as he could, then bolted for the door. It was hotter than a whorehouse on Saturday night inside the church, and not just because the minister's sermon seemed directed at him, as usual.

He pulled at his shirt collar. Damn if he knew what the problem was.

Once he was outside, Heath tapped his shoulder. "I know you're the guest of honor today, but give us a hand, will you?"

Connor followed Heath inside the fellowship hall, glad for something to do. Somebody had decided they should eat outside, so all the tables and benches had to be carried to the shade trees in the church-yard.

Women swarmed everywhere, carrying plates, cups and tableware. The fellowship hall filled with the aroma of all sorts of foods. Connor caught a glimpse of Elizabeth through the doorway to the back room.

She'd gotten the worst job in the kitchen. Elizabeth stood over the stove frying three pans of chicken, with smoke in her face and grease popping on her.

As he watched, she lifted the hem of her apron and dabbed her forehead. Connor's chest tightened. Even standing in a hot kitchen, Elizabeth Hill seemed delicate and proper. She made sweating look good.

"Hey, Connor, let's go," Heath called.

He grabbed the other end of the table and they carried it outside.

When everything was settled in place under the trees, the men stood around and talked while the meal was being prepared. The only woman outside sat on one of the benches, wearing a sour look on her face and arguing with her husband. Not that Connor blamed her; her belly looked ready to pop open with a baby.

Connor sidled up next to Heath and nodded across the churchyard. "Who's that fella over there talking to the mayor?" he asked.

Heath craned his neck. "Garrett Whitmore."

Connor had seen the man escort Elizabeth into the church this morning. "Looks like a dandy," he said.

Garrett Whitmore was close to forty, from the looks of him, dressed in a fine suit of clothes with a cravat and a beaver hat.

"Garrett owns the hotel and the feed store," Heath said. "Along with a chunk of the land around Sterling."

"Big man around here, huh?"

"Pretty big," Heath said, and frowned. "Pompous old windbag, if you ask me."

Connor moseyed across the churchyard. When Mayor Rogers saw him, he interrupted his conversation and introduced Connor to Garrett Whitmore, then moved on.

"Glad to know you," Garrett said, and pumped Connor's hand. "Sterling owes you a debt of thanks for your quick thinking at the bank robbery, and I want to thank you personally for what you did for my Elizabeth.''

Connor's spine stiffened. ''*Your* Elizabeth? I didn't know she'd been spoken for.''

''We have an understanding, Elizabeth and I,'' Garrett said, as if that explained everything.

But for Connor, it created more questions.

''I know what you're thinking,'' Garrett said, nodding generously. ''She wouldn't make much of a wife, what with her being so far past her prime and all. But Elizabeth's got some good points.''

''Is that so?''

''She's a strong woman. Doesn't require much fussing over,'' Garrett said. ''She's got a good head on her shoulders. Owns property, too. Prime property.''

''Is that a fact?''

''And,'' Garrett continued, ''she's the third prettiest woman in Sterling.''

Connor frowned. ''She's what?''

''Third prettiest woman in town,'' Garrett said. He shrugged. ''The top two are a lot younger.''

Connor had heard horse traders say kinder things about old nags they were trying to unload.

''Well, thanks again. Glad to have you in Sterling,'' Garrett patted Connor's shoulder and moved along.

Connor mumbled a curse, then clamped his lips together, remembering he was standing in a churchyard. But whether he'd said it aloud or not, he meant it.

The mayor's wife appeared in the doorway of the fellowship hall and made a big production of inviting everyone inside to fill their plates. Connor moved along with the crowd. He was hungry. But just as he got near the steps he caught sight of Elizabeth coming out the back door.

Connor watched as she disappeared around the corner. On impulse, he followed. He found her at the pump, leaning over the trough, splashing cold water on her face.

For a moment he watched her, enjoying this private moment when she thought no one was around.

Her dress had hiked up in the back, just enough that he got a glimpse of her calves. Leaning over as she was, her breasts filled out the front of her dress. And of course, her bottom was sticking out.

A strong tremor passed through Connor, warming him. And surprising him, too. Other thoughts—pleasurable thoughts—followed quickly.

Connor shook himself. This was not what he'd come to Sterling for.

"Miss Hill?"

She jerked upright, sending little droplets of water flying, and spun to face him.

"Mr. Wade!"

Elizabeth swiped at the rivulets steaming down her cheeks. How embarrassing to be caught in such an unladylike posture—bending over the water trough. What must Mr. Wade think of her?

But Elizabeth's embarrassment turned to something different as she gauged the look on his face. He didn't seem to think less of her. In fact, he seemed to enjoy it.

A whole new wave of emotions warred inside Elizabeth. Strange feelings, much too confusing to analyze.

Connor pulled the handkerchief from his hip pocket and offered it to her.

Elizabeth eyed it, but even though water moistened her face and dripped from her hands, she didn't reach for it.

"It's okay," Connor said, holding it out. "It's clean."

Elizabeth's back stiffened. "That's not the point. It's not proper for me to take a personal item of yours."

"Oh." Connor glanced back over his shoulder, then leaned a little closer. "I won't tell anybody if you won't."

Elizabeth still refused to take his handkerchief.

"Either that," Connor said, "or you can stand there and keep dripping."

She huffed and snatched the handkerchief from his hand. Carefully, she patted her cheeks and forehead, then looked up at him.

"Did you want something?" she asked.

"Well...yes," Connor said.

But all he could do was stand there and think how fresh and dewy Elizabeth looked. How pretty she was when her cheeks were flushed like this. And her lips. He'd never seen lips like hers. Full and pink. She'd probably never been kissed. Kissed right, anyway.

"Mr. Wade?"

Connor shifted and cleared his throat. "It's time to eat," he said, which was stupid. If anybody knew the meal had been served, it was Elizabeth, who'd been standing in the kitchen the whole time.

But instead of frowning at him and telling him she knew perfectly well it was time to eat, Elizabeth smiled. "Why, thank you, Mr. Wade. It's kind of you to think of me."

Connor's chest swelled a little. It wasn't an offer for a roll in the hay, and she did seem a little formal, but she sounded like she meant it.

He moved aside and gestured, then fell in step beside her.

Abigail Rogers rushed forward when they turned the corner into the churchyard, and caught Connor's arm.

"There you are, Mr. Wade. Come along now, come along, you must eat with the mayor."

Abigail dragged him up the steps and cut in front of everyone else waiting in line to get their food. No one seemed to mind.

The women in the serving line filled Connor's plate to overflowing, then Abigail hustled him outside and sat him down beside the mayor.

Connor knew most of the people seated at the table with him. Besides the mayor and his wife, the Reverend and Mrs. Brady were there, along with the minister's niece Dixie, who ended up seated next to Connor.

Dixie wasn't much more than seventeen, Connor guessed, with blond hair and slender hips. He wondered if this was one of the two women in Sterling whom Garrett Whitmore considered prettier than Elizabeth.

All morning long, everyone at church had praised his actions at the shoot-out and called him a hero. Hardly a soul he'd talked to hadn't thanked him for what he'd done. And he'd sure gotten more than his share of stares in the last two days.

Connor was grateful for all the kind words everyone in town had showered on him. He appreciated the trouble everyone had gone to organizing the social, even after he'd told Abigail Rogers that he didn't want the honor.

But now Connor had had enough. The whole idea that he was some sort of a hero was ridiculous.

If only the townspeople knew just how ridiculous.

Right now, all Connor wanted was to eat his meal in peace, have a few minutes to himself, and find someone who could make Dixie Brady quit batting her eyelashes at him.

None of those things seemed likely to happen anytime soon.

The food was good, though, and Connor ate his fill. Dixie went back inside twice and heaped his plate for him, and fussed over his napkin when it fell to the ground.

"The ladies here in Sterling sure can cook," Connor said, finishing off another chicken leg.

"You'll have to save room for dessert," Abigail said. "Mrs. Canter makes a delightful cherry cobbler, and Elizabeth Hill is known for her apple pie. You met Mrs. Canter a little earlier. Ike's wife. And of course you know Elizabeth."

Connor leaned slightly to the right and saw Elizabeth seated at the next table. Her back was to him, giving him a lovely view of her waist and hips, and her bottom seated on the bench. Little tendrils of her dark hair curled around her neck.

He watched her lift her fork while keeping her little finger extended. She carefully dabbed at her lips with her napkin. Artful, feminine movements. Movements of a woman with a fine upbringing and good manners.

Connor took his elbows off the table.

Then, annoyed with himself, he pushed his plate aside.

Enough of this nonsense. He had business to take care of. He had to find a way to get Elizabeth Hill alone, and get on with the reason he'd come to Sterling.

Chapter Five

Apparently, not much noteworthy happened in Sterling, and that's why the townsfolk made such a big deal out of Connor stopping the bank robbery. The mayor and his wife took the opportunity to wring every drop of drama out of the incident, much to Connor's dismay.

Seated on a hard bench under a tree in the church-yard, flanked by the mayor and his wife, Connor had to struggle to keep his mind from drifting away as the mayor got up to start the so-called festivities.

Mayor Rogers began the event by declaring what a wonderful town Sterling was, how great its citizens were, how the community effort made the town run. He thanked the ladies of Sterling for the fine food they'd prepared, then called on Reverend Brady for a prayer.

Ike Canter got up next and told the story of the shoot-out. It was the sixth time Connor had heard the man tell the tale; he couldn't guess how many times Ike had actually repeated it himself.

But everybody in the churchyard seemed to enjoy it. Some sat on benches, others on blankets spread out on the grass. Connor wished the whole thing would hurry up and be over with.

Finally, the mayor rose and took charge of the ceremony again.

"Let's get Elizabeth up here," Mayor Rogers called. He looked out over the crowd. "Elizabeth? Come on up here, Elizabeth."

She was seated with Gena Blake and several other people Connor didn't know. He'd spotted her as soon as the ceremony began. Elizabeth got to her feet, straightened her dress and walked to the front of the group; she looked like she didn't want to be there any more than he did.

"We all know what Elizabeth has been through in the last little while," Mayor Rogers announced. "Her father passed away, leaving our town without a doctor. And, of course, we all know about her brother. But we're glad to have her here with us, just the same."

Mayor Rogers waved Connor to the front of the group, then continued. "Connor, we want to thank you for saving Elizabeth's life, no matter what."

Mrs. Rogers passed a box to Elizabeth and whispered something to her. Elizabeth, in turn, passed it along to Connor.

Their hands touched. Her fingers were cold, ice cold. Connor caught her gaze. She was trying hard to put on a brave face.

Connor's mind swept back to the shoot-out in

front of the bank and the moment when their gazes had met. He'd seen the terror in her eyes. Now, at this moment, he saw much the same thing. Then, as now, he was overwhelmed with the need to help her.

And the best way to do that was to get this ceremony over with.

Connor accepted the box from her, pried off the lid and removed an engraved silver plate. He held it up and applause broke out in the crowd. Mayor and Mrs. Rogers smiled, altogether pleased with themselves.

"I appreciate how welcome you've all made me feel," Connor said, when the applause died down. "Sterling is a fine town, with lots of fine people. I'm glad I could help out. Thank you."

Applause rose from the townspeople again; Mayor Rogers shook Connor's hand and slapped him on the back.

"Let's all enjoy an afternoon of fellowship," Mrs. Rogers announced, "and those lovely desserts, too."

The applause continued. Connor headed for Elizabeth, who was darting toward the rear of the gathering. He didn't get very far, though. More people crowded around him, somebody took his engraved plate and a dozen or so people shook his hand.

"Looks like lots of good things are happening in Sterling," Ike Canter said, standing at Connor's elbow. "I heard the town council's got somebody interested in taking up medicine here."

"Praise the Lord," Reverend Brady intoned.

Garrett Whitmore elbowed his way into the group. "A doctor? Coming to Sterling? Is he young or old?"

Gerald Gunther, owner of the general store, pulled on his long mustache. "What difference does that make?"

Garrett frowned, deep in thought. "Makes a big difference," he said, then left the group again.

Gradually, the lure of the desserts overcame most everyone, and Connor was left alone. Or so he thought. Dixie Brady sidled up next to him.

"How about if I get you some pie?" she asked.

Connor managed to smile. "Thank you, Miss Brady."

She batted her lashes. "I told you to call me Dixie," she said, and headed for the fellowship hall.

Connor was tired. Tired of smiling, tired of being nice to people. Tired of pretending.

He spotted Elizabeth standing by herself under one of the trees. She looked tense, troubled, as if she were anxious to leave, too. He didn't blame her, not after that speech the mayor had given.

Connor walked over. "I don't know about you, but I've had about all the socializing I can take for one day."

Elizabeth spun around, stunned to see Connor Wade standing next to her. Bad enough what she'd just endured in front of the whole town—another humiliation. But did this man have to draw attention to her again?

"I take it you don't come to church often, Mr.

Wade?'' she asked, and didn't bother keeping the note of disapproval from her voice.

''As often as I can,'' Connor said. ''Of course, it didn't used to be that way. I used to think I'd done so many bad things in my life I wasn't worthy to set foot in the house of the Lord.''

She'd suspected as much, but was surprised to hear him admit it. ''What changed your mind?'' she asked.

Connor grinned. ''I figured I'm just the kind of man God wants here the most.''

Elizabeth giggled. Out loud. Right there in the churchyard. She slapped her fingers across her lips to hold her laughter inside.

Connor glanced around, then leaned closer and lowered his voice. ''What do you think the good people of Sterling would do if they found out the real reason I stopped that bank robbery?''

Elizabeth leaned in. ''The real reason?''

''The owner of the restaurant was so caught up watching the shoot-out she wouldn't bring my coffee. All I wanted was another cup to finish off my dessert.''

Elizabeth reeled back. ''Coffee! You risked your life for a cup of coffee?''

''Yep. Got me a nice engraved silver plate, but still no coffee.'' Connor grinned. ''Do you think we should tell everybody the truth?''

''Oh, Mr. Wade...'' Elizabeth burst out laughing. Her whole face lit up. Her eyes danced. Connor chuckled along with her. She giggled until she hic-cuped, then pressed her fingers to her lips.

"How about it, Miss Hill?" Connor said softly. "Will you keep my secret?"

Elizabeth sobered. Connor stopped laughing. He gazed into her eyes, those big blue eyes of hers, and for a moment he was lost. She seemed lost, too. And in those fleeting seconds, what a wonderful feeling it was to be lost with a woman as fine as Elizabeth Hill.

She didn't know what had come over her. Laughing, sharing a secret with a man she hardly knew. It felt so good, it surely must be sinful.

But how could something as wonderful as this be a sin?

Elizabeth didn't get a chance to ponder the question, because Freddie Brewster interrupted them, shaking his head fitfully.

"Oh, goodness, Miss Elizabeth," Freddie said. "You got to do something."

"What's wrong, Freddie?"

"I've done gone and made Betsy cry," Freddie wailed. "I didn't mean to. She wanted a slice of your apple pie, but it was all gone by the time I got inside. So I brought her some cherry cobbler and she busted out crying."

Elizabeth glanced past Freddie and saw Betsy seated at the table, sobbing into her hands. Two other women huddled around her, trying to console her.

"It's not your fault," Elizabeth said. "It's just the baby."

Freddie shook his head miserably. "She's either snapping at me or she's crying. Yesterday, she looked at the baby's booties she'd knitted and busted out crying over that."

"All perfectly normal," Elizabeth said. "She'll be back to her old self once the baby comes. Just go sit by her and hold her hand."

"Well, okay. If you say so, Miss Elizabeth," Freddie said, and headed back to his wife.

"The joys of motherhood," Elizabeth mused.

Connor didn't think the woman looked like she was enjoying much of anything, certainly not her impending motherhood.

Then another unwelcome sight appeared. Garrett Whitmore.

"Elizabeth, did you hear the news?" he asked, inserting himself between her and Connor.

She took a step back. "What news is that?"

"We're getting a doctor in town," Garrett said. "I just talked to the mayor and it looks like it's all set."

Her stomach wound into a knot.

"A new doctor?" Elizabeth asked. "To replace Papa?"

Garrett nodded quickly. "And the best part is that he's a young fella. Brand-new doctor from Philadelphia."

"But—"

"Don't you see, Elizabeth? Now you can get rid

of that medical equipment that's taking up all that room in your house."

She touched her hand to her throat. "Sell Papa's things?"

"Of course," Garrett said. "It's only right, Elizabeth. You can't expect a new doctor to bring all that equipment with him."

"Well, no, I don't suppose. But—"

"Besides, you need the money," Garrett said. He frowned at her. "I saw you brought two pies to the social today, Elizabeth. Did you bake more while you were at it?"

"No. I was in a hurry, and—"

"Now, Elizabeth, we've talked about this before. You have to bake those pies to sell to the restaurants. That's money in your pocket."

"Yes, Garrett," Elizabeth said wearily, "I'm very aware of that."

"I don't think you are," Garrett insisted. "Now, just listen a minute—"

"I have a few plans of my own," Elizabeth told him.

Garrett glanced at Connor and chuckled indulgently. "Of course you do, Elizabeth. Now, just let me tell you—"

"I've decided to convert my home into a boardinghouse."

A wave of nausea passed through Elizabeth as the words popped out of her mouth. She hadn't meant to tell anyone yet, certainly not Garrett.

He had been a close friend of her father, and in

the last year, Garrett had taken it upon himself to give her financial advice. He meant well, of course. He had the best of intentions. Still, he annoyed Elizabeth at times.

Garrett rubbed his chin and nodded thoughtfully, mulling over the boardinghouse proposal she'd blurted out. "That's a good idea, Elizabeth," he said at last.

"Do you think so?" she asked, pleased that he approved.

"You've got good property," he said. "You need to put it to use."

"A lot has to be done first, of course," Elizabeth said. "And I'm not sure where I'll get the money."

"Get to baking those pies," Garrett advised. He slapped Connor on the shoulder and grinned. "Darned if they don't fool you sometimes and come up with an idea. Women. Who'd have figured?"

Connor's temper simmered. His hand curled into a fist. He would have liked nothing more than to drive it straight into Garrett Whitmore's face.

"Miss Elizabeth?" a young woman called. She stood a few feet away, as if reluctant to disturb them.

"Yes, Sadie?" Elizabeth asked.

She glanced at Connor and Garrett, then dipped her lashes. "Could I talk with you? Private-like?"

Elizabeth and the young woman headed for a deserted spot in the churchyard.

"Elizabeth fancies herself some kind of a doctor," Garrett said to Connor. "It's not real doctoring she does, of course. We've got the undertaker who handles the busted bones and gunshots. Elizabeth just takes care of women stuff.''

Punching Garrett Whitmore in the nose seemed like a better and better idea with each minute that passed, Connor decided. Maybe if he did, the town would take back that fancy engraved silver plate and leave him alone.

Tempting, very tempting. And it would feel good. Connor hadn't punched anybody in a long time.

His anger flared again, deeper and stronger with the realization that none of it was any of his business. Garrett and Elizabeth had an understanding, as Garrett had put it.

Connor fumed silently and left Garrett standing by himself.

He paced around for a while to walk off his foul mood and to discourage any more of Sterling's good-hearted citizens from thanking him for stopping the bank robbery. After he'd cooled down, Connor plopped down on a bench next to Heath Wheeler.

Heath was working on a slice of peach pie and a steaming cup of coffee. Most everyone else was finished, and the women were clearing the tables.

''I'll come down to the stable to pick up my horse in the morning,'' Connor said.

Heath gulped down a bite of pie. ''You're leaving Sterling?''

For a moment, Connor considered the possibility. Just leave. Head out. Go someplace where no one knew him.

That's what he'd intended when he'd come to Sterling. Connor swore a silent oath. He should have minded his own business when he'd seen those yahoos trying to rob the bank.

His gut tightened as Elizabeth flashed into his mind. That robber might have killed her if he hadn't stepped in. Connor couldn't bear the thought.

But since the robbery, the good folks of Sterling—with the best of intentions—had turned him into something he wasn't. What would they say if they knew the truth?

His gut tightened. More importantly, what would Elizabeth say?

It would be easier to move along. In fact, he probably should do just that. But Connor had a plan. He needed Elizabeth to make that plan work. He couldn't leave.

"No, I'm not leaving," Connor said to Heath. "I've got to find me a place to live. Can't stay in the hotel forever."

"Here's your pie, Connor," Dixie Brady crooned sweetly.

Connor looked up at the minister's niece standing over him holding a plate and a cup of coffee. She placed both on the table in front of him, batted her lashes and smiled down at him.

"Thank you, Miss Brady," he said.

Dixie gave him a long lazy look, like a cat appraising a mouse, then tapped her fingers against his wrist. "Didn't I ask you to call me Dixie?"

Connor nodded. "Yes, sure thing. Dixie."

She stayed where she was, making no effort to leave.

"Thank you," Connor said again, and finally Dixie moved on.

"Where are you planning to look for a place to live? The rooming house?" Heath asked, and pushed away his empty plate.

"I've got an idea I'm working on."

Gena Blake walked over. "Can I take your empty plate?" she asked Heath.

His eyes got big as he looked up at her standing on the other side of the table. He opened his mouth, but a moment passed before any words came out.

"Yes, ma'am, Mrs. Blake," Heath said. "Thank you, ma'am."

When he reached for his plate to pass to her, Heath bumped his cup, sending his coffee spilling across the table.

"Jesus..." Heath's face turned bright red. "Oh, sorry, ma'am. I didn't mean to—"

"It's all right," Gena said, smiling sweetly.

Heath turned redder while Gena mopped up the coffee with a napkin. She took his empty plate and cup and disappeared into the fellowship hall.

"Christ..." Heath swore again and dragged his palms down his face. "Every time I get around that woman I get so damn butterfingered I can't do nothing. Nothing but make a fool of myself, that is."

Connor chuckled. "Maybe you ought to stick to horses."

Heath grunted. ''If I could get my arms all the way around one at night, I just might do that.''

Elizabeth popped into Connor's mind. She wasn't one of those small women, but he could get his arms around her easily. He could do a lot more than hold her. And would—often—if he had the chance.

A hot current surged through Connor, arrowing through his belly, diving lower. There it bloomed with predictable results.

Connor tried to ignore what was happening to him, but it was downright impossible in view of the fact that Elizabeth stood only a few yards away, bending and stretching as she did her part to gather the dirty linens and dishes from the tables.

Connor watched every move, every turn she made. Little wisps of hair blew around her face. Her sleeves pulled back when she reached for something, displaying her delicate wrists.

With a long sigh, Connor enjoyed this moment with her, albeit from a distance.

Because tomorrow morning he was going to her house to tell her why he'd come to Sterling after her.

Chapter Six

Elizabeth Hill owned a fine house.

Probably the finest in Sterling.

Connor pushed his hat back on his head as he stopped at the front steps. Surely the finest house he'd ever seen.

The morning sun shone on the glass panes of the two-story house and reflected off its white paint. Green shutters hung by every window. A porch stretched the width of the house, decorated with pots of flowers; a swing suspended by chains hung at one end.

Glancing down at the market basket in his hand, Connor pulled in a deep breath. A woman who packed a china plate, silver cutlery and a linen napkin just to serve a piece of pie was bound to live in a fancy house. Still…

Connor squared his shoulders and climbed onto Elizabeth's front porch. He clanged the brass knocker. After a moment the curtain was pulled back at the window and Elizabeth peered out.

She didn't smile. If anything, she looked none too pleased to see him.

The curtain fell shut and a second later the door opened. She had on a brown skirt this morning, and a pale blue blouse that deepened the shade of her eyes.

"Morning, Miss Hill," Connor said, and as an afterthought, pulled off his hat.

Elizabeth glanced past him, up and down the road in both directions, then settled her gaze on him.

"Good morning, Mr. Wade."

She made no move to invite him inside.

"I brought back your basket," Connor said, and thrust it at her.

"Oh. I'd forgotten," Elizabeth said, and took it.

"You were right about your pie," Connor said. That remark earned him the first smile of the morning, so he kept going. "Best tasting apple pie I've ever had."

"Thank you."

"'Course, now, it might have been a fluke," Connor told her. "I'd have to have a couple more pieces to say for certain."

Elizabeth's spine stiffened. "Mr. Wade, I assure you, my pie is the finest—"

She stopped, seeing the little grin pulling at his lips. He was only teasing her. Elizabeth smiled, too.

"That's one of the reasons I came by, Miss Hill, other than to return your basket," Connor said.

Her eyes widened. "You'd like to buy one of my pies?"

"No, not exactly," Connor said. "I have some business to discuss with you."

Her brows pulled together. "What sort of business?"

"Would it be all right if I came inside?"

Elizabeth hesitated. She didn't budge from the door, just stood there looking at him for a long time. Finally she glanced up and down the road again and stepped back.

"Well, I suppose it would be all right," she said. "For a few minutes."

Connor walked inside and she closed the door behind him. The cool of the foyer closed in around him. Somewhere, a clock ticked.

In front of him was a wide staircase leading up to the second floor. Off to his right was the dining room. A huge walnut table that seated ten sat in the middle of the room. Against the back wall was a hutch with beveled glass doors, and inside were the pink china dishes with the little white doves he'd eaten his pie off of. The whole thing sparkled in the morning sunlight streaming through the window.

Connor had never seen anything so fine in his whole life.

"Would you like to sit down?" Elizabeth asked.

He nodded. "Sure."

Elizabeth took his hat and hung it on the peg beside the front door, then set her market basket on the table beneath it. She led the way to the parlor.

The parlor held a green settee, cushioned chairs, a rocker, tables with carved legs and crystal lanterns.

A piano sat against one wall. Lace curtains hung at the windows, and paintings decorated the walls. Delicate figurines sat on the tabletops. A floral rug covered most of the floor.

There was a still, settled feel to the room. Connor became conscious of the dust on his boots, and of how big he was amid the dainty furnishings.

But Elizabeth looked comfortable here, like she belonged in this elegant setting.

Connor paused in front of the bookcase that stretched to the ceiling. Volumes of leather-bound books were squeezed into every shelf.

''Are these your books, Miss Hill?'' he asked.

Elizabeth tilted her head back, studying them. ''They belong to my father and me.''

''You've read all these?''

She glanced up at him as if she didn't understand why he'd ask such a thing. ''Of course.'' She sat down in one of the chairs and pointed to the settee. ''Make yourself comfortable, Mr. Wade.''

As if he could be comfortable in a room such as this.

Connor did as he was told and took a seat. He wished she'd left him his hat; at least then he'd have something to do with his hands. He plastered them on his knees and sat up straight.

''Would you care for refreshment?'' Elizabeth asked.

Connor wasn't exactly sure what ''refreshment'' might entail in a home as fine as this. But visions of having to sit here and attempt to balance some little teacup on his lap kept him from accepting her offer.

Still, it didn't escape him that Miss Elizabeth Hill was treating him like a guest in her home. An honest-to-goodness guest. She'd seated him in her parlor, offered to serve him something—off those thin little pink plates of hers, no doubt. Elizabeth probably served the mayor's wife off those same dishes when she came over.

Connor's chest tightened. He'd never been treated like this before. Never imagined he would be, and certainly not by a refined lady like Elizabeth Hill.

"You said you'd like to discuss business?" Elizabeth asked.

Now was his chance. He had her alone. He'd thought and planned and plotted. He'd ridden for weeks. All for this moment. This moment with Elizabeth.

Words formed in his mind. He'd decided what to say to her, decided it weeks ago in a dark alley in Kansas City. He knew exactly what he wanted.

But he'd never expected Elizabeth Hill to be the woman sitting before him now. Never expected she'd be so pretty, so dignified, so elegant.

Never expected that he would feel so ashamed.

Connor had no delusions about who he was or where he came from. That's why it surprised him that now, at this critical moment, his pride got the best of him.

"Yes, Miss Hill. I've come to discuss business with you." Connor cleared his voice, changing his mind, making an offer he'd not come here to present. "I'd like to extend my carpentry skills to you to renovate your place into a boarding home."

She rocked forward in her chair and her mouth opened. A breathy little gasp slipped out. Connor couldn't tell if she was shocked from happiness or just plain shocked.

"But Mr. Wade, I—I couldn't accept your services for free."

"I never said it would be free."

Her brows pulled together in a suspicious frown. "What did you have in mind?"

In only a moment it came to him. "Room and board, here, in exchange for the work."

Heat rushed up from deep inside Elizabeth, tingling her skin and burning her cheeks. Connor Wade living here? In her home? With her cooking for him? Cleaning up after him? Seeing him throughout the day? Every day? Every…night?

A myriad of emotions boiled inside Elizabeth. She didn't even know what most of them meant, but they frightened her, just the same.

She touched her fingers to her forehead. "Mr. Wade, I don't think that would be proper."

Connor shrugged. "It's just business, Miss Hill. Nothing personal."

"Oh, well, of course." Her cheeks flamed again. She felt foolish and…disappointed? Certainly there would be nothing personal in the arrangement. Why had she even thought such a thing? A woman her age. An old maid. A spinster. The woman the whole town knew would never have a man interested in her. The last woman ever to find a husband.

"I see you've got a barn out back," Connor said. "I'll live there and take my meals there. I'll work on your place and keep to myself. You won't even know I'm around."

"Oh." Elizabeth twisted her fingers together, not sure why she felt disappointed.

"You do want your boardinghouse, don't you?"

"Certainly."

"I didn't mean to pry," Connor said, "but yesterday at church I got the idea your cash was low right now."

"Yes, that's true."

"I figured this would help us both," Connor said. "You need the work done and I need a job."

"But this wouldn't be a job, really," Elizabeth. "I mean, I can't pay you."

"I know. But I need a place to live and I need to eat until I can find a job."

"Mr. Wade, there are lots of people in Sterling who would gladly give you a job—any job you wanted—after what you did for the town."

Connor pulled on the back of his neck and sighed heavily. "Yeah, I reckon you're right about that. But, honestly, I've heard all I can stand to hear about that bank robbery and what a good thing I did."

He looked up at her. "I figure you've had your fill of it, too, Miss Hill."

A little something inside Elizabeth tugged her toward Connor Wade, and she felt a kinship with him she'd never imagined.

Goodness knows, she'd certainly heard enough about the bank robbery and been held up to public scrutiny long enough.

Elizabeth smiled. "Yes, I see your point."

"The way I figure it, that makes you and me just about perfect for each other," Connor said. "Businesswise, of course."

"Of course...businesswise."

"So, what do you say?"

Elizabeth's stomach had started tingling awhile ago and just wouldn't stop. She didn't know how to interpret that. Did it mean she should refuse Mr. Wade's offer? Or take him up on it?

"I hardly know you, Mr. Wade," Elizabeth said. "You're a complete stranger, really."

Connor spread out his arms. "What do you want to know about me?"

She hadn't expected this kind of openness and it startled her. Naturally, there had been a lot of speculation about Connor among the townspeople. The ladies at the social yesterday had chattered endlessly, proposing all sorts of possibilities. And, Elizabeth admitted, she was a little curious herself.

"Well, where are you from?" Elizabeth asked.

"Missouri. I was born there. My pa died when I was a kid, so it was just me and my mama looking out for each other. When she passed on, I headed out to see what was over the next hill. I worked a lot of different jobs, lived in a lot of different places.''

He delivered his personal history matter-of-factly, with no hesitation.

''You have no family?'' Elizabeth asked.

Connor shook his head. ''Nope.''

''What brings you to Sterling?''

Connor shifted on the settee. ''Like I said, Miss Hill, I spent most of my life moving around. That's over with now. I've got a plan I'm working on.''

''What sort of plan?''

''It's time to put down some roots,'' Connor said. ''I'm going to find work, then start my own business.''

''That's very ambitious, Mr. Wade.''

''So how about it, Miss Hill? Do you want me working on your boardinghouse or not?''

Elizabeth's heart ached a little at the thought of an endless string of lonely days and nights in the house stretching out before her. Gena had thought the boardinghouse idea a good one. Garrett had said the same at church yesterday. Elizabeth really wanted to do it.

But people would talk.

''I—I don't know, Mr. Wade,'' Elizabeth said.

''Something about the arrangement not to your liking?'' Connor asked.

''It's—it's just that, well, you see, I'm an unmarried woman, and...''

''And you're worried about what people might say.''

"Well, yes," she admitted.

Connor sighed. "I've found that people are always going to talk, Miss Hill. But just because people are talking, that doesn't mean what they're saying is right. And it sure as hell doesn't mean they're worth listening to."

Elizabeth fidgeted. "That's true, of course. But..."

"You've got to do what you think is best," Connor said. "If you don't want your boardinghouse—"

"But I do," Elizabeth said. "Yesterday in church I prayed for guidance."

Connor chuckled. His crooked grin widened to a genuine smile. "I don't believe I've ever been anyone's answer to prayer before, Miss Hill," he said. "But here I am."

She gasped. Connor Wade? An answer to her prayer? Gracious, maybe she ought to be more careful what she prayed for from now on.

"So, you want me to start?" Connor asked.

"Well..."

"Then you want me to wait?"

"No, but..."

Connor looked at her thoughtfully, then pulled on his neck. "As I see it, Miss Hill, what you've got to ask yourself is which is more important to you— keeping the town from gossiping about you or having what you want."

"It's not that easy," Elizabeth said. "There are things you don't know about. Things you don't understand."

"Then tell me."

Elizabeth was momentarily taken aback. First, because Connor Wade had asked to hear her personal difficulties, and second, because she could have told him so easily.

He made it sound so simple. Just tell him. Open her heart and soul and pour out all the burdens she carried, all the trials she'd been through in the last year. Lay them on him. He'd manage them.

Elizabeth's stomach turned mushy. Connor Wade had a strength that went deeper than his forceful appearance, his wide shoulders, his big chest and arms. Deeper even than the strength it took to walk into the street of a town he'd never been in, stop a bank robbery and save the life of a woman he didn't know.

Small wonder he'd been the topic of conversation among the women in the fellowship hall kitchen yesterday. Small wonder the town revered him.

It was hard to imagine Connor Wade as an answer to a prayer, though. Yesterday in church, she'd prayed for guidance in her decision to open a boardinghouse, prayed for the funds to accomplish it. And today Connor Wade showed up on her doorstep, saying things that made sense and offering to work for free.

Elizabeth didn't think she could very well say no. And really, she didn't want to.

"All right, Mr. Wade," Elizabeth said. "I'll accept your offer."

He rose from the settee. "You're sure?"

"I'm positive." Elizabeth extended her hand. "We have a deal."

"Deal," Connor said, and took her hand.

His knees weakened. Damnation, had *that* been a mistake.

Chapter Seven

"I suppose we should get started right away," Elizabeth said. "If that's all right with you."

Connor nodded. "Suits me fine."

Elizabeth led the way out of the parlor, down the hallway beside the staircase and into the kitchen, her slippers making soft brushing sounds on the hardwood floors. Connor's heavy footsteps followed.

Now that she'd made the decision to go ahead with her boardinghouse she was excited, anxious to get the project underway.

"The pantry should be expanded," Elizabeth said, opening the door to the little room inside the kitchen. "It's not nearly big enough for all the food I'll need to properly serve my boarders."

Connor stepped inside and studied the shelves. She didn't have much in the way of foodstuffs. But a woman living alone wouldn't require much.

"Better shelves are all you need," Connor said.

"Do you think so?" Elizabeth stepped into the

pantry with him, craning her neck, rising up on her toes trying to see around him. He was so big.

"I can put these shelves in the center section closer together, then add some new ones on the other two walls," Connor said, pointing. "If that's all right with you."

"Yes, I think that would be..."

Elizabeth's voice trailed off as she realized how close she stood to Connor in the confined space of the pantry. An awareness of his height, his strength overwhelmed her.

She dared to lift her gaze to his and found him watching her. No, studying her, was more the feeling. She should have been shocked, or at least annoyed. Instead, it pleased her.

"So you like my shelf idea, Miss Hill?" Connor asked softly.

"Your what?"

He gestured. "My idea to change your shelves."

"Oh, the shelves. Of course." Elizabeth forced herself to turn away from him, and made a great show of studying the pantry, pressing her lips together, tapping her finger against her jaw.

"Yes, that sounds as if it will work quite nicely," she finally declared.

Connor stepped out of the pantry and nodded to a closed door at the back of the kitchen. "Is that a storage room?" he asked.

"It was, at one time. It's a classroom now. I'll show you," Elizabeth said.

She opened the door and they walked inside. A

table and two chairs sat in the middle of the room. On one wall hung a chalkboard. Above it were bright-colored placards illustrating the alphabet. Along another wall stood a bookcase crammed full of books.

"This is where I tutor my students," Elizabeth said.

Connor looked around the room. "Sterling doesn't have a school?"

"Of course. But sometimes a child needs extra help. Some fall behind the rest of the class because of illness." Elizabeth smiled. "One little girl I tutor is much smarter than the other children. The teacher can't keep her busy. So her mother brings her here."

Connor walked slowly around the room, eyeing the books, the placards above the chalkboard.

"I guess it doesn't look like much," Elizabeth said, twisting her fingers together.

He turned sharply. "It looks just fine. Like a real schoolhouse. I was just thinking that I could put a window in this wall and get a better breeze through here. It wouldn't cost much."

"That sounds like a good idea," Elizabeth said, and clasped her hands together in front of her. "Well, that's the extent of the renovations. The roof needs some work and the porch swing needs fixing. I haven't used the barn in quite some time, so it may need something done to it. And…and maybe the surgery."

"What about upstairs?" Connor asked, gesturing toward the ceiling. "What about the bedrooms?"

"The rooms are quite lovely, actually," Elizabeth said. "Very spacious. My father built them to be large, purposely. Any boarder would be thrilled to live up there."

"Maybe you could divide up a few of them?" Connor suggested. "You could get more people in here that way."

"I hadn't considered that," Elizabeth said, frowning.

"Mind if I take a look?"

"No, that's fine."

Elizabeth turned to lead the way upstairs, but stopped suddenly. "I should get you some paper so you can write these things down."

"No," Connor said. "No need. I can remember."

They climbed the staircase, and when they reached the second floor, Elizabeth's stomach began to tingle again. Good gracious, she was upstairs with a man. A man she didn't really know. And they were about to go looking at bedrooms.

The vision of Connor standing in his hotel room swept into her mind again. Goodness, she'd only known this man four days and already she'd found herself in more intimate settings with him than with any other man in all her years put together.

Elizabeth stopped outside the first bedroom on the right, but didn't go inside. She couldn't. It was positively scandalous.

"This room is very large," she said. "Could it be made into two rooms?"

A bureau, washstand and small writing desk filled

the room. A sunny yellow coverlet spread across the bed, and braided rugs warmed the floor.

Connor walked inside. The room that had looked so big a few seconds ago seemed to shrink. He stood in the center, studying it from all angles, then rapped on the walls with his knuckles, listening.

"Papa built so many bedrooms into the house," Elizabeth said. "He wanted his whole family to live with him. This room was seldom used. Only three times, when Papa's relatives came out from the East for a visit."

Connor paced, nodding and looking around.

"The room next door is the same," Elizabeth said.

He ambled past her into the next bedroom. It was furnished much the same as the other one, but decorated in soft blues. Connor studied, rapped on the walls and listened. Elizabeth watched from the doorway.

"Most of these things belonged to my mother," Elizabeth said, and pointed to the bureau. "That's her music box. She brought it with her when she and Papa came west. Mama died when I was a child. I don't remember much about her, except how she loved music. I suppose that's why I love it so much, too. She used to let me sit with her when she played the piano. It's one of my fondest memories."

Connor gazed around the room, then turned to Elizabeth. Heat fanned her cheeks. Mercy, the man must think her a silly goose, prattling on like this.

"I can turn these two rooms into four," Connor

said, stepping into the hallway again. He looked down at her. "Anything else up here you want me to see?"

There was, but the upstairs seemed airless at the moment, unusually warm. Connor must have felt it, too, because Elizabeth saw little beads of perspiration on his temples.

"No," Elizabeth said. She turned quickly and headed down the stairs.

"I guess that's about it," she said, twisting her fingers together, standing at the front door.

"Not exactly." Connor frowned down at her. "Are you sure you want to do this, Elizabeth?"

It was the first time he'd used her given name. It startled Elizabeth, but didn't displease her.

"Yes, I'm sure."

Connor shook his head. "This house is special to you, and rightly so. It's your home. You've got a whole lifetime of memories wrapped up in this place. Are you sure you want to go changing it around? Have strangers living here?"

A little knot rose into Elizabeth's throat. But it wasn't the idea of opening her home to strangers that brought it on, it was the fact that Connor had listened to her talk about the house. Listened and understood. She hadn't expected that of him.

Elizabeth gulped down the lump in her chest. "It's lonely here."

Connor pressed his lips together. "I understand lonely."

"Then you understand why I'm willing to sacrifice my past for my future."

Connor nodded. "Better than you know."

His gaze on her was intense, warming her inside and out.

The mantel clock ticked in the parlor, reminding Elizabeth that time was passing and she was standing in the hallway making eyes at Connor Wade. She stepped away and picked at a tiny speck of lint on her sleeve.

"Anything else need doing around here?" Connor asked.

"No, I don't think so. Unless..." Elizabeth looked up at him and frowned. "There's my father's surgery," she said again.

Connor followed her down the hallway beside the staircase and turned left through another door.

"This was my father's office and waiting room," Elizabeth said, and stepped aside.

A big desk sat in one corner, flanked by two bookshelves and a row of cupboards. Chairs were scattered around the room. A door, now bolted, opened to the outside.

Elizabeth crossed the room and gestured. "This is—was—my father's surgery."

Leaning inside the adjoining room, Connor saw an examination table, cabinets with glass doors, books, bottles and all sorts of gadgets he'd just as soon not know any details about.

"There's another room on the other side of the

surgery," Elizabeth said, pointing, "where severely ill or injured patients stay—stayed."

"Your pa must have been a fine man," Connor said. "The town still speaks highly of him."

Elizabeth smiled proudly. "He was a wonderful doctor. I used to help him. I took care of the business portion of his practice, keeping the books, handling his accounts. I assisted with the patients, too. Some of them."

"That must have pleased him."

"Yes, I think it did. Papa was so good about explaining things. I read his journals and medical books, and we discussed new procedures. I enjoyed it so much." Elizabeth's smile faded. "But, actually, he wanted my brother to follow in his footsteps."

"Seems natural, a son following along after his pa."

Elizabeth drew in a deep breath and turned to Connor. "I guess you've heard about my brother."

"Heard what?"

It surprised her that no one had told Connor, the newcomer in town, what her brother had done. Still, she didn't for a moment believe the town had forgotten the incident.

"I should tell you the truth about him," Elizabeth said. "It may affect your decision to work here."

She squared her shoulders. It wasn't easy to tell this story. Even now, after all this time, she still felt the shame of what her brother had done.

"Raymond was a clerk at the Sterling bank. He embezzled five thousand dollars. He's in prison."

Connor shrugged. "Why would that keep me from working for you?"

"Because he's my brother and he deceived the entire town. He stole from them. The money was never recovered. He was sent to prison," Elizabeth said.

"Did you help him steal the money?"

"Of course not!"

"Then it's got nothing to do with you."

"It certainly does," Elizabeth said. "My brother's shame is my shame."

Connor watched her closely, frowning down at her, then said, "That's not the way I see it. And it's got nothing to do with me working here."

"Well, all right, if you're sure."

"I'm sure."

Elizabeth blew out a breath, relieved. "Good."

"So what do you want done in here?"

"These rooms can be used by boarders, too, I suppose. There won't be any need for me to keep Papa's equipment once the new doctor gets here."

"Why not?"

"Because the new doctor will need it. I'll have to sell it all to him."

"Hell with the new doctor," Connor said. "If you want to keep your papa's things, then keep them."

Elizabeth huffed. "You simply do not understand the situation, Mr. Wade."

"I understand it better than you think I do, Miss Hill."

They glared at each other, making Elizabeth more annoyed with each passing second. How dare this man criticize her? He was a stranger. He didn't know her. He knew nothing of what she had gone through.

And how could this stranger keep stirring up all sorts of emotions in her?

Elizabeth put her nose in the air and spun away.

"That's all for this room," she announced, and marched out of the surgery.

"Yes, ma'am," Connor drawled, and followed her.

Elizabeth set a brisk pace down the hallway to the front door, then waited there, tapping her foot until Connor caught up.

"I'll expect you first thing in the morning," Elizabeth told him. "You can begin by—"

Shouts from outside and the clatter of footsteps on the porch stopped Elizabeth. She yanked open the front door. Freddie Brewster was on her porch, wringing his hat. Betsy was in the wagon, holding her belly and moaning.

"It's time, Miss Elizabeth!" Freddie hopped on his toes, pointing toward the wagon. "It's time!"

"Freddie!" Betsy reeled back in the seat. "Don't leave me!"

"I'm coming right back, darlin'," Freddie called. "Hurry up, Miss Elizabeth. She's hurting something terrible."

"Freddie!"

"All right," Elizabeth said. "Just stay calm."

"Yes, ma'am," Freddie said, and hurried off the porch after Elizabeth.

Betsy moaned and rocked back and forth on the wagon seat.

"Help her down," Elizabeth said. "We need to get her inside right away."

Freddie reached up for his wife. "Just come on down from there, sugar. Come on down. I got you now. Don't worry. Just—"

"Oh, shut up, Freddie!"

"All right, darlin'. I will."

Freddie assisted Betsy to the ground, then looped his arm around her and steered her toward the porch. Elizabeth got on the other side of her.

"When did it start?" Elizabeth asked.

"About an hour ago," Betsy said. She pulled away from Elizabeth and clutched Freddie with both hands. Big tears suddenly rolled down her cheeks. "Oh, Freddie, I love you so much. I don't want to die having this baby."

"Now, Betsy, don't go talking like that," Freddie said, trying to look brave. "Miss Elizabeth is gonna take good care of you."

"I know that!" Betsy yelled. "Do you think I'm some kind of an idiot, Freddie Brewster?"

"No, honey pie, I don't think that at all. It's just that—"

"Ohh!" Betsy moaned and clutched her belly with both hands.

"Let's get her inside," Elizabeth said.

Together, she and Freddie got Betsy up the steps onto the porch. Connor jumped ahead of them and opened the door, his face white and his eyes wide.

"Open the surgery," Elizabeth said to Connor. He took off down the hallway.

When they arrived in the surgery, Elizabeth eased Freddie's arms from around his wife.

"I'll take it from here, Freddie," she said.

"But—" Freddie gulped. "Don't you want me to do something? Boil water, or something?"

Elizabeth gave him a smile. "No, we're fine."

"But—"

Elizabeth turned to Connor. "Can you take Freddie to the kitchen for some coffee?"

"Sure thing," Connor said, anxious to be out of there.

"But Miss Elizabeth," Freddie said, "I can't leave Betsy. Not when she's—"

"Oh, Freddie, just go on!" Betsy shouted.

Connor caught Freddie's arm and pulled him out of the room. The door shut in their faces. Both men stood there, staring at it.

Connor's stomach twisted in a knot. He didn't know anything about having babies, but the whole idea scared him. Scared the hell out of him. Freddie look scared, too. But more than that, he looked worried.

"You reckon she's gonna be all right?" Freddie asked.

Connor didn't have the slightest idea. But Freddie looked so miserable he had to say something.

"Elizabeth knows all about this sort of thing. She'll take good care of your wife."

Freddie frowned, considering his words. "Yep. I reckon you're right about that. Why, even when Doc Hill was alive most of the women went to Miss Elizabeth for their...womanly things, if you get my meaning."

Connor didn't want to think about womanly things requiring a doctor's attention.

"Let's go see if we can find some coffee," he said.

"I still think we ought to boil some water."

"All right, then," Connor said, "we'll boil water."

In the kitchen, the men hunted through the cupboards until they found pots, filled them from the pump, stoked the fire and put them on the stove. Once that was done, Freddie still looked like he was worried sick, and Connor didn't think he should walk off and leave him.

"I've got a few things to tend to in the barn," Connor said. "How about giving me a hand?"

Freddie glanced in the direction of the surgery. "I don't think I ought to leave. Betsy might need me. Miss Elizabeth might want me to bring her something."

"The surgery is on the back of the house," Connor said. "If Elizabeth needs anything she can open the window and give a yell."

Freddie mulled this over, then finally nodded. "Well, I reckon it's all right."

They left by the kitchen door at the side of the house and walked to the barn out back. It hadn't been used in a while. Boards had come loose from the adjoining paddock. Weeds sprouted.

Connor pushed open the big barn doors, letting the warm breeze blow in. Dust motes took flight. Bits of straw swirled across the dirt floor.

A row of stalls ran the length of the barn on the right side. The left, where feed and equipment might have been, was bare. Overhead was the loft.

"Looks kind of empty," Freddie mused, following Connor through the dim interior. "As I hear it, Garrett Whitmore bought all of Miss Elizabeth's stock, supplies and equipment after her pa passed on. Even bought the buggy Doc Hill used to visit his patients."

"Is that so?"

"I reckon he was just trying to help," Freddie said. "But the way I hear it, Whitmore turned around and sold that stuff and made himself a tidy profit off it. That just don't seem right to me."

Connor mumbled a curse, not bothering to hide it from Freddie.

"Doc Hill used to have a fella working here for him, looking after the place." Freddie pointed to the corner of the overhead loft. "That's where he used to live."

Connor climbed the steep, narrow staircase and opened the door to a single room. The floorboards creaked as he walked around. A bunk with a bare mattress stood in the corner, alongside a little bureau and washstand. Everything was covered with dust and grime.

"Must have been awhile since anybody lived here," Connor said.

Freddie ran his finger through the dust along the ledge of the bureau. "Looks like it."

Connor wiped a circle in the window and pressed his face close to the glass. About thirty yards separated the barn from the back of the house. He saw that the window in the surgery was open, and he thought about Elizabeth. She was one brave woman. No amount of money on this earth could get *him* inside that room right now.

He spent awhile longer poking around the room, the barn, the other outbuildings, with Freddie trailing along behind him. Connor tried to keep Freddie occupied, keep his mind off his wife, but he was about out of things to do and things to talk about. They headed back to the house.

As they approached, the kitchen door opened and both Elizabeth and Betsy walked outside.

"False alarm," Elizabeth announced when she saw them.

Freddie ran to his wife. "Are you all right, honey?"

"I'm all right, Freddie," Betsy told him, and leaned her head against his shoulder. "I just feel dumb as a tick on a dead dog for rushing over here all in a hurry, bothering Miss Elizabeth."

"It's no bother," Elizabeth assured her. "Take her home, Freddie. Let me know how things go."

"Sure thing, Miss Elizabeth." Freddie took Betsy's arm and led her away.

Connor sidled up beside Elizabeth as the young couple disappeared around the corner of the house.

"I've got to admire you for keeping a cool head, Elizabeth," he said.

She smiled up at him. "I've delivered quite a few babies in Sterling."

Connor shook his head. "You ought to be the new town doctor."

She rolled her eyes. "Don't be silly."

"What's so silly about it?"

"For one thing, I've never been to medical school," Elizabeth said, and dismissed the whole idea with a wave of her hand.

"I found the room in the barn," Connor said. "I'll fetch my horse and get moved in."

Elizabeth tucked a stray wisp of hair behind her ear.

"And this evens things between us," she said.

Connor frowned at her. "Evens things?"

A little knot tightened in Elizabeth's stomach. "That day when I came to your hotel room to thank you, you said I still owed you something for saving my life."

"I haven't forgotten," Connor said.

"Well, we're even now."

Connor shook his head. "We're not even. Not by a long shot."

"But—"

"Don't worry, Miss Hill. I'll let you know what I want...in due time."

He grinned down at her and sauntered away.

Chapter Eight

"Afternoon, Heath," Connor called, as he walked into the livery stable.

Heath looked up from the hay he was raking and leaned his pitchfork against the boards of the stall. "Come to check on your horse?" he asked.

"Come to take him off your hands," Connor said.

Heath brushed straw from his face. "Found a place to live, did you?"

Connor nodded. "Yeah. And a job."

"Glad to hear you're staying on." Heath dragged his sleeve across his sweaty forehead. "Where are you working?"

"Miss Hill's place."

Heath's eyes widened. "Elizabeth Hill? You're working for Elizabeth?"

"Living there, too."

Heath pulled on his chin. "Town's going to be talking, you know."

"I'm just a hired hand," Connor said. "Elizabeth

decided she wants to turn that big house of hers into a boardinghouse, so I'm doing the renovations for her. I'm living in the barn.''

"There'll still be tongues wagging." Heath grinned. "The ladies of Sterling will be glad to know you're staying. The way I hear it, they've about decided Dixie Brady is best suited for you."

"Who?"

"Dixie. The preacher's niece."

Connor grunted and changed the subject. "I need to rent a wagon for a few hours. I've got to pick up some supplies. You want to ride along?"

"No, I don't need anything."

"I'm going by Gunther's store."

Heath stopped short, then shrugged casually. "Well, maybe I could use a couple of things, seeing as how you're going that way."

While Connor hitched a team to the wagon, Heath scooped a bucket of water from the rain barrel, washed, combed his hair and put on a clean shirt.

Connor grinned when Heath climbed up in the seat beside him. "I appreciate you getting all duded up just to go to town with me."

Heath glared at him. "I didn't get duded up for you."

"That must mean all this is for Gena Blake."

Heath shifted on the seat. "There's nothing wrong with a man wanting to look presentable when he goes into town."

Connor flicked the reins and the team pulled away

from the livery stable. "Gena's a fine-looking woman."

"I just wish she'd get over that husband of hers," Heath grumbled. "It's hard competing with a dead man."

"Looks to me like that would give you the advantage," Connor said.

Heath grunted. "That tells you how good I am with women."

Main Street was quiet as Connor pulled the wagon to a stop in front of Gunther's General Store. He tied off the reins, set the brake and jumped down. Heath paused on the boardwalk, checked his reflection in the glass window, hitched up his trousers and followed Connor inside.

Shelves covered two walls of the store, crammed with everything from trousers to matchsticks. Displays of copper pots, cooking utensils, blankets and tools filled the aisles. A potbellied stove sat in one corner with a couple of chairs beside it.

Two people were in the store and Connor recognized them both. Jane Gunther, a younger, smaller version of her sister Gena, stood in the far corner talking to Boyd Sherman, the man she was supposed to marry. Connor wondered how much prewedded bliss they were experiencing because at the moment neither Jane nor Boyd looked very happy. In fact, Boyd looked downright mad.

Connor and Heath both stopped beside the copper pots, their attention drawn to the couple. Boyd grabbed Jane's arm and shook her hard.

"Hey!" Heath's voice boomed as he crossed the store. He shoved Boyd backward into the shelves. Canned goods clattered to the floor. Connor put himself between Jane and the two men.

"Keep your hands off her!" Heath said.

Boyd righted himself, his face red with anger. "This is none of your business!"

"I'm making it my business," Heath told him.

"No, please, it's my fault," Jane murmured, tears in her eyes.

Connor stayed in front of her, keeping her away from Boyd.

Heath pointed his finger at Boyd. "Don't you ever lay a hand on her again."

Boyd glared at Heath and Connor, then stomped out of the store.

"Boyd!" Jane called. "Boyd, wait!"

"Jane!"

Gena hurried down the aisle from the back of the store and gathered her sister in her arms.

"Oh, Gena," Jane sobbed. "Boyd—Boyd's so mad at me."

"Everything will be all right," Gena said, and patted her shoulder.

"But what if he doesn't want to marry me now?" Jane cried.

"Boyd still wants to marry you," Gena told her. "Now, go upstairs and wash your face. I'll come up and talk to you in a bit."

Jane sniffled and hurried away.

Gena watched her sister disappear through the

curtain into the back room of the store, then turned to Heath and Connor.

Heath shifted his weight from one foot to the other and cleared his throat. "Sorry about the mess," he said, and nodded toward the tins littering the floor behind them. "I know it was none of my business, but I couldn't stand by and let that happen. No man ought to ever lay a hand on a woman like that, whether they're getting married or not."

Gena looked back and forth between Heath and Connor, then grinned. "It seems Sterling is overrun with heroes these days," she said. "And thankfully so."

She moved past them and knelt to pick up the canned goods.

"Let me get that." Heath dropped to one knee alongside her and loaded the tins into his arms. When they rose, Gena touched his shoulder.

"Thank you, Heath, for helping my sister."

Startled by her touch, Heath jumped, and the cans spilled onto the floor again.

"Dammit—" Heath's face turned redder. "Sorry, ma'am. Excuse my language."

"Believe me," Gena said, "I've wanted to say far worse myself, at times."

Connor headed toward the front of the store, leaving Heath and Gena on the floor together, picking up cans and trying not to look at each other.

Elizabeth's barn had been stripped bare of any sort of tools or equipment, thanks to Garrett Whitmore, so Connor picked out what he'd need to get the renovations started. He bought some supplies, too, and placed everything on the counter.

"Do you need anything else today?" Gena asked, as she began tallying his order.

Connor pulled on his chin. "Seems like I'm forgetting something."

"Next time, make a list and drop it off. I'll fill it for you while you're in town." Gena smiled. "It's a special service we offer our special customers."

"Yes, ma'am, I'll do that," Connor said.

"Same goes for you, Heath," Gena said.

Heath knocked over the glass jar of peppermint sticks on the counter, righted it and shoved his hands in his pockets.

They loaded the supplies and equipment into the wagon, and Connor climbed up into the seat. "You going back to your shop?" he asked.

Heath shook his head. "No, I think I'll hang around town awhile."

"I'll bring back your wagon."

"Keep it as long as you need it."

Connor nodded his thanks, jangled the reins and headed the team toward Elizabeth's house. Halfway down the street, he glanced back. Heath was still standing outside Gunther's General Store.

Elizabeth sneezed, the sound echoing in the silent little room in the barn. She wiped her nose on her handkerchief, shoved it in the pocket of her skirt and stood back to admire her work.

And work it had been. She hadn't thought so

much dust and dirt could accumulate in so short a time. But maybe it hadn't been that short a time, after all. Elizabeth counted up the months since her papa died and the hired hand had left. Time was slipping past.

She'd certainly put in a full afternoon, though. Elizabeth couldn't allow Connor Wade to come to work for her and live in this little room when it was so dirty. So she'd knocked down the cobwebs, washed the walls and floors, scrubbed the window, beat the mattress and polished the furniture. She'd added a few touches to make the place seem more like home.

A lot of work to go to just for a hired hand. Elizabeth decided not to think too hard on why she'd done it.

She gathered her mop, broom, cleaning rags and bucket of dirty water and descended the steps from the room, reminding herself that was all Connor Wade meant to her. A hired hand. Nothing more. Absolutely nothing more.

A wagon swung into the driveway beside the house as Elizabeth left the barn. A smile came to her lips as she recognized Connor holding the reins.

She forced her smile away. One should not smile at one's hired help. Not even hired help as handsome as Connor Wade.

Elizabeth bit into her lower lip. *Especially* not hired help as handsome as Connor Wade.

He stopped the team and jumped to the ground.

"What have you been doing?" he asked, and took the bucket of water from her hand.

Elizabeth smoothed a stray lock of hair behind her ear, realizing that she must look a mess. She had on the old green gingham dress she always wore when she cleaned, and a scarf wrapped around her head.

"Cleaning your room," she said, and nodded toward the barn.

"I didn't want you to do that," Connor declared, and tossed the dirty water into the grass. "You've got enough to do already."

Elizabeth peered over the side of the wagon. "You bought supplies? I'm supposed to provide meals. That's our arrangement."

"I got a look at your pantry, Miss Hill. You eat like a bird." Connor hoisted a sack of flour onto his shoulder and went into the kitchen.

Elizabeth followed him inside and put the supplies away as he made trip after trip into the house. Her pantry and cupboard filled up quickly. She hadn't had so much food in the house since her father and brother lived there.

When they finished, Connor drove the wagon to the barn, unloaded the building supplies, then called to Elizabeth as he once again pulled the team to a stop outside the kitchen door. She stuck her head out.

"I'm taking Heath's wagon back," Connor said. "Do you need anything from town?"

"I can't imagine anything we could possibly

need, after all this shopping you've done today,'' Elizabeth said with a smile.

Connor paused. ''You want to ride along?''

Elizabeth's breath caught. Yes, yes she wanted to ride along. She'd almost bolted for the wagon when the image of faces glaring up at her from the board-walk stopped her still in her tracks. Gracious, people would certainly talk if they saw her parading herself through town with Connor Wade.

''No, no thank you,'' Elizabeth said. ''I'd better not.''

''Suit yourself. I'll be back in a while.'' Connor flicked the reins and drove away.

Elizabeth stood in the kitchen doorway, watching until he'd driven out of sight.

Consoling herself with the thought that she'd done the right thing, Elizabeth went up to her room, washed and changed into a dark blue dress. She went back to the kitchen. Seemed she had supper to prepare. She had a hired hand to feed.

Elizabeth debated how many potatoes to cook. For herself, she'd need only one. But how much would Connor eat? She didn't want to run short, but she didn't want to waste food, either.

He was a big man and probably had a hearty ap-petite. Elizabeth laid out three more potatoes, then went back to the pantry.

After much thought, she fried chicken and boiled potatoes and carrots. Elizabeth couldn't remember when she'd made such a big meal. When her father was alive, they'd had guests over often. He liked company, and they had social obligations. Since his death, Elizabeth served refreshments to an occasional guest, or the ladies when they got together to plan a social. But she never cooked a full meal. Certainly not a meal for a man—hired hand or not.

Humming as she worked, Elizabeth found herself looking forward to supper tonight. She usually dreaded her evening meal, alone in the quiet house, with empty hours ahead of her until she went to bed. A smile came to her lips. Tonight she wouldn't be alone. This hired hand idea was a good one.

Just as she was cutting out the biscuits, Connor rode past the kitchen window toward the barn on his horse, retrieved from the livery stable. A few minutes later, he knocked on the back door.

"You're just in time," Elizabeth said, opening the door. "Biscuits are hot out of the oven. Come inside."

Connor shook his head. "I'll eat in the barn."

Elizabeth looked down at him standing at the bottom of the steps, disappointment tightening her chest.

"That's our arrangement," Connor said.

"Well, yes. Of course."

Elizabeth heaped a plate full of food and covered it with a linen towel.

"There's more, if you want," she said, and passed it down to him.

"This will be fine." Connor tipped his hat politely and headed for the barn.

Elizabeth shut the door, then leaned back against it and squeezed her eyes closed.

Connor paused in the doorway to his room in the barn. Just enough light from the setting sun filtered through the window to give him a good look at his new home. He recognized Elizabeth's touch. She'd done a lot more than clean the place.

White linens were on the bunk, topped by a yellow coverlet. Priscilla curtains covered the window. She'd somehow managed to get a small table and chair up here and had wedged them into the corner. A plate, cup and saucer, and cutlery were stacked neatly on the table. A coffeepot sat on the little stove.

Connor grinned. A vase of flowers sat on the windowsill.

He leaned forward and sniffed the blooms. He had no idea what kind they were. To anyone else they would have smelled like flowers, but Connor was sure they smelled like Elizabeth.

Seated at the table, Connor ate the meal Elizabeth had prepared. He ate slowly, savoring each bite, thinking of her inside the house, eating by herself at the table in the kitchen.

When he finished, he stripped off his clothes, washed, then settled between the linen sheets Elizabeth had put on his bed. He propped himself up against the two pillows she'd brought him and folded his hands behind his head.

Through the window beside his bed, Connor saw lantern light appear in one of the rooms on the second floor. He sat forward.

Elizabeth's bedroom.

Though the shade was pulled down tight, he imagined her inside her room, going through her nightly ritual before bed. Taking off her shoes, her dress, all those undergarments women wore. Peeling them away, one by one, until she was naked, her pale skin glowing in the lantern light. Plucking the pins from her hair, one by one, letting it fall loose around her bare shoulders.

Did she stand in front of a mirror and brush it out? he wondered. Did she sleep with it down? Proper women put their hair up at night. But since Elizabeth lived alone, did she allow herself that one scandalous act?

Heat simmered inside Connor, building with each new imagined scene. He didn't usually fantasize about women, didn't usually need to. But there was something about Elizabeth...

Connor's chest tightened a little as he wondered what Elizabeth would do if she knew the truth about him. What would the prim and proper Elizabeth Hill say if she found out he'd been in prison?

Connor scrubbed his palms over his face, knowing he'd be better off avoiding all these conjured up scenes of a naked Elizabeth, and sticking to business. The business that had brought him to Sterling in the first place.

His damned pride had caused him to change his tactics some, but his reason for coming here hadn't changed. He had access to the house now. He'd get what he'd come here for, one way or the other.

Chapter Nine

The thud of hammer against wood brought Elizabeth from under the coverlet, squinting at the morning sunlight. She rubbed her eyes as she stumbled to the window and raised the shade.

At the corral beside the barn, Connor nailed loose boards in place. Elizabeth sank to her knees, looking out the window, watching the play of his muscles through his shirt, his long arms as he swung the hammer, his fingers as they gripped the handle.

What a sight to awaken to.

Elizabeth rested her palms on the windowsill. She'd seen that the corral fence needed fixing months ago, but lacked the expertise to repair it herself. Now Connor was doing it, and she hadn't even asked him to.

How nice to have a hired hand. How nice to have Connor.

He spun around quickly, searching the rear of the house before his gaze settled on her bedroom window. Elizabeth jumped back and plopped down on the floor. Gracious, had he seen her watching him?

She sat up, pushing her hair off her face. Well, he was her hired hand and she could watch him if she wanted to. Couldn't she?

On hands and knees, Elizabeth crept to the window, reached up and yanked the shade down. Maybe she needed more time to get used to the idea of having a hired hand around the place.

A little tremor passed through her. No, she needed to get used to having Connor Wade around.

If that were possible.

Elizabeth washed, dressed and twisted her hair atop her head, then went downstairs. She put on coffee, and as it bubbled on the stove, she fried bacon and eggs. A knock sounded on the back door just as she pulled biscuits from the oven. She opened the door and found Connor standing on her porch. He looked hale and hearty from the work he'd been doing this morning.

"I was just coming for you," Elizabeth said. "Breakfast is ready."

"I know." Connor grinned. "I smelled it cooking."

"Come in," Elizabeth said.

Connor hesitated. "I'll eat outside."

"It's just a quick meal. You may as well eat in here." And really, it made perfect sense that he did. Just this once. Just for breakfast.

Elizabeth put two place settings on the table as Connor ambled inside. He filled their cups while

Elizabeth brought platters of food to the table. Connor held out her chair. She gave him an awkward smile and sat down.

"You're up working bright and early this morning," Elizabeth said, passing him the eggs.

"I wanted to get the corral fixed so my horse can exercise," Connor said, buttering a biscuit. "He doesn't like staying cooped up in the stall."

"Not much has been done around here since my brother...left."

"Went to prison, you mean?"

"Yes...went to prison," Elizabeth said. "Anyway, I appreciate your fixing the corral."

"I saw a few other things around here that need attention. I can take care of them, if you want."

"It's not part of our deal," Elizabeth said. "I don't want you to think I'm taking advantage of you."

Connor paused, his fork halfway to his mouth. "Feel free to take advantage of me anytime the mood strikes you, Miss Hill."

A warm shudder whipped through Elizabeth. She kept her eyes on her plate, afraid she'd blush.

"To tell you the truth, I think I'm getting the better part of this deal." Connor waved his fork over his plate. "This is the best food I've had in a long time."

Elizabeth smiled. "Thank you. I'm making my apple pie for the Founders' Day festival."

"I see another first prize ribbon coming your way," Connor said.

"Was your room comfortable?" Elizabeth asked. "Did you sleep well last night?"

Connor had hardly slept a wink last night, but it wasn't because his bunk was uncomfortable. Images of Elizabeth had kept him flopping around like a fish on a riverbank.

A knock sounded at the back door before he could give Elizabeth an answer to her question. She got up and answered.

"Oh." Elizabeth glanced back at Connor, then stepped away from the door.

Garrett Whitmore strode into the kitchen, glaring down at Elizabeth.

"I just heard a rumor in town, Elizabeth," he said. "I heard that Connor Wade was living here with you, and I don't have to tell you that—"

"Morning, Whitmore," Connor called. He lifted his cup from the saucer. "Have some coffee with us?"

Garrett's spine stiffened. His frown deepened and he turned back to Elizabeth.

She twisted her fingers together. "Mr. Wade is working here for me."

"Working?" Garrett cast a doubtful glance at Connor.

"Yes," Elizabeth told him. "I'm turning my home into a boardinghouse. I discussed it with you on Sunday, remember?"

"Well, yes, of course I remember. But—"

"Mr. Wade was gracious enough to agree to do the work in exchange for room and board," Elizabeth said. "In light of my financial situation, I didn't see how I could refuse his offer."

Garrett glared at Connor as if he could think of a thousand ways Elizabeth could have refused that offer.

"Maybe you'd like to kick in the cost of the labor?" Connor suggested. "Pay me outright?"

Garrett tugged on his vest, ignoring Connor. "Well, as long as it's for a good cause," he said. "How many pies are you baking today, Elizabeth?"

"Pies? Goodness, I hadn't really thought about it."

"You'd better get on it. The restaurants will be waiting," Garrett said. "And the new doctor will arrive in a few days. I'll bring him over right away to look at your father's equipment."

Elizabeth's shoulders sagged a little. "All right."

Connor raised his cup again. "Sure you won't have some coffee with us?"

Garrett opened the back door. "I'll be back later on to check on you, Elizabeth."

"I'm perfectly all right."

"I'll come back, just in case." Garret cast a glance at Connor, then left.

Elizabeth closed the door. "I knew this would happen."

"What's that?"

"The talk. It certainly didn't take long for the town to know what I'm doing—and start talking about me again."

"You had to figure Whitmore would come over,"

Connor said. "Seeing as how you two have that *understanding.*"

"Understanding?" Elizabeth turned to him. "What understanding?"

"The understanding that you two are getting married."

"Married!" Elizabeth's mouth flew open. "Who told you that?"

"Whitmore," Connor said, and rose from his chair.

"Of all the nerve." Elizabeth flatted her arms at her sides. "I have no intention of marrying Garrett Whitmore."

"So, what? You're just leading him on?"

Elizabeth's eyes widened. "Of course not! I never said—never even hinted—that I was remotely interested in Garrett."

Connor shrugged. "He thinks you are."

"Well, I'm not."

"Maybe you're giving him that impression, when you really don't mean to?"

Elizabeth gasped and looked up at Connor. "Could I be doing that? I mean, do you think I am?"

Connor gazed at her face. Carefully, he caught a strand of her hair and brushed it off her cheek.

"A woman like you, Elizabeth, is liable to make a man think all sorts of thoughts."

Her heart beat a little faster at the feel of Connor's fingertips lingering on her cheek. She could have lost herself in that feel, lost herself completely.

"I try hard to be a proper lady," Elizabeth said softly.

"You're a fine lady." Connor stroked his fingers through the loose hair at the back of her neck. "But you don't have to be a lady every minute of every day."

Elizabeth gazed up at him. "That sounds like something men say when they want to have their way with a woman."

Connor eased closer. "There's no denying I'd like to kiss you, Elizabeth."

She was surprised by his honesty, and his boldness. He'd told her. Said it out loud. Right to her face.

And now that he had, Elizabeth's mouth went dry. No man had kissed her before, not the way a man kissed a woman. Not with passion. Somehow, she knew that's how Connor Wade would kiss her.

Her whole body burned from the nearness of him. She could almost taste his lips, they were so close.

"Are you going to kiss me?" she whispered.

"Do you want me to?

"Well..."

"If you're not sure, I won't kiss you." Connor's hand stilled on the back of her neck.

"Wait." Elizabeth caught his arm. "Do you want to kiss me?"

A big smile spread over his lips. "I've wanted to kiss you since the day I laid eyes on you outside the bank."

"But I punched you in the stomach."

"I know," Connor said. "I figured any woman with that much spirit was a woman I just had to kiss."

Her stomach quivered. "Really?"

"Really." Connor leaned close again. "So, can I kiss you?"

"Well…"

"Is that a yes or a no?"

"Well…"

Connor looped his arm around her waist. "How about if I give you just a little kiss? I'll stop when you tell me to."

"How can I tell you to stop if you're kissing me?"

"Just punch me in the gut again. I'll get the message."

Elizabeth giggled. "All right."

Connor lowered his head and brushed his lips against hers in a quick, easy motion.

Elizabeth frowned. "That really was a little kiss. I was expecting something…bigger."

"I can do that, too," Connor said.

"Really?"

"Really. Do you want me to?"

"Well…"

"I'll take it as a yes."

Connor tightened his arms around Elizabeth and pulled her closer, then covered her lips with his. Gently he plied her, moving slowly until she relaxed. Connor groaned and deepened their kiss. Elizabeth went limp in his arms.

She'd never imagined anything so wonderful. Connor's strong arms around her, the feel of his chest brushing her breasts. And his mouth, warm and soft, devouring hers so pleasurably. Her head spun.

When he lifted his head, ending their kiss, she didn't move, just stayed in his arms.

"Is that...all?" she asked.

Connor gazed down at her and grinned. "Didn't you like it?"

"Oh, yes, very much," she said quickly.

Connor heaved a sigh and released Elizabeth. "I'd better get out of here or nothing will get done today."

He left the kitchen. Elizabeth watched out the window as he disappeared into the barn.

She floated through the morning, doing her chores, thinking about Connor. She still tasted his kiss on her lips, felt his arms around her.

By noon the day had grown warmer. Elizabeth opened the windows as she prepared their meal. She warmed ham steaks, heated potatoes and carrots from last night's supper and what was left of this morning's biscuits, listening to the steady ring of the hammer pounding away behind the house. She loaded everything onto a serving tray along with a glass of lemonade and left the kitchen.

Elizabeth's steps slowed as she approached the barn and saw Connor working in the corral. His shirt was off. Beads of perspiration rolled down his big bare back. When he turned, she saw the hair on his chest glistening wet in the sunlight.

The sun overhead seemed to have heated up another few degrees as Elizabeth watched him working. She gave herself a little shake and started walking again.

Goodness, she was acting crazy. She'd seen a man's bare chest before. In fact, she'd seen her brother without his shirt more times than she could count, when they were children, after they were grown. And Connor Wade's chest was just like her brother's.

Except for his wide shoulders. And his hard muscles. And, of course, his big arms.

Slipping through the gate, she rounded the corner of the barn and froze. Connor wasn't alone in the corral. Dixie Brady was with him. Apparently, Elizabeth had been so busy in the house this morning she hadn't seen the preacher's niece walk by.

Dixie Brady, young, pretty, stood in the shade twirling her parasol, smiling at Connor as he worked. She had on a pink dress with lace at the cuffs, and her blond hair was artfully arranged under a sassy little hat. Connor must have been more humorous than Elizabeth ever realized, because Dixie giggled with every word he spoke.

"I brought your meal," Elizabeth announced.

Connor and Dixie both stopped and looked up at her. Dixie, at least, had the good grace to look uncomfortable.

"Hello, Elizabeth," she said, smiling and twirling her parasol.

Elizabeth placed the tray on the bench at the side of the barn and yanked Connor's shirt off the fence post where he'd left it. She thrust it at him.

"Put this on," she said. "You'll be more comfortable out of the sun."

Connor looked at her for a moment, then took the shirt and pulled it on over his hot, sticky body. The heavy material clung to him as he pulled it in place and fastened the buttons.

"Thank you, Miss Hill," he said, eyeing her and tugging at the collar. "This is so much better."

"Eat, before it gets cold," Elizabeth said. She turned to Dixie. "So, what brings you out here?"

"Just being neighborly," Dixie said, glancing around her at Connor. "I guess I'd better be getting back to town. Bye, Connor."

He tipped his hat before settling onto the bench beside the tray of food. Elizabeth watched Dixie until her lacy parasol disappeared around the corner of the house, then turned to Connor, who was holding his plate and eating as if nothing were wrong.

For a moment, Elizabeth didn't know whether to be hurt or angry. After another moment, she settled for anger.

Only hours ago, in the middle of her kitchen, Connor had taken her in his arms. He'd kissed her. Really kissed her. The way a man kissed a woman. And now she'd walked out to her barn to find him keeping company with the likes of Dixie Brady.

Elizabeth stomped over to him. "I think I deserve some kind of explanation."

Connor paused, a forkful of carrots hovering over his plate. "For what?"

"For you being back here alone with that Dixie Brady."

Connor chewed and swallowed, then shrugged. "She just came by to visit."

"Visit! You call that visiting, the way she was ogling you?"

"I was working on the fence," Connor said, waving his fork across the corral.

"You have got some kind of nerve, Connor Wade. Kissing me, then keeping company with another woman right under my nose."

Connor's brows drew together in a frown. "What the hell are you talking about?"

Elizabeth marched over and yanked the plate from his hand.

"Make your own food from now on."

"Hey—"

She snatched up his cup of lemonade and dumped it on the ground, splattering his boots. "Better still, just forget everything. Our deal is off."

Dumbfounded, Connor looked down at his boots, then up at her. "Elizabeth—"

She spun away, then turned back and jerked the fork from his hand.

"And your chest *does so* look like my brother's!"

Elizabeth put her nose in the air and stomped away.

Connor caught up with her halfway across the yard. He put himself in front of her, and when she ducked around him, he grasped her arm with just enough pressure to stop her in her tracks.

"Look, Elizabeth, you've got this all wrong," he said. "That woman just stopped by to visit."

"I didn't see it that way." Elizabeth pulled against him.

Connor didn't let go. Instead, he wrapped his arms around her and crushed her to his chest. Plate, food and cup fell to the ground.

"You didn't see me do this to her, did you?"

Connor's mouth covered Elizabeth's, hot and full. He worked his lips against hers with a command she hadn't felt this morning in the kitchen. Heat bloomed deep inside her, bringing life to places she'd never felt before. He feathered his tongue against her lips until she parted them, then he filled her mouth.

Elizabeth moaned. The fire inside her flamed. *This* was a real kiss.

Unable, and unwilling, to stop him, Elizabeth curled her fingers into his shirt and clung to Connor as his tongue continued to work its magic. She did the same to him. Some force inside her made her respond. Made her press herself closer until her thighs touched his, her breasts contacted his chest.

Connor broke off their kiss and held her arms, stepping back to break contact.

"Our deal isn't off," he told her. "I'm not leaving."

He released her. Elizabeth staggered a step or two, weak without his strong arms to hold her upright. Connor stalked away.

Inside the barn, Connor paced, slamming his fist into his open palm. He'd wanted to kiss Elizabeth Hill. Hell, he'd wanted to do a lot more than kiss her since he'd first laid eyes on her. Well, he'd done it. He'd kissed her. Now he couldn't stop.

Somehow, he had to. This wasn't what he'd come here for. This wasn't what he wanted her for.

Connor cursed in the silent barn. But there was no turning back now.

Chapter Ten

Two days now and Elizabeth still hadn't spoken to him.

Connor left his room in the barn, wondering if things would be any better this morning. He hadn't seen her since he'd kissed her in the corral, except when he'd gotten his meals from her. Then, she'd refused to talk to him, just fed him out the back door like a stray dog.

No, he decided, Elizabeth would have treated a stray dog better.

Connor approached the house, hoping she'd gotten over whatever was bothering her. He also hoped the gray clouds overhead weren't an omen.

Of course, he could have said to hell with Elizabeth Hill and gone into town at any time over these past few days, had a beer or found himself a woman. But none of that seemed appealing.

Instead, he'd lain in his bunk on the linens that smelled like Elizabeth, looking at her bedroom window every night, letting his imagination run away with him.

But all the thoughts in his head weren't his imagination. He'd held Elizabeth in his arms. He'd kissed her. She'd kissed him back.

Connor didn't pretend to understand women. Consequently, he didn't know exactly why Elizabeth was mad at him. He could take a guess, though.

He'd done the polite thing and asked if he could kiss her—something he'd never done before with any woman. She'd said yes. That shouldn't be what was upsetting her, but maybe it was.

And just what was so all fired wrong with Dixie Brady talking to him at the barn he didn't know, either, but Elizabeth had been pretty upset about that, too.

Connor shoved his hands into his trouser pockets. Of course, he hadn't asked Elizabeth if he could kiss her in the corral. He'd just done it. He'd really kissed her, too, and there'd been nothing polite about it.

Maybe that's what Elizabeth was mad about. If so, her anger was building up a steady head of steam these past couple of days. She hadn't spoken to him. His meal portions kept growing smaller. He'd smelled apple pie baking, but a slice never appeared on his plate.

Connor paused outside the back door and blew out a heavy breath. Elizabeth was going to talk to him today, whether she wanted to or not.

He rapped on the door. After a moment the curtain over the window in the door pulled back and Elizabeth's face appeared. She glared at him, hostile and cold. But all Connor could think was how pretty she looked.

Finally, she opened the door. ''Breakfast isn't ready. Come back later.''

''Miss Hill—'' The door slammed shut.

Connor stared at the closed door for a few seconds, then yanked his hat lower on his head and knocked again. A full minute dragged by without so much as her face appearing at the window. Connor made a fist and banged on the door. He pounded and pounded until finally it was jerked open.

''Would you just stop that?'' she demanded, glaring down at him.

''No, I won't. Not until—''

She pushed the door closed, but Connor braced his arm against it, holding it open. Elizabeth threw her weight into the effort, but got nowhere. She planted herself in the doorway and crossed her arms in front of her.

''I have nothing to say to you.''

''That suits me fine because I'm not in the mood to listen to anything you have to say,'' Connor said. ''I came to tell you something, not listen to you talk.''

''Of all the nerve—''

''First off, I'm done with the work in the barn. I need to get started on the house today,'' Connor told her. ''And second, I need something from your pa's surgery.''

"Papa's surgery? What's wrong?"

A tiny bit of concern showed in her expression, the only thing vaguely resembling civility he'd seen from her in days.

"I got a sliver of wood stuck in my hand a couple of days ago and I can't get it out."

"Let me see."

Connor held out his left hand. Elizabeth took it, turned it toward the light and leaned closer.

"This has already started to fester." She looked up at him. "Why did you wait so long? You should have told me when it happened."

"You weren't speaking to me."

"I'm not speaking to you now, either, yet here you are." She dropped his hand. "Come along."

Connor hung his hat on the peg beside the back door, then trailed after her through the house toward her father's surgery. He walked slowly, not in much of a hurry to get there. Not when he could watch Elizabeth's bustle bobbing ahead of him down the hallway.

She had on a black skirt and white blouse this morning, and her hair was done up on top of her head, as usual. Elizabeth didn't look fancy, just pretty. And touchable. Very touchable.

Connor wanted to touch her. Two nights of thinking about their kiss had only made him yearn to do it again. And somehow the fact that she didn't seem to want him around made him desire her even more.

Elizabeth opened the door to her father's surgery and led the way into the examination room. Efficiently, she rifled through glass cabinets and assembled items on the examination table.

"Let me have your hand," she said.

Connor waited in the doorway. "I don't usually go to the doctor."

"Most men don't," Elizabeth said.

"Women come here a lot," Connor said. "I noticed them coming and going the last few days."

"Women are smart when it comes to medical matters." Though she hadn't said it, it was clear Elizabeth considered men just the opposite.

He nodded toward the books on the shelf. "Have you read all of those?"

"Most of them."

"They belong to your pa?"

"You're stalling."

Connor shifted his weight from one foot to the other. "No, I was just—"

"Stalling."

He looked at his hand. "Now that I think on it a little more, it's not that bad. Maybe I should just—"

"You may as well get it over with," Elizabeth said. She crossed the room, caught his wrist and led him to the examination table, then circled to the other side.

Connor eyed the medical paraphernalia and his stomach rolled. "Is this going to hurt?" he asked.

"Of course." Elizabeth glanced up at him and a hint of a smile touched her lips. "But I give peppermint sticks to all the brave little boys who come in here."

Connor frowned. ''I don't especially like peppermint.''

''Then I'm sure I have something you'll like.''

She already had something he liked, but Connor doubted seriously she'd give out samples of that today.

Elizabeth gently patted the back of his hand. ''Just relax. This won't take a minute.''

She unfastened the button on his cuff and rolled it back, then held his hand in hers over the basin she'd set out.

''You might not want to watch this,'' Elizabeth said.

He didn't want to watch any kind of medical procedure. But he wanted to watch Elizabeth, so that's what he did.

He'd thought so much about her, lying in his bunk at night and working in the barn during the day, that it felt wonderful to see her again. As if he'd been thirsty for a long time and now could drink his fill.

And better yet, she was touching him. Her hands were soft and gentle. She smelled good. Even inside the surgery, where all sort of odors warred, Connor only smelled Elizabeth.

Why did he have to meet her now? he wondered. Why couldn't she have come along earlier in his life? Things might have turned out so differently for him with a woman like Elizabeth at his side.

Why meet her now when she could only be disappointed in him?

Connor's chest ached a little at the thought. He

knew he couldn't go back and change the things that had happened, change the things he'd done.

He couldn't change the things he still intended to do. And that made his chest hurt worse.

Connor watched the little frown lines in Elizabeth's forehead as she concentrated on plucking the wood splinters from his finger. Watched the way her lips pressed together, her eyes as they focused on the task.

He glanced at the books that she'd read and studied. Such a smart woman. Pretty, too. And desirable. Connor felt that desire stirring in him.

"This might sting a bit," Elizabeth said.

"I didn't feel a—yeow!"

So much for desire.

He pulled away, but Elizabeth held his hand over the basin as she poured a smelly brown liquid over his finger. She smiled up at him and set the bottle aside.

"All done," she said, and dried his finger with a fresh cloth.

Connor grumbled silently, studying his hand, while Elizabeth unrolled a length of bandage. She wrapped his wound and tied it snugly, and Connor decided he was no worse for the experience.

"You're a good doctor," he said. "I don't know what the town needs with that new one they've got coming."

"He's trained at a medical school, for one thing," Elizabeth said. "He's a real doctor."

"You could go to one of those medical schools," Connor said. "Didn't you ever think about it?"

"I used to. A long time ago when I was young." Elizabeth smiled at the memory. "I used to dream that I'd go off somewhere to a little town that had no doctor, and heal the sick, take care of the wounded."

Connor followed her to the cabinet and stood behind her as she returned the bottles to their shelves.

"So why didn't you do that?" he asked.

Elizabeth shrugged. "There aren't many women who are doctors. People aren't very accepting of the few that are. And medical school costs a great deal of money."

"Your pa would have paid for your schooling," Connor said.

"Maybe." Elizabeth shook her head. "But can you imagine what everyone in town would have said about it?"

She busied herself cleaning up the surgery, putting things away. Connor didn't ordinarily like a doctor's office, but couldn't bring himself to leave.

"I guess I owe you an apology," he said.

She looked up at him. "An apology? For what?"

"Kissing you like that."

Right before his eyes she turned stiff and frosty.

"We kissed? Oh, I'd forgotten," she said, and went on with her work.

"You *forgot?*" Connor pulled on the back of his neck. "Damn... And that was the best kiss I ever gave a woman."

She whirled. "It was?"

Connor glared at her. "I knew you remembered."

Elizabeth's cheeks pinkened. "Our kiss? It was the best you've given?"

"So far." Connor edge a little closer. "I can do a lot better, though. I haven't had much practice lately."

She dipped her lashes. "But you're sorry you kissed me?"

"Hell, no," Connor told her. "I said I apologize. I never said I was sorry."

Connor touched her chin and tilted her face up. "Are you sorry I kissed you, Elizabeth?"

That kiss of his had caused her to feel a lot of things in the past two days, but *sorry* wasn't one of them. She'd thought about it, played it over and over in her mind, tasted it again and again. Her body had tingled where he'd touched her. The whole thing had been positively scandalous. Positively…wonderful.

"I'm not sorry," Elizabeth said. "But it's not proper for a man and woman to kiss like that."

"Who said so?"

"Well…" Elizabeth pursed her lips. "Well, nobody said it. Everyone just *knows* it."

"Nobody ever told me."

Elizabeth smiled. "That's because you're not trying to be a lady."

"You're a fine lady, Elizabeth." Connor touched his hand to her arm, gently stroking his fingers against her sleeve. "But don't you think it's all right to be a woman sometimes?"

She frowned. "Well, I don't know…"

Connor moved closer until their bodies almost touched.

"Because if you were a woman sometimes, not just a lady, I could keep practicing my kisses. Keep improving."

Warmth arrowed through Elizabeth, raced down her limbs, swelled her heart. Connor inched nearer. His warm breath fanned her mouth.

"I—I don't think you need any more practice," she whispered.

"You're sure?"

"Well…no, not entirely."

Connor grinned. "I'll give you one more kiss to help you make up your mind."

He didn't wait for her answer, and it was just as well. She didn't have enough air in her lungs to say anything.

His lips came down on hers, sealing them together. Her knees weakened. She clamped on to his shoulders to keep herself upright.

Connor groaned and pressed deeper. Elizabeth parted her lips for him. Two days ago—and in the days that followed—it had seemed outrageous, scandalous that he should touch her so intimately. Now it seemed familiar. She welcomed him inside her and greeted him in the same way.

He raised his head, his breath hot against her face.

"Well?" he asked. "Was that better than the kiss in the corral?"

"No, honestly, I don't think so."

Connor frowned. "Damn, woman..."

He kissed her again. This time he wrapped both arms around her and pulled her full against him. With one hand he dug into the hair at the nape of her neck. With the other he pressed the small of her back until she leaned backward over the examination table.

When he released her, Elizabeth collapsed onto the table, catching herself with her elbows.

"Oh, yes..." She breathed heavily, trying to stay on her feet. "That one was definitely better."

Connor braced his arms against the table, panting. "Yep. I'd say so."

They both stayed that way for a few moments, their heavy breathing the only sound in the room.

Finally, Elizabeth righted herself and nervously straightened her clothes. She glanced at Connor, at his trousers, and blushed bright red.

He stepped behind the examination table, but it was too late. There was no way he could hide that.

"We...we shouldn't do this anymore," Elizabeth said, brushing at her sleeves.

"You're probably right," Connor said, dragging his arm across his forehead.

"I'll go fix breakfast now."

"I'll be here a few more minutes," Connor said.

Elizabeth edged toward the door, but couldn't help looking back at him. Determinedly she kept her gaze on his face, but at the last second it dipped to his fly.

Elizabeth's face turned brighter red and she raced from the room.

He paced around in the surgery, trying to get himself under control. Elizabeth was right. He shouldn't kiss her anymore. Stopping was proving too difficult. And kissing was becoming not quite enough.

Images of Elizabeth sprang into his mind, and Connor had to struggle to force them away. He'd never be fit to walk out of the surgery, at this rate.

As a last resort, Connor opened one of the medicine bottles in the cabinet and took a big whiff. He reeled back at the stench.

Connor shoved the bottle back inside. That sure as hell took the desire out of him. Most of it, anyway.

He closed the door to the surgery and headed through the house. He planned to work off the rest of his desire in the barnyard, but voices drew him toward the front door. He waited in the hallway, out of sight, listening.

Mrs. Canter, Ike's wife, was talking to Elizabeth, and Elizabeth was apologizing profusely.

"Gracious, Mrs. Canter, I'd forgotten all about our meeting this morning," Elizabeth said. "I'm so sorry. Really I am. I—I don't know where my mind was all morning long."

"Abigail is expecting us," Mrs. Canter said. "We have to finalize the plans for Founders' Day. There's much to be done and little time left."

"I'll just get my wrap and we can go," Elizabeth said.

Connor heard her footsteps to the kitchen and back, then voices again, and finally the front door closed. At the parlor window, he peeked out and saw Elizabeth and Mrs. Canter heading toward town. For several moments he watched the women as they walked down the dusty road, then disappeared from sight.

Connor stepped back, the silence of the still rooms enveloping him. Had Elizabeth forgotten he was in the house? Or did she already trust him enough that she didn't give it a thought?

Connor stood there for a while waiting, just in case. He heard no voices, no footsteps on the front porch. No sign the women had returned.

At last he was satisfied Elizabeth was gone.

And finally, he had the house to himself.

Chapter Eleven

All the ladies at the meeting predicted this Founders' Day celebration would be the best one ever. But Elizabeth could do no more than smile and nod in agreement, because she hadn't paid the least bit of attention to the plans being made today.

Seated in Abigail Rogers's parlor, Elizabeth struggled to keep her mind on the conversation, the suggestions, the disagreements—and there were plenty of each. The four other women seated around her seldom got through a committee meeting without some controversy, and today was no exception.

But instead of adding her opinion, Elizabeth said little. How could she join in? She couldn't keep up with the meeting. All she could think of was Connor.

A little tremor rippled through Elizabeth, causing the teacup in her hand to clatter. Quickly, she glanced around, saw the other women still talking, and set the cup aside.

Elizabeth's cheeks warmed. Everything warmed, in fact. The memory of the kiss Connor had given her in her father's surgery this morning played over and over in her mind. Her body reacted each time.

Could the other women see the difference in her? Did they suspect what she'd done just minutes before coming to the mayor's house? Was it obvious she'd been kissed—really kissed? And had liked it?

Kissed by Connor Wade. The mysterious stranger in Sterling. The town hero. Her hired hand.

When she'd arrived at this morning's meeting, the minister's wife had confided to the group that Dixie Brady was quite taken with Connor. She wasn't alone, Mrs. Canter had countered. Nearly every young woman who'd seen or heard about Connor was interested in him.

No one in the room suggested Elizabeth was one of those women. Certainly not at her age. Given her situation, Elizabeth was glad.

Founders' Day was over a week away. Planning had gone on for months, but much still needed doing. Each woman reported on her area of responsibility—Elizabeth managed to sound intelligent when called on—and Abigail Rogers nodded thoughtfully. The meeting was finally adjourned.

Anxious to leave, Elizabeth headed for the door, but Abigail called to her. "I need to speak with you, Elizabeth."

A lump knotted in Elizabeth's stomach. Had she imagined the disapproving tone in the mayor's wife's voice? Did the woman know she'd been kissing Connor Wade? At that instant it flashed in her mind that perhaps Dixie Brady had sneaked back to the house and seen them kissing in the corral. Was Elizabeth about to become grist for the town's gossip mill—again?

She pressed her lips together, fearful she might start to perspire.

The other women gave her curious glances as they left Abigail's parlor. Elizabeth smiled politely as they filed by, trying her darnedest to look innocent.

Abigail closed the door behind the other women. She looked hard at Elizabeth for a moment.

Elizabeth felt dampness on her forehead.

Abigail straightened her shoulders. "There is a matter which I feel I must discuss with you, Elizabeth."

She tried harder to look innocent. "Yes, Mrs. Rogers?"

"I've heard a rumor," Abigail said. She frowned slightly. "A rumor about you."

"Oh?" The word came out as a squeak. A guilty squeak.

"Is it true that you intend to convert your home to a boardinghouse?"

Relief weakened Elizabeth's knees. It took all her strength not to collapse.

"Yes, it's true," she said. "I have all those rooms, and I need the income, and Sterling could use a respectable place for boarders, and—"

Elizabeth stopped, realizing that she was running

on. Realizing, too, that Abigail Rogers was still frowning.

"Some people in Sterling don't think it's a good idea," Abigail said, her brows drawn together in a deep scowl. "Not a good idea at all, what with you being an unmarried woman, living alone."

Elizabeth held her breath waiting for Abigail to finish.

"I agree with them," the mayor's wife said. "I suggest you watch yourself, Elizabeth. You'd be wise to consider the consequences of your actions. The last thing Sterling needs is another scandal."

Elizabeth's family had already provided plenty of that.

"I intend to be very careful about who I rent rooms to," Elizabeth assured her.

She thought she was off the hook now, but Abigail's gaze still drilled into her. "The other ladies and I intend to keep an eye on your situation."

"You have nothing to worry about," Elizabeth promised.

Abigail folded her hands in front of her. "Nor would we want anything unseemly going on at your home *now,*" she said. "I understand Mr. Wade is living there."

Elizabeth's stomach heaved and her heartbeat quickened as visions of Connor filled her head. Connor and all the kissing that had been going on at her house.

"Mr. Wade is doing the renovations," Elizabeth

said, "in exchange for room and board. He's living in the barn."

Abigail's expression softened marginally and she leaned a little closer. "Mr. Wade has caused quite a stir among the young women of our town, as I'm sure you know. I trust you'll keep an eye on things, make certain nothing untoward goes on."

Elizabeth gulped, realizing what Abigail meant. She wanted Elizabeth to make certain nothing went on between Connor and any of the young women in town.

But instead of being relieved, she felt a new sort of hurt come over her. It had never occurred to Abigail that anything might go on between herself and Connor. Elizabeth, the town spinster. The old maid. The very last woman expected to find a husband. Why would Connor Wade be interested in her?

"I'll keep an eye on things," Elizabeth said, and left Abigail's house.

The clouds in the sky had grown darker while Elizabeth had been inside, hinting that a storm was on its way. She glanced at the horizon, her insides churning like the gray clouds.

What had she been thinking, kissing Connor Wade? Fancying herself a young girl, giddy over a little flirtation.

But she wasn't a young girl. She was a spinster. Twenty-seven years old, unmarried, without even the faintest prospect of a husband on the horizon.

Elizabeth had forgotten her status for a bit. The ladies of Sterling had reminded her.

She'd been courted when she was young, called on by some of the men in town. But none of them had ever seemed special to her, and *she'd* never seemed special to any of them, apparently. So she'd concentrated on running the family home, helping her father, involving herself with church and civic matters, leaving her where she was today. A spinster. Which everyone in Sterling made sure she remembered.

When she arrived home, Elizabeth hung her shawl, hat and handbag beside the front door. In her rush to leave this morning she hadn't had breakfast. She was hungry. Elizabeth was sure her hired hand was, too.

A sound caught her ear as she stepped into the kitchen. She stopped and listened. None of the children she tutored was expected today, but she was certain she heard the sound of papers rustling.

Elizabeth walked to the room where she tutored her students and looked inside. To her surprise, Connor sat at the table, bent over a book.

She smiled, feeling her spirits lift at the sight of him—spinster or not.

"Brings back memories, doesn't it?" she asked.

His head jerked up, and when he saw her Connor bolted to his feet so fast he banged his knee on the table and knocked the chair backward.

"Sorry," Elizabeth said, coming forward. "I didn't mean to startle you."

"I was just starting to work on the window." He waved toward the tools assembled on the floor.

She picked up the child's reader from the table and flipped through the pages. "I like to look back at these old books, too, sometimes. So many memories of growing up."

Elizabeth slid the book into place on the shelf and turned to Connor. "If you're bored in your room at night you can take one of Papa's books to read."

Connor righted the chair he'd knocked over, rubbing his knee. "I'm pretty tired at night."

She pointed through the house toward the parlor. "Why don't you take something, just in case?"

Connor slid his fingers into his back pockets. "I'll do that."

"You must be hungry," Elizabeth said. "I'll fix us something to eat."

Connor followed her into the kitchen. "How was your meeting?"

She rolled her eyes as she tied on an apron. "It wouldn't surprise me if an all-out fight broke out someday."

Connor grinned. "Yeah? Maybe I'll start going to those meetings. I'd like to see that."

"If you came, you'd spoil everyone's fun," Elizabeth said. "The ladies couldn't talk about you if you were there."

"I don't know that I've ever been the topic of ladies' conversation before."

"Well, you certainly are now." Elizabeth pulled a frying pan from the bottom cupboard. "You're the most eligible bachelor in Sterling. Everyone is wondering which woman will catch you."

"Anybody got their money on you?"

Elizabeth stopped and looked at him. "Hardly. I'm much too old to find a husband. I'll be the last bride in the whole state of Texas. And if you don't believe me, just ask anyone in town."

"Too old, huh?" Connor shook his head. "See? That's something else I didn't know."

"You, on the other hand, can have your pick of any of the young women in town."

"What if I don't want one of them?"

Elizabeth glanced back at him. "Then you'll certainly disappoint a lot of people in Sterling."

"Doesn't matter to me if they're disappointed or not," Connor said, and ambled over to the stove.

Elizabeth looked up at him. "You really mean that, don't you?"

"Damn right," he said. "What are you fixing?"

"Ham again. Is that all right?"

"I'll eat anything you cook."

"I'll put a chicken in to roast this afternoon," Elizabeth said, setting out potatoes. "We'll have to eat early. I have choir practice tonight."

Connor eased up beside her and helped himself to a slice of the potato she'd just peeled.

"I guess those fine Christian ladies have got you frying chicken for that Founders' Day thing."

Elizabeth glanced up at him. "How did you know?"

"Worst job in the kitchen," Connor said, and crunched into another slice of potato. "Figures they'd give it to you."

Elizabeth lifted her chin. "I happen to make very good fried chicken."

"You can tell yourself that if you want to, Elizabeth. But it's plain as day they give you that job because it's the worst one."

She looked up at him. "And why would they do that?"

"Because you let them."

Elizabeth stopped slicing. "What is that supposed to mean?"

Connor shrugged his wide shoulders. "You've taken it in your head that somehow you share the blame for your brother stealing from the bank. You even feel guilty that your pa died, leaving the town with no doctor."

"They are my family. Why shouldn't I feel that way?"

"Because you didn't do anything wrong," Connor told her. "But you let the town make you feel like you did. You let them treat you bad."

"And what am I supposed to do?" Elizabeth asked. "Just say 'who cares what the town thinks' and turn my back on all of them?"

Connor nodded. "You'd probably feel better about yourself if you did."

Elizabeth turned away. "You don't know what you're talking about."

"All I'm saying, Elizabeth, is that you deserve better treatment than what you're getting from this town."

"I have friends here," she insisted. "A lot of friends."

Connor just looked at her for a moment, then drew in a breath and changed the subject.

"Can you make some corn bread?" he asked. "You make the best corn bread I ever tasted."

Elizabeth smiled. "Of course."

Since Connor had worked on the window in the classroom all afternoon, he ate supper in the kitchen with Elizabeth, then gathered his tools and headed back to the barn. He came back a short while later.

"Thought I'd help you clean up, since you've got choir practice," he said, stepping into the kitchen.

As he picked up a towel to dry the dishes, Elizabeth noticed that he'd changed his shirt and trousers. His hair was damp and slicked back on the sides.

"Are you going somewhere tonight?" she asked, handing him a dripping plate.

"I figured I'd go into town," Connor said. "You don't mind if I walk along with you, do you?"

"Well…"

"I know you don't want anybody getting the wrong idea about us," Connor told her. "But like you said, who'd figure anything would be going on? What with you being so old and all."

Elizabeth looked up and saw a grin twitching his lips. Even though the town considered her too old to marry, she didn't feel old. Not at all. And at the moment, Elizabeth felt very young.

"I'll see if I can make it all the way to the church tonight without my cane," she said.

Connor looked down at her and they both laughed.

They finished the dishes and Elizabeth hurried upstairs. In front of the mirror she pinned her hat in place, pinched a little color into her cheeks, then went downstairs and grabbed her shawl and handbag.

Connor waited patiently on the front porch.

"Looks like it might rain," he said, nodding toward the sky.

Elizabeth pulled her shawl around her shoulders. "Maybe the Lord will hold it off until after choir practice."

Clouds darkened the sky, all but covering what was left of the sun. Lanterns burned in the shop windows as Elizabeth and Connor walked through town. Few people were on the street.

When they reached the church, several of the choir members congregated in the yard; the front door stood open.

"There's Jane," Elizabeth said, as they crossed the churchyard. "Gena's sister."

Connor recognized her. Recognized, too, the man with her.

"Jane used to be a regular member of the choir," Elizabeth said. "She's helping out this Sunday because we have two other members out ill."

Connor didn't think Jane looked too happy about

being there. But that was probably because the man with her—Boyd Sherman—wasn't very happy.

They were standing off to themselves in the churchyard, and Boyd was obviously displeased with Jane. Even in the dim light, Connor saw the tight expression on his face. Finally, Boyd spun around and left. Jane went after him, but he kept going.

"Jane!" Elizabeth called, and walked over. "Is something wrong?"

Jane glanced at Elizabeth and Connor, then shook her head quickly. "No, nothing's wrong." She hurried inside the church.

"I don't know what Jane sees in that man," Elizabeth said.

"He's no good, if you ask me," Connor said, glaring down the road after Sherman. "Somebody ought to—"

"Connor," Elizabeth admonished. "I'm sure Boyd Sherman has some redeeming qualities."

Connor nodded toward the church. "You'd better get on inside, Elizabeth."

She hesitated. Something about the look on his face made her reluctant to leave.

"Connor, you're not thinking about—"

"Practice is starting," Connor said. "Go on, now. You don't want to be late."

Elizabeth climbed the stairs and stepped inside the church. She turned and looked out again in time to see Connor striding across the churchyard, in the same direction Boyd Sherman had taken.

Chapter Twelve

Heath Wheeler closed the big double doors of the livery stable just as Connor walked up.

"You look like you could use a beer," Connor said.

Heath grinned. "You buying?"

"I'm buying," Connor said. They headed for town.

"How's the job?" Heath asked.

"Coming along," Connor said. "The place needs some work. Nobody's done anything since Elizabeth's brother left."

"It's a big place for her to keep up on her own," Heath said. "Fact is, I—"

Connor stopped on the boardwalk, seeing that Heath had suddenly taken root and was staring across the street at Gunther's General Store. The shades were drawn, but lanterns burned inside. Shadows moved across the windows.

"Why don't you go talk to her?" Connor asked.

Heath pondered the question, then shook his head. "I already made a fool of myself the last time I did that, nearly coming to blows with that bastard Boyd Sherman right there in her pa's store."

"Sherman's a bastard, all right," Connor said.

"Besides, I don't want to look like I'm rushing her, what with her husband just dying and all," Heath said. He stood on the boardwalk a moment longer, gazing at the store, until Connor elbowed him.

"Let's get a beer," Connor said. Heath relented, and they walked down to the Foxtail.

A good-size crowd of men filled the saloon, some seated at the gaming tables, a few strung out along the bar. Connor knew most of them. He nodded and exchanged greetings as he and Heath ordered beer.

"Well, speak of the devil," Heath said, and nodded toward the back of the saloon.

Connor leaned against the bar and saw Boyd Sherman playing poker with three other men.

"I ought to go bust him in the face, just for the hell of it," Heath said.

"Probably make you feel better," Connor agreed. "Wouldn't mind doing it myself."

Connor sipped his beer while he and Heath talked. He hadn't been in the saloon, hadn't had anything stronger to drink than Elizabeth's coffee, in a long time. At one point in his life, Connor had whiled away most of his waking hours in one saloon or another, getting drunk and starting fights.

But all of that had changed, and Connor was

happy that it had. With the possible exception of busting Boyd Sherman's nose, Connor's old way of life didn't have any appeal right now. Being in the saloon was just a comfortable way of catching up on news, talking with friends. But even that ran a distant second to sitting with Elizabeth in her kitchen.

Connor was finishing his second beer when Sheriff Parker came through the bat-wing doors. He paused, surveyed the saloon, then let his gaze fall on Connor. They glared at each other for a few seconds, neither flinching, neither blinking an eye. Finally, the sheriff moved on.

"I'd better get going," Connor said, as he drained his glass. "Elizabeth is finished with choir practice by now."

Heath raised an eyebrow. "I didn't know your job as hired hand included escorting Miss Hill around town."

Connor grinned. "It does now."

"Maybe I'll walk along with you," Heath said.

Connor flipped coins onto the bar and they left. He didn't have to look to know Sheriff Parker's gaze followed him out the door.

The wind had picked up and the air had grown cooler by the time Connor and Heath arrived at church. It was dark now. Yellow light shone from the windows. The choir was still singing when Connor and Heath went inside.

"Mr. Wheeler? Just the man we need."

Abigail Rogers left a small gathering of women

in the back of the church and planted herself in front of Heath and Connor. She'd greeted them pleasantly enough, but Connor couldn't shake the feeling they'd been cornered.

"As you know, our Founders' Day festival is coming up shortly," Abigail said. "We have just discovered that many of our booths suffered water damage over the winter and must be repaired immediately."

"Well, uh…" Heath ducked his head.

"If our festival is going to be a success, those booths must be repaired," Abigail said. "Can you do this for us?"

"Well—" Heath began.

"Sure he can," Connor said. "He'd be glad to."

Heath threw Connor a sour look.

"Excellent!" Abigail declared.

"And Connor here will help me," Heath said, and slapped him on the back.

"Wonderful," Abigail said. "You can pick up the booths from the storage shed behind my barn tomorrow morning."

Abigail moved on, leaving Heath and Connor to stare after her. They gave each other a long look, then moved along, too.

Elizabeth seemed surprised to see him when choir practice ended. Surprised and pleased. To Connor's way of thinking, that made getting stuck rebuilding booths for the Founders' Day festival worth it.

"I didn't expect to see you," Elizabeth said, wrapping her shawl around her shoulders.

"I didn't like the idea of you walking home in the dark," Connor said.

"But I walk home in the dark every week after choir practice."

"Well, this week you don't have to," Connor said.

Elizabeth smiled. "No, I don't suppose I do."

Everyone said their good-nights as they moved outside, and Reverend Brady locked up the church.

Connor eased up next to Heath. "Maybe you ought to walk Jane home."

Heath spotted her crossing the churchyard alone. "That would be the neighborly thing to do, wouldn't it?"

"Real neighborly," Connor agreed.

"Damn neighborly." Heath headed across the yard.

In the oaks that ringed the churchyard, leaves rustled and limbs swayed in the wind. The air smelled clean and damp.

"We'd better go. That storm's about to hit." Connor caught Elizabeth's elbow and they headed toward home. "How was practice?" he asked.

"Not bad," Elizabeth said, "considering that Mr. and Mrs. Bloomfield weren't speaking and refused to sing at the same time, and Jane Gunther cried through half of practice."

"The spirit of brotherly love, huh?"

Elizabeth giggled. "Reverend Brady offered a prayer, but it didn't help much."

A gust of wind blew in their faces, bringing fat

raindrops with it. More fell, spattering the ground, tapping on the tin roofs of the businesses along Main Street.

Connor grabbed Elizabeth's hand. She hiked up her skirt and they started to run. The house was in sight when another gust of wind whipped Elizabeth's shawl from her shoulders and sent it flying. Connor dashed back, snatched it off the ground, then caught Elizabeth's hand again and pulled her to the safety of her front porch.

"Gracious," Elizabeth said, breathing heavily, dabbing at her face with her handkerchief.

"Looks like we beat the worst of it," Connor said, gazing out at the rain pouring down on the yard.

Elizabeth shivered. "Come inside and warm up. I'll make some coffee."

Connor looked down at himself. His clothes weren't much more than damp, but warming by the fire sounded good. He pulled off his boots and followed Elizabeth into the house.

She'd taken off her shoes, too. They both went into the kitchen and sat them neatly by the stove. Connor's big boots, her little slippers, side by side.

"Looks like your shawl got ruined," Connor said, holding up her soiled wrap.

Elizabeth unpinned her hat and sat it aside. "Oh, dear. I've had the worst luck with shawls lately. Maybe it will come clean."

Connor picked up the bucket beside the back door

and pumped water into it. Elizabeth immersed her shawl.

"At least this wasn't my favorite." She smiled. "And you don't have to get punched in the stomach over it."

"What are you talking about?"

Elizabeth wiped her hands on a towel. "When I punched you after the bank robbery it was because I was upset about my shawl."

Connor raised an eyebrow. "I got sucker punched because of your shawl?"

"It was a gift from Papa. The last thing he ever gave me," Elizabeth said. "When you shot that bank robber his blood got on my shawl and ruined it. I was upset, so I punched you in the stomach. Silly, isn't it?"

Connor shook his head. "No, not really."

"I shouldn't have hit you."

"As long as it made you feel better, it's all right."

"You always make me feel better, Connor," Elizabeth said. The words slipped out. She hadn't meant to say them. But Connor smiled and she was glad that she had. Besides, it was true. He did make her feel better.

They stayed near the stove as Connor stoked the fire and Elizabeth heated the coffee. Outside, rain pattered against the windows. Gusts of wind buffeted the house.

"Would you like to sit in the parlor?" Elizabeth asked.

"Sure," Connor said. "I'll go start the fire."

By the time he got the kindling lit and the logs had caught, Elizabeth had carried the tray into the parlor and set it on the little table in front of the settee. She poured coffee and served.

Connor settled onto the settee. Lantern light cast the parlor in soft hues. The little stove in the corner warmed the room. Connor sipped coffee from the delicate pink-and-white cup and looked over at Elizabeth seated in the chair to his right, both of them in their stocking feet.

He'd never seen a woman so pretty before. A few wisps of her hair had blown loose in the wind and curled around her face. Her cheeks were slightly flushed.

For a moment Connor wished he could capture this instant, somehow hold it here forever. The image of Elizabeth, the smell of her, the two of them safe in this warm, sturdy house, and the storm outside. His heart ached with the want to have these things, have them belong to him, forever.

He would have something like them, something similar, someday. Connor was sure of that. And he was equally sure Elizabeth could never be part of it.

Not after she found out. Connor didn't know how he would bear the look on Elizabeth's face when she learned the truth about him. The real truth.

For a moment he considered telling her about his being in prison. If she knew, she'd understand. Maybe then she wouldn't be so disappointed when she found out the rest.

Connor sipped his coffee and looked around the

parlor again. Hell, he didn't know how he'd ever tell her now.

"Papa and I used to do this sometimes," Elizabeth said. "We'd sit in the parlor in the evenings and talk. We'd play checkers or cards. Sometimes we'd read. Did you and your mother do that, after your father died?"

Connor shifted on the settee. "My ma was sick. She didn't feel much like doing that sort of thing."

"I'm sure she appreciated you taking care of her," Elizabeth said.

"I expect so," Connor said. "I heard in town tonight that new doctor's due in tomorrow."

Elizabeth's shoulders slumped. "I know I should be glad Sterling is getting a doctor, but..."

"Look, Elizabeth, if you don't want to sell your pa's equipment, you don't have to."

"It's the right thing to do," Elizabeth said. She drew in a breath. "The new doctor needs it."

"How are you going to tend to the women who come to you for help?"

Elizabeth shook her head. "They'll go to the new doctor, once he sets up his practice."

"I wouldn't be so sure about that," Connor said.

"Please, Connor, this is hard enough without you disagreeing with me."

"If you think I'm going to tell you what you do for those women doesn't mean anything to them, you're wrong, Elizabeth."

She just looked at him for a few minutes, then

smiled. "See what I mean? You always make me feel better."

"I'm just telling the truth," Connor said.

"Would you like to read something?" Elizabeth asked.

She got up from her chair and went to the bookcase. Connor stayed on the settee, suddenly fascinated by her stocking feet crossing the floor. With her back to him, she studied the books, rose on her toes to see the higher shelves, turned sideways reading the spines below. Her dress swirled around her legs, giving him a peek at her white petticoat.

"What sounds good?" Elizabeth asked, looking back at him. "Something historical? Romantic? Adventuresome?"

"Better stick with an adventure," Connor said.

"Then how about Mr. Jules Verne's *Twenty Thousand Leagues Under the Sea?* It seems appropriate on a rainy night. Have you read it too many times already?"

Connor shook his head. "No."

Elizabeth settled into the chair again, curled her legs under her and pulled her hem down over her feet. She stopped, and offered him the book.

"Papa always liked me to read to him. Would you prefer to read yourself?"

"I like the sound of your voice, Elizabeth."

She smiled, then opened the book and began to read. Connor sank deeper into the settee, closed his eyes and listened. Elizabeth's voice was like music.

When she finished the first chapter, she closed the book. "I suppose that's enough for one night."

Connor glanced at the clock. "I ought to go."

But he didn't get up. Neither did Elizabeth.

Instead, she started talking. About nothing special, really, just things as they popped into her mind. Her father, her brother, the house, things she wanted to do to fix up the place for her boarders. She talked about the people of Sterling, too. A little gossip, what scandal she knew.

When she finally ran down, Connor still seemed interested and not the least anxious to leave. But it was late, they'd drunk all the coffee and the rain had stopped. Elizabeth didn't want him to go, but couldn't ask him to stay.

They went into the kitchen, where Connor stood by the back door and pulled on his boots. He hesitated for a moment before going outside. Elizabeth stood beside him and caught herself wondering if he would kiss her again. Caught herself hoping that he would.

He didn't.

"Good night," Elizabeth said.

"'Night," Connor said, going down the back steps. "Be sure to lock up."

Elizabeth did as he asked, then extinguished the lanterns and went upstairs to her room. The air was chilly. She changed into her nightgown and let down her hair. But instead of crawling into bed, she blew out the lantern at her bedside and raised the window shade.

Across the barnyard she saw the light burning in Connor's room. Elizabeth dropped to her knees at the window, watching his shadow move behind the curtains.

There was something comforting about having Connor around. He was strong, capable. He'd done so many repairs around her house, things that had needed doing for a long time. And he made it all look so easy.

Tonight, how nice it had been that he'd started the fire in the parlor. One less thing she'd otherwise have done herself. In fact, without Connor there, she'd have probably just gone up to bed.

Instead, she'd had a lovely evening. They'd talked. Well, she'd done most of the talking. Connor had listened. Something else he was good at.

Yet for all her chattering, he seemed to enjoy the evening, too. She was sure he'd been reluctant to leave. She'd been reluctant to see him go.

Connor had a way about him. He saw things more clearly than she. All day she'd given thought to the things he'd told her. Maybe she did feel shame over what her brother had done. Maybe she did feel guilty that her father had died, leaving Sterling with no doctor.

Maybe, just maybe, none of that was her fault.

And maybe the town did make her feel as if it were. More likely, as Connor had said, she'd allowed that to happen.

The lamp burned in his room for a long time, and Elizabeth wondered what he was doing. Undressing?

Washing? Shaving? Did men shave at night? Her father and brother didn't.

It occurred to Elizabeth that she should have given him the book they'd been reading in the parlor. Connor might have wanted to read more of the story tonight.

Elizabeth's heart started to beat a little faster. Maybe she should take the book to him in the barn right now.

Chapter Thirteen

Clouds blew in front of the moon, sending strange shadows across Elizabeth's path. She lifted the lantern higher as she closed the kitchen door behind her and headed toward the barn.

Mr. Jules Verne's epic adventure in her hand seemed to suddenly weigh a hundred pounds. Or maybe it was her conscience dragging her down.

Determinedly, Elizabeth pressed on. She wasn't doing anything wrong, really. Simply offering the book to her hired hand for the evening. What was so terrible about that?

Well, for one thing she was dressed in her nightgown and robe. And her hair was down. And it was dark.

And he was Connor Wade.

At the barn door Elizabeth stopped and glanced behind her at the house. Should she go back? Was this a foolish errand? Tomorrow could she write her own book: *Twenty Thousand Ways to Look Like a Harlot?*

A harlot, indeed. Elizabeth jerked her chin. Why had she even thought such a thing? Connor had no interest in her. Everyone in town knew it. Wouldn't she be the last woman in Sterling ever to find a husband?

Elizabeth glanced up at Connor's window and saw that it still glowed yellow. He was awake. She pushed open the barn door and went inside.

The smell of the horse, leather and the hard-packed dirt floor swirled around Elizabeth as she held the lantern higher and climbed the narrow, creaking staircase to Connor's room. Unexpectedly, the light seeping around the edges of his door disappeared. He'd extinguished his lantern.

Elizabeth paused a half-dozen steps from the top. Was Connor ready to sleep now? Maybe she should leave. Maybe he was—

The door burst open and banged against the wall. Connor lurched into the doorway in a half crouch.

Elizabeth screamed. But not because of the gun in his hand. Not because it pointed straight at her.

Because he was naked.

They both froze. Light from Elizabeth's lantern bathed him, threw shadows across his body.

What big feet he had. The thought blazed through Elizabeth's mind. Long, long legs. Hair and muscles and bulges and—

She jerked her head away, heat raging inside her, and thrust the book at him.

"I thought you might want to—" Elizabeth glanced at him again and a little mewl slipped through her lips. "I'm sorry," she whispered, and took off down the stairs.

"No, Elizabeth, wait!"

She didn't wait. She flew down the steps, her feet barely skimming the risers. Behind her, she heard a thunk, a curse, and Connor calling her name again. Still she didn't stop.

At the bottom of the stairs she glanced up to see Connor rattling down the steps after her, hopping into his trousers. Another groan vibrated in her throat. Elizabeth dashed through the barn.

He *couldn't* catch her. She *couldn't* let him. Elizabeth knew she'd die on the spot if she had to look him in the face right now.

She was almost to the barn door when his hand closed around her arm.

"Elizabeth, wait."

She pulled against him, but he didn't let go.

"Wait!"

Her arm stretched out, Elizabeth stopped, leaning away from him as far as he'd allow. Shame and humiliation burned inside her. She refused to look up at him.

"I'm sorry," he said softly.

"No," she said, drawing in a few breaths to calm herself. "I'm the one who should apologize."

"When I heard footsteps coming up the stairs I didn't know what to expect," Connor said. "It never occurred to me it would be…you."

Elizabeth's face burned, sending flames fanning through her whole body.

"I shouldn't have," she said. "I mean, I thought you might like to…"

Words died in her throat as she waved the book between them. A few silent seconds passed and finally she lifted her gaze to look at him. Harsh, tense lines tightened his face. Lines she knew had nothing to do with Jules Verne's epic adventure.

"I need to talk to you," he said.

He didn't wait for her to agree or protest, just took her elbow and led her to the little bench outside the barn. She sat, the wood beneath her dry, protected from the rain by the overhanging roof. Connor took the lantern from her and blew out the flame. He pulled on the shirt he'd brought with him, but fastened only the center button, then plopped down beside her.

The night breeze tugged at Elizabeth's robe, her hair, Connor's loose sleeves and the tail of his shirt. The air smelled sweet, washed clean by the rain.

For a long time Connor sat there leaning forward, forearms resting on his knees. Faint light from the moon allowed Elizabeth to see his face, but she read nothing from his expression.

"I'm sorry," she said, when she couldn't stand the silence any longer. "This is all my fault. I shouldn't have come out here. I just thought you might like to read a little more."

He turned to her then. "Is that the only reason you came out here?"

"Of course," Elizabeth said, smoothing down the skirt of her robe. "I mean, what other reason would there be? Everyone in the whole blessed town knows I'm not much of a catch and that Dixie Brady—''

''I don't give a damn about Dixie Brady!'' Connor sprang from the bench, glaring down at her. ''She's not worth half of you, Elizabeth! And neither is any other woman in this town!''

Elizabeth stared up at him, unsure which was more alarming, his sudden anger or the words he'd spoken.

''Connor—''

''Just listen,'' he said, letting go of his anger with a large sigh. He paced back and forth in front of her for a few minutes, then pushed his fingers through his hair and sat down beside her again.

More minutes dragged by. Whatever Connor wanted to say to her wasn't easy for him. Elizabeth had the idea he didn't quite know where to start.

''Connor—''

''I was in prison.''

She blinked at him in the darkness, not sure she'd heard him right. ''You were in—''

''Prison.''

Elizabeth sat there, stunned, unsure of where this topic of conversation had come from, and why.

''I don't understand,'' she finally managed to say.

Connor leaned back against the barn, shifting his shoulders. ''I should have told you right from the start, Elizabeth. I just...I just wanted to start over fresh here in Sterling. I didn't want everybody to know.''

Well, she certainly couldn't argue with that reasoning. She imagined her brother, when released from prison in a few months, would feel much the same.

"What happened? Why were you sent to prison?" He'd brought it up so she felt she could ask.

"Because I was stupid." Connor spat the words. They came out with an ache, a regret and with no excuses.

"That's all, Elizabeth," Connor said. "I was stupid. I'm not going to blame what happened on anybody but myself. It was me, all me."

Another minute crawled by before he spoke again. "I got caught robbing a train."

Elizabeth studied him in the dim light, trying to match this new information with what she already knew about Connor.

He'd robbed a train? Been in prison? This man who'd stopped a bank robbery, rescued a stranger, saved a town? This man who'd offered free carpentry service, repaired festival booths, consoled a young man whose wife was in labor? This man who'd listened to her, to every word and worry, who'd talked to her, encouraged her?

He'd been a criminal?

"I don't understand," Elizabeth said softly. "Why did you do it?"

"I got no excuses."

Elizabeth never understood why her brother had embezzled from Sterling's bank, either. He didn't need the money. He had a good home, a family, a respectable job.

She'd asked her father that question, but he hadn't had an answer. Wise as he was, all he could say was that sometimes men did foolish things when they were young.

Maybe Connor was one of those men. Or had been.

"Have you robbed any trains since then?" Elizabeth asked.

He swung around on the bench and looked her square in the eye. "No, ma'am. I swear to you, Elizabeth, I've not broken the law since that happened. And I'm never going to do anything like that again. I told you, I've got me a plan for a business of my own. And a real home. A family."

Connor sat back against the barn. "Anyway, I wanted you to know. And if you don't want me here anymore, I'll move along."

A little wave of panic swept through Elizabeth. Connor gone? She couldn't imagine it. She couldn't imagine waking up and not finding him on her doorstep, or sitting across the supper table from her. Not seeing his window glow with lantern light every night before she went to bed.

Besides, her own brother—whom she loved dearly—had done the identical thing. Turning her back on Connor would be tantamount to doing the same to Raymond.

They'd both committed a crime and been caught. They'd served their time. Paid their debt to society.

It wasn't Elizabeth's place to judge them, nor punish them further.

"My brother will be released from prison in a few months," she said.

"You heard from him?"

"No. Raymond won't write to me. He never has. Not one letter since he left," Elizabeth said. "But when he's released in a few months, I'd like to think that wherever he goes, whatever he does, he'll be given a fresh start, and his past won't be held against him."

Connor's big hand closed over hers, folding his fingers around her, warming her skin.

"The last thing I'd ever want to do is cause you any heartache, Elizabeth."

He already caused her heart to ache, but whether it was a good or a bad ache she wasn't sure. What she did know for sure was that she couldn't hold his past against him. Just as she wouldn't turn away from her brother because of what he'd done.

"I don't want you to leave," Elizabeth said. "You made a mistake in your past. You paid for it. That's the end, as far as I'm concerned."

Still, Connor didn't seem completely relieved by what she'd told him. In the moonlight she saw that his face was still tense.

"Was there something else you wanted to tell me?" she asked.

Connor looked hard at her for a while. His fingers tightened around her hand.

"Yes?" she prompted.

He let out the breath he'd been holding and released her hand. "No, that's it."

"I don't believe you," she said. "You could have told me about your past tomorrow morning at breakfast. Why now?"

He raised an eyebrow at her and shifted uneasily on the wooden bench.

"I don't imagine you come outside in your night-clothes too often," Connor said, his gaze zipping from her throat down to her toes.

Elizabeth warmed under his gaze, as if he'd actually touched her, as if he knew her errand to his room tonight was motivated by something more than literary interests.

"Especially," he added, "to deliver a book to somebody like me."

She squirmed. Humiliation bubbled inside her.

Connor touched her chin and turned her to face him. "You honor me, Elizabeth."

Her embarrassment melted away...along with her heart.

"That's why I didn't want you thinking I was something I wasn't," he said.

Connor gazed into her eyes, and Elizabeth thought again how handsome he was.

And how it must have hurt him to tell her about his past. Men were so prideful. He'd told no one else. He'd wanted to keep it a secret. But he'd confided in her. Only her.

"You'd better go," Connor said after a moment.

She wanted to stay, but knew he was right. Rising

from the bench, she realized that she still held the book in her hand. "Would you like to read this?"

"No," he said, rising slowly. "I'm pretty well worn-out tonight."

Elizabeth nodded. He looked it.

Connor walked her back to the house and waited as she went inside and closed the kitchen door behind her. With a heavy heart, he headed back to the barn.

He'd known Elizabeth wouldn't hold it against him that he'd been in prison. That's just the kind of woman she was.

A little curse tumbled from Connor's lips. No, she hadn't been put off by his prison record.

But what would Elizabeth do when she found out the rest?

Elizabeth had just gotten to the kitchen the next morning when a knock sounded on the back door. She knew it was Connor.

Was he naked?

The notion flashed in her mind unbidden, bringing with it memories of last night, and a flush to her cheeks.

Gracious, such thoughts. Elizabeth chided herself as she walked to the door. She stopped suddenly. Why had that been her first recollection about last night, rather than his confession that he'd been in prison?

Because it really—really—didn't matter to her.

Elizabeth opened the door. Connor, fully clothed, waited on the porch.

"I'm starting breakfast now," she told him.

"No rush," he said. "I'm going to pick up those booths from the mayor's place this morning and get a few supplies while I'm in town."

"More supplies?" Elizabeth asked. "Let me give you some money."

"No need," Connor said. "We'll settle up later. I'll be back in about an hour."

"I'll have breakfast ready then," Elizabeth said.

"Do you need anything while I'm in town?"

"Well, yes, if you don't mind." Elizabeth disappeared from the doorway for a moment, then passed an envelope to him. "It's a letter to my brother. Could you drop it by the express office?"

Connor tucked it inside his shirt pocket, then smiled and walked away. She stood at the door, watching him go, thinking how glad she was that things were still comfortable between them. After last night, it could have been quite different.

Elizabeth turned back to the stove. She'd have to remember to write down what she owed Connor for supplies when he got back. He'd already bought building materials and stocked her pantry.

Elizabeth paused. She hadn't given him any money, and as far as she knew he hadn't worked at a paying job since arriving in Sterling.

Where did Connor get his money?

Connor caught Heath just as he opened the livery for the day, and reminded him of their errand this morning.

"Damn, I forgot all about it," Heath said.

"Like hell you did," Connor said.

Heath grinned. "No, I swear, it slipped my mind."

The two men hitched a team to one of Heath's wagons and drove toward the mayor's house on the other side of town. Mrs. Gunther swept the board-walk in front of their store as they drove by. She waved, and both men tipped their hats.

"I don't know how many more neighborly acts of kindness I've got left in me," Heath said. "I walked Jane Gunther home from choir practice last night. She cried the whole way."

"What did you do to her?"

"I didn't do one damn thing," Heath said.

"Why was she crying?"

Heath shook his head. "I've got my suspicions."

More than likely it was because of Boyd Sherman. Connor remembered them arguing before choir practice.

"At least I got to see Gena a few minutes when I finally got to the store," Heath said.

Abigail Rogers came out onto her front porch when they drove up with the wagon. Connor and Heath sat there for a full five minutes listening to the mayor's wife talk before she finally directed them to the storage shed behind her house. They made quick work of loading the booths despite Abigail standing beside the wagon explaining what was wrong with each booth and how it should be repaired, as if they couldn't see that for themselves. They endured another five minutes of thank-yous, then finally pulled away from the house.

"I've got to pick up some supplies from Gunther's before I head home," Connor said. "You want to stop by?"

"I can't look Jane in the face this morning. Not after seeing her cry last night because Sherman had upset her and she was so in love with him and getting married." Heath looked at Connor. "This morning I saw that bastard coming out of Miss Hester's parlor house. That just didn't sit right with me."

Connor left Heath at the livery and drove the wagon back to Gunther's General Store. He and Mr. Gunther talked about the weather as he bought the supplies he needed. Connor was glad everyone had stopped talking about the bank robbery.

Gena came out from the back room just as Connor was about to leave. He took a moment to have a word with her, then left the store.

Outside on the boardwalk, Connor loaded the supplies into the wagon, and was ready to climb aboard when he remembered the letter Elizabeth had given him.

Connor pulled it from his shirt pocket and looked at Elizabeth's graceful handwriting. Fine, delicate lettering, with lots of curves and swirls. The envelope was thick. She must have written several pages to her brother.

Too bad he'd never get to read it.

In his mind Connor saw Raymond Hill sitting in that stinking prison cell, waiting for Elizabeth's letter. A solitary bright spot in an endless succession of dreary, life-draining days.

Connor tore the letter into tiny pieces, dropped them in the trash barrel beside the store, then climbed into the wagon and drove away.

Chapter Fourteen

Elizabeth's place was a welcome sight when Connor turned the team down the lane beside the house. Driving past the kitchen, he saw Elizabeth's face at the window. She smiled and waved. The smell of bacon and biscuits wafted out. Connor stopped the team and jumped down.

Coming here felt like home, or what he guessed having a home would feel like. It was what he'd always imagined.

Connor stopped at the foot of the back steps and looked up at Elizabeth's smiling face at the door. He ought to do what he'd come here to do. Either that or move on.

But right now, looking at Elizabeth, Connor could do neither.

"Hungry?" Elizabeth asked, stepping back.

"Starved." Connor hung his hat by the door and washed his hands in the basin by the pump. The kitchen was warm. It smelled good. Elizabeth stood at the stove in her white ruffled apron. Connor's chest started to ache.

"You may as well eat in here this morning," Elizabeth said.

Connor noticed she'd already set the table for two. He filled their coffee cups while she served the food. They'd done this so many times now the routine felt familiar. He held her chair; they sat across from each other and talked as they ate.

Their meal lasted longer than it should have, but Connor didn't mind. He couldn't think of one other place he'd rather be. Elizabeth seemed content, too, and that pleased him.

They'd finished washing and drying the breakfast dishes when a knock sounded on the back door. Garrett Whitmore bustled inside when Elizabeth opened it, and waved another man in with him.

"Elizabeth, I've got just the man you've been wanting to meet," Garrett said. "Dr. Tom Avery, Sterling's new physician."

"Oh…"

"Morning, Miss Hill," Dr. Avery said, removing his hat.

The new doctor looked to be in his late twenties, fresh faced, handsome with brown wavy hair and blue eyes. He smiled and dimples showed in his cheeks.

"Nice to meet you, Dr. Avery," Elizabeth said.

Connor stepped forward and introduced himself; they shook hands.

Garrett rubbed his palms together. "Well, let's

get on with what we came here for. Elizabeth, you want to show Dr. Avery your father's equipment?''

"Well..." Elizabeth glanced at Connor.

"The doc here doesn't have all day, now, Elizabeth," Garrett said.

"Well...all right."

She led the way toward the surgery. Connor didn't follow. He left the kitchen.

He drove the team to the barn, unloaded the booths and supplies and went to work. It wasn't long before the barn door opened and Elizabeth came inside.

Connor stepped back from the booth he'd been pulling rotted boards off of. "Sure as hell didn't take Whitmore long to get the new doctor over here," he said. "Must have brought him straight from the depot."

"Garrett is just trying to help," Elizabeth answered.

Connor snorted and hooked his claw hammer into another board. "So, does he want the equipment?"

"I think so," Elizabeth said softly.

Connor looked at her. "Are you going to sell it?"

"Of course," Elizabeth said quickly. "I have to."

"No, you don't."

"Stop saying that!" She turned on him, her fists clenched. "I have to sell. Can you imagine what the town would think of me if I didn't? Do you know how they'll look at me?"

"I've got a pretty good idea," Connor said. "But so what?"

The commotion of feelings in Elizabeth hardened into anger. "You don't understand," she told him. "You don't know how awful it is to have everyone talk about you. Point at you on the street. Whisper behind your back."

Connor felt his own anger growing. "Maybe I do, Elizabeth. Maybe I know exactly what it feels like. But is that reason enough to let other people run your life?"

"They're not running my life!"

"Yes, they are. You're scared to make a move, fearing what everybody will have to say about it."

Quickly, unexpectedly, Elizabeth's anger turned and tears sprang into her eyes. "What else can I do? I have no father, no brother. No husband. No family of my own. What will I do if the whole town turns against me? Tell me, what else can I do?"

He'd seen her cry once before, the day of the bank robbery. But those were big, racking sobs, borne of frustration and fear.

These were tiny tears, welling in her eyes, trickling down her cheeks. Anguished tears of sadness and loneliness.

Connor wanted to smother her against his chest, hold her tight and make everything all right for her. Somehow, that would make everything all right for him, too. But he had to tell her the truth, tell her what was in his heart.

He took a step closer. "Standing up to the town, defying them, wouldn't be easy. I'll grant you that.

But if you do it, Elizabeth, at least you'd be your own person. And you'd be a hell of a lot happier.''

"I was happy! Perfectly happy until you came along, Connor Wade! Just don't talk to me anymore!''

Elizabeth bolted from the barn. Connor let her go.

Elizabeth threw herself on her bed and cried. She cried for her dead father, for the mother she barely remembered, for her brother in prison. She cried over the sale of her father's medical equipment. With it gone, he would be gone, too, completely. Elizabeth cried until she couldn't cry anymore.

Sitting up, she wiped at her tears and sniffed. Her gaze settled on the book at her bedside. Last night she'd taken it to the barn for Connor to read. Now she might go out there and hit him over the head with it.

She wasn't sure why his words in the barn just now had hurt her so. Except that what he thought mattered to her. And she didn't like it when they disagreed. And he probably was right.

Pouring fresh water into the basin, Elizabeth splashed her face. She combed out her hair and twisted it atop her head again. The reflection in the mirror could have looked better, Elizabeth decided. Her eyes were puffy and her nose was red.

But so what? If Connor Wade thought she shouldn't have a care what anybody thought of her, she could start with him.

Elizabeth headed downstairs with the intention of

inventorying her father's surgery. Dr. Avery had been impressed with the equipment and supplies. He wanted to think it over and come back later with an offer. Garrett had wanted to close the sale on the spot, but Dr. Avery had been firm.

But no matter what he offered, Elizabeth would sell. She saw no benefit in haggling or waiting. She didn't want the process drawn out any longer than necessary. It was already painful enough.

A voice wailing on the porch brought Elizabeth to the front door. She opened it and found Betsy Brewster sitting on the steps clutching her big belly.

"Oh, my Lordy, Miss Elizabeth, it's *time!*"

Elizabeth rushed outside. "It could be another false alarm. Come in—"

"No, this is it. Look." Betsy lifted the hem of her skirt and tapped her shoes together. "See? The baby's leaking out of me."

Elizabeth saw the stains on Betsy's stocking and shoes. The baby was on its way. "When did this happen?"

"Awhile ago," Betsy said. "I got here quick as I could."

"You came alone?" Elizabeth looked around. "Where's Freddie?"

"He's been hanging on me like a wet towel on a nail. I got so dang tired of it I told him to get out of the house before I—" Betsy's face contorted with pain. She locked her arms around her belly and groaned.

"Come on, Betsy, let's get you in the house," Elizabeth said.

"I can't. I can't get up," Betsy wailed. "I'm just going to have this baby right here on the porch."

Elizabeth maneuvered behind her and tried to lift her. "Betsy, you can't have the baby out here. Come on—"

"No! I can't! Oh, Miss Elizabeth, I can't."

"All right." Elizabeth leaned her against the porch railing. "I'll be right back."

Betsy groaned again as Elizabeth took off around the house. She wasn't about to let Betsy have her baby on the front porch. She had to get her inside. And to do that she needed Connor.

Elizabeth ran to the barn and pushed open the door. Connor was exactly where she'd left him earlier, working on the Founders' Day booths.

"Connor, come quick. I need you."

Hammer in hand, he propped it against his hip. "I thought you didn't want me to talk to you."

"Do you have to pick now to listen to me?" Elizabeth grabbed the hammer from his hand and tossed it away. "It's an emergency. Come on."

Connor headed toward the door with her. "What's wrong?"

"Betsy's having her baby. I need you to—"

Connor dug in his heels. "Hold on, now. I don't want any part of this."

Elizabeth planted her hands on her hips. "If you think you're going to pick this moment to collect on whatever it is you think I *owe* you, Connor Wade, you can just forget it.''

His eyes narrowed as he looked her up and down. ''I'm not about to waste *that* on this situation.''

''Then come on,'' Elizabeth said.

Still he hesitated. ''I don't know anything about having babies.''

Elizabeth grabbed his arm and tugged. ''I need you to carry her into the house. That's all.''

He glared down at her. ''That's all?''

''Yes, that's all. Now, come on.''

They hurried to the front of the house and found Betsy sitting on the steps, holding her belly and moaning.

''Betsy,'' Elizabeth said, kneeling beside her, ''Connor is going to take you into the house.''

''No! Just let me die out here where I can see the sky!'' Betsy said.

''You're not dying,'' Elizabeth insisted. She turned to Connor. ''Carry her into the surgery. I'll get things together and be right there.''

''Wait. Don't—''

''Hurry,'' she told him. ''We don't have much time.''

Connor watched helplessly as Elizabeth disappeared into the house. He looked down at Betsy, who was still moaning. All he had to do was carry her into the house, but she was already in so much pain he was afraid to touch her. What if he did it wrong? What if he hurt her? Despite her big belly, Betsy was just a little bit of a thing.

He gulped and wiped his hands on his shirt, then bent down to lift her into his arms. Betsy's hand shot out and clamped on to his.

"Ohh..." she cried.

"Ohh..." Connor cried along with her, sinking to his knees while Betsy squeezed his fingers. She clamped down tighter and tighter until the contraction eased. Connor jerked his hand away.

"Freddie! Where's Freddie?" she asked.

Connor backed off a step, flexing his fingers. "I don't know."

"I need Freddie!"

"All right," Connor said, trying to decide whether it was safe to get within arm's length of her again. "I'll find him."

He moved in and tried to lift Betsy, but she flung her hand out, smacking him across the chin, sending his hat sailing.

"Now! I need Freddie now!"

"All right, all right," Connor said, trying to catch her flailing arms. "Calm down. I'll—"

"Calm down? You expect me to calm down when I'm about to die in childbirth and my own husband isn't even here?"

"I'll find him. I swear. Just let me get you inside."

"Ohh..."

Another contraction claimed her. Connor scooped her up. Betsy grabbed the front of his shirt as he carried her into the house.

"Elizabeth!" he called from the foyer. Where

was she? What was he supposed to do with this woman now?

Betsy twisted her fingers deeper into his shirt, catching a handful of chest hairs. Connor stifled a yelp and hurried to the surgery.

No sign of Elizabeth. Where the hell was she?

Connor carried Betsy to the little room next to the examination room and laid her gently on the bed. But before he could straighten up, Betsy yanked his shirt so hard he went down on his knees at the bedside.

"Find Freddie! Tell him to get over here! Now!"

Connor nodded quickly. "Yes, ma'am. Don't worry. I'll get him here."

"Well, hurry up!"

Connor touched her fingers, trying to untangle them from his shirt. "All right, I will. Just let go of me."

Betsy jerked him closer, ripping the shoulder seam, her eyes wide and blazing. "You tell Freddie that if he doesn't get over here, I'm going to— Ohh..."

Her eyes rolled back as another pain claimed her. Connor pulled her fingers from his shirt. She clawed at him blindly. He leaned left, dodging her. Betsy's other hand shot out and latched on to a handful of his hair.

"Yeow!" Connor cried.

She pulled his head down, banging it against the mattress, groaning and writhing in pain.

"Elizabeth!"

"Ohh…!"

"Elizabeth!"

A few moments later, Betsy relaxed. Connor scrambled away, rammed his shoulder into the wall, staggered to get to his feet, then scurried to the bottom of the bed, out of Betsy's reach.

Elizabeth breezed into the room carrying a stack of folded linens.

"Connor, please," she said. "Don't shout. Betsy is in a delicate condition and I don't want her upset."

"Delicate?" Connor flexed his fingers and rubbed the top of his head.

"Run along," Elizabeth said. "Find Freddie."

Connor looked at Betsy, then at Elizabeth. "I'm afraid to leave you here alone with her. It's not safe."

"Not safe?" Elizabeth gave a quick laugh. "Honestly, where do you men come up with these silly ideas?"

"But—"

Elizabeth set the linens on the bureau, then took a closer look at him. "Connor, you've torn your shirt. Really, you should be more careful."

He touched the tender spot on his head. "Yeah, I'll do that."

"Run along, now."

He left.

Connor retrieved his hat from the front porch where Betsy—in her delicate condition—had knocked it off his head. He knew he needed to find Freddie, but at the same time he was afraid to leave Elizabeth alone. Still, he didn't know what he could do to help her, considering that he didn't like the idea of going back into the surgery again. Already he'd come as close to childbirth as he ever wanted to be.

Connor mumbled a curse, pulled on his hat and headed for town. He went from shop to shop looking for Freddie, asking if anybody had seen him. Nobody had. Connor kept looking.

More than anything, he wanted to get back to Elizabeth. The whole idea of women giving birth wasn't something he'd thought much about. Seeing Betsy, helping her, brought it closer. Knowing Elizabeth had taken the responsibility of delivering the baby brought it closer still.

He searched his way down Main Street before finally spotting Freddie hiking toward town with a fishing pole over his shoulder and a wicker basket in his hand. Connor relaxed, glad his involvement was done.

"Oh, my Lord. It's time, isn't it," Freddie said, taking one look at Connor. Instead of happy and excited, Freddie looked worried. He looked scared. Women died in childbirth. Freddie knew that. Connor did, too, but had never given it any real thought until now.

"Betsy's all right? I mean, so far?"

Connor nodded. "She's fine. Let's go."

They hurried through town to Elizabeth's house and went inside. Betsy's moans greeted them as they reached the door to the surgery. Freddie gulped and his face went white.

Connor knocked gently. Elizabeth came to the door, her sleeves rolled back.

"I found Freddie," Connor said.

Elizabeth peered around Connor and gave him a confident smile. "Everything's going fine, Freddie."

"Thank you, Miss Elizabeth."

Elizabeth leaned closer to Connor. "It will be awhile still. Keep Freddie occupied, will you?"

"All right, I can do that," Connor said. "Do you need anything?"

She shook her head. "No, we're fine."

"Give a holler if you do," Connor said.

Elizabeth smiled and disappeared into the room again.

Connor stared at the closed door for a few minutes, listened to Betsy's groans, then turned to Freddie. He looked as if he were about to give birth to the baby himself.

"Let's go out to the barn," Connor said. "It will be awhile."

Freddie didn't budge. He stared at the door until Connor stepped in front of him and nodded toward the outside door. Finally, Freddie left.

A lot of work needed doing inside the house and Connor had barely started it. But he couldn't see hammering and banging away at the renovations Elizabeth wanted done while Betsy was in the surgery having a baby. He took Freddie out to the barn and they worked on the booths for a while. Freddie didn't have his mind on the work, and really, neither did Connor. Nothing seemed important when, inside the house, a woman might give up her life bringing a baby into the world.

The barn grew warm after a while, so Connor gathered up tools and headed for the front of the house. The swing on the porch needed fixing, and since it was shady there and cooler, it seemed like a good job for the two of them to tackle.

"You reckon everything's going to be all right?" Freddie asked.

He'd put that question to Connor a couple dozen times already today. Connor didn't know the answer, of course, so he gave the only response he was positive about.

"Elizabeth knows what she's doing."

Freddie nodded thoughtfully and they went to work on the porch swing. Connor tried to keep a conversation going, keep Freddie from worrying about his wife and baby. He could only imagine how he'd feel himself, in Freddie's position.

Finally, Elizabeth opened the front door and stepped onto the porch. Both men whirled.

"It's a boy," Elizabeth said, smiling broadly. "They're both fine. You can go see them now, Freddie."

He let out a whoop and rushed inside the house.

Connor wanted to give a yell, too, relieved as much as anyone that everything had turned out all right.

"The baby has red hair, like Freddie," Elizabeth said. "He's beautiful."

Connor thought Elizabeth was the beautiful one. Her collar was open, her sleeves turned back. She looked hot and tired. Yes, very beautiful.

"Why don't you sit down and rest a bit?" Connor offered. "I fixed the swing."

She gazed at the chain, now securely fastened to the ceiling of the porch, and smiled. "We've both been busy."

"You get the prize for the day, Elizabeth," Connor said. "I'll go make us something to eat."

"I'll come with you," Elizabeth said.

He shook his head. "You need to rest."

"Actually, I'd rather be with you."

Connor smiled. "I'd rather have you with me."

They made supper. Elizabeth took a tray in to Betsy, enough for two. Freddie stayed with her, helped her eat, held his son until Betsy fell asleep.

"How long before I can take them home?" Freddie asked when he walked into the kitchen a short time later cradling the baby awkwardly in his arms.

Elizabeth passed the last dripping dish to Connor. "I don't want her moved for several days."

"That long?" Freddie asked.

Elizabeth dried her hands on a towel. "You can come over and see her as often as you like. I'll take good care of her."

"Yes, ma'am, Miss Elizabeth. I know that." Freddie looked down at the little baby swaddled in a white blanket. "I guess I'll see you tomorrow, little fella."

He passed the baby to Elizabeth. Connor dried the last dish and they all walked to the front door together. Freddie said good-night and left.

"How about if we try out that swing you fixed?" Elizabeth suggested.

"Sounds good. I can use some rest," Connor said. "I don't mind telling you that baby being born today about wore me out."

Elizabeth grinned and followed him out onto the porch.

Night had fallen, bringing a cool breeze with it. Faint moonlight lit the porch. In the distance, lanterns from town shone. Elizabeth took a seat on the swing, holding the baby in her arms. Connor sat beside her.

"That was a hell of a day," Connor said softly.

Elizabeth smiled. "It certainly was."

He planted one foot on the floor and set the swing in motion, rocking them gently.

"The baby's not going to start crying, is it?" he asked.

"If he does, we'll just take him right back to his mother," Elizabeth said. "That's the best part about being a doctor."

Connor grinned and leaned a little closer. His shoulder touched Elizabeth's but she didn't move away.

"Kind of a cute little thing," Connor said. "Even with the red hair."

"He's adorable," Elizabeth said, holding the baby closer to her breast.

"I'm going to have me a few of those, one day," Connor said.

She looked up at him, surprised. "Really?"

"You bet. I'm going to have a wife, a home and some kids."

"You sound sure of yourself."

"Damn right," Connor said.

"I wouldn't mind having a few of these, too."

Elizabeth's gaze returned to the baby and Connor thought she looked a little sad. Then he remembered that she thought herself too old to get married, and wished he hadn't brought up the subject.

"I owe you an apology," Connor said.

She turned to him again. "For what?"

"For being so hard on you about selling your pa's medical equipment. You've done your share of standing up to the town already, by turning your place into a boarding home and taking the chance on letting me live here," Connor said. "I guess I should have kept my mouth shut."

"You were only trying to help," Elizabeth murmured.

"I can't seem to mind my own business when it comes to you, Elizabeth." Connor gazed out into the darkened yard for a few seconds, then turned back to her. "I'm not going to apologize for that."

Elizabeth laughed gently. "I didn't expect you to."

Connor smiled, pleased at how well they'd gotten

to know each other. How comfortable they were together.

He shifted on the swing, raised his arm and stretched it along the back.

"Are you going to try to kiss me?" Elizabeth asked.

He froze and knew he looked guilty, because that's exactly what he had in mind.

"You sound like you know what you're talking about," Connor said. "Have you been kissed in a porch swing before?"

"When I was fourteen Billy Fitzpatrick tried to kiss me right in this very swing."

"Did you let him?"

"Yes."

Connor eased a little closer. "So I guess that makes you an experienced woman."

"I suppose. It wasn't much of a kiss."

Connor shifted his arm, looping it around her shoulder. She tilted her face up and he touched his lips to hers. Elizabeth moaned softly and leaned into him. Connor groaned and deepened their kiss.

Such comfort he felt. Elizabeth's mouth on his was exciting, but it was more than that. It was familiar. Waves of contentment washed through him, more compelling than the thrill of their kiss. His body reacted, wanting more. But for now, this moment was enough.

The baby started to fuss and Elizabeth pulled away from Connor. She didn't break contact completely, but lingered for a few seconds longer.

"I'd better take him to his mother," she whispered.

"I'd better go, too," Connor said.

"I'll be right back," Elizabeth said. "You can—"

"No. I'd better go."

Elizabeth nodded. She understood.

"'Night," Connor said, and walked off the porch into the darkness.

Chapter Fifteen

Elizabeth dashed around the kitchen, afraid she'd be late. Not because she'd overslept—which would have felt good—but because she had so much to do this Sunday morning.

She wasn't used to having a patient in the surgery to care for, a large breakfast to prepare, a house to tidy up—all while getting ready for church.

Elizabeth didn't even want to think about what lay ahead in the next week. She had music lessons to give and tutoring sessions to prepare. Tempting though it was, she couldn't cancel the lessons and let her students down. Also, she couldn't afford to do without the fees their lessons generated.

There were pies to bake, too, for the restaurants in town, and of course, the final preparations for the Founders' Day celebration.

Heaving a heavy sigh, Elizabeth pushed an errant strand of hair from her face. Somehow, she'd have to manage all those things.

A knock sounded at the back door and Elizabeth saw Connor through the window. He'd come for breakfast, and he was early.

She could have been annoyed at finding Connor on her back porch early, before he was supposed to arrive, annoyed that she had a dozen things to do this morning, that she was behind on all of them, and now he added to her problems. But instead, Elizabeth felt her load lift a little at the sight of him.

"You're just in time," she said, swinging the back door open. "Come in. I've—"

She stopped because Connor stopped. He didn't come inside. He didn't move at all. Connor stood rooted to her back porch, staring at her. His gaze dipped quickly, taking her in from head to toe.

Elizabeth gasped as she realized she'd flung the door open and invited Connor inside—and she was wearing her robe and her hair was loose around her shoulders. "Oh..." She stepped back and felt her cheeks flush. She ran her hand down the front of her robe as if that might disguise the fact that she wore only her nightgown underneath.

He'd seen her dressed this way before, the night she'd gone out to his room in the barn. But it had been dark then. Not like now, with the sunlight blazing in through every window and door in the house.

Elizabeth's face flushed hotter as she saw Connor's chest expand with the quick intake of his breath. She knew what he was thinking.

"I—I'm running late this morning," she said. "Freddie's here already—since daybreak. He's asked a dozen questions. I have breakfast to cook, and the baby was up most of the night, so I hardly got any sleep at all. Betsy is having another crying fit, and—and I can't be late for church.''

Connor pulled his hat lower on his forehead and shouldered his way into the kitchen, averting his eyes. Elizabeth pulled the sash on her robe tighter, her hands shaking, her knees quivering.

She should have been glad he was gentleman enough not to ogle her in this compromising state. But Connor looked handsome this morning, dressed in the white shirt, dark vest and string tie she'd seen him wear to services last Sunday, and something— Elizabeth didn't know what—drew her to him anyway.

''I figured you'd have your hands full this morning,'' he said. ''That's why I came early.''

She followed him to the stove. ''I'll get breakfast on the table and then tend to Betsy. She's crying something awful this morning. Once Freddie and the baby are settled, I'll get dressed. I can't be late for church.''

''Freddie can take care of Betsy,'' Connor said, keeping his back to her as he rummaged through the cupboard for the skillet. ''Between the two of them, they'll take care of the baby. I'll get breakfast made. You go upstairs and get ready for church.''

''But I can't leave you here to do all the cooking by yourself. I'll—''

''Go, Elizabeth.'' Connor turned to her, his expression dark. "Go now. Or I can guarantee you won't make it to church on time."

Heat bloomed in Elizabeth, rushing from deep within her straight up to her cheeks. But she couldn't turn away. Connor's smoldering gaze held her captive, right there in the middle of her kitchen, tempting her—daring her—to stay where she was.

What was it about this man? Only a moment ago finding him at her back door had brought relief to her. She'd been glad to see him. Comforted by his nearness. Now, he caused her pulse to race and naughty thoughts to dance in her head—simply by looking at her. By the suggestion of a few words.

Elizabeth swallowed hard, forcing her dry throat to work. Connor stood a few feet away, big, sturdy and strong. He'd held her in his arms before, kissed her the way a man kisses a woman. What would it be like, she wondered, to step into his embrace again? To have him in her kitchen each morning and know the freedom to touch him at her leisure? To live as a man and a woman, a husband and wife, lived? To be late for church every Sunday morning?

Visions of Reverend Brady, the choir and the entire Sterling congregation seated in church while she dashed in late—Connor trailing along behind her— jarred Elizabeth from her thoughts.

"I'd better go," she whispered.

"I believe I said that already."

"Yes, you did." Elizabeth smiled faintly and backed across the room. She paused in the doorway for one last look at Connor standing at her stove, holding her skillet. The desire to run to him surged through her again, but instead, Elizabeth hurried from the room.

Connor watched the empty space Elizabeth had just occupied in the doorway for a long moment, picturing her in her robe, smelling her scent, feeling the pressure behind his fly. He'd had lots of women in his time, nameless, faceless whores who'd known their business and done it well. But he'd never been more aroused than right now after seeing Elizabeth in her plain robe, covered from ankle to neck to wrist, buttoned in and cinched up tight.

For a moment Connor seriously considered following her up the stairs. He was tempted. Oh, he was tempted. Just climb the steps, slip down the hallway into her bedroom.

Would Elizabeth turn him away? If she had good sense she would. But he'd seen the look on her face this morning. He knew she felt what he felt, though probably not to the same degree.

But Connor could fix that.

Connor could while away this fine Sunday morning showing Miss Elizabeth Hill the delights a man and a woman could share. Visions played out in his head, not unlike so many others he'd had concerning Elizabeth. Yes, he could spend every morning, every day of his life showing her those things.

Connor growled under his breath and banged the skillet down on the stove. Enough of those thoughts. He wouldn't be showing Elizabeth—or anybody—

anything this morning. And if he didn't get himself under control, he wouldn't be fit to walk into church.

Forcing his thoughts onto breakfast, Connor popped the biscuits Elizabeth had made into the oven, then scrambled a dozen eggs. It was a simple breakfast, but he doubted anyone in the house would complain.

He poured coffee and loaded the cups and saucers on a tray with two heaping plates of eggs and buttery biscuits, then headed for the surgery in the back of the house. Even before he knocked, he heard Betsy crying.

The door opened quickly and Freddie stood in front of him, wringing his hands as the sounds of Betsy's sobbing grew louder.

"I brought breakfast," Connor said, and handed him the tray.

"You got to go get Miss Elizabeth," Freddie said, gripping the tray so hard the cups rattled in their saucers.

"She's getting ready for church."

Freddie winced. "But something's wrong with Betsy. She keeps crying and crying and she won't stop. What am I supposed to do with her?"

Connor reeled back. "How the hell should I know?"

"I got to do something," Freddie said.

"What did Elizabeth say?"

"She said it was normal, and all, but I can't just stand around and let Betsy cry like that. I've got to do something. What am I supposed to do? Go ask Miss Elizabeth to come down here, will you?''

Hearing Betsy's wailing should have taken the desire right out of Connor, but instead, it made him want to go upstairs and find Elizabeth. Find her and keep her up there. All morning. All afternoon. All—

''Connor?''

''What? Oh.'' Connor heaved a sigh. ''Freddie, I told you Elizabeth is getting dressed and I haven't got any idea what you should do.''

Freddie winced again as Betsy's sobs grew louder. ''Well, what would you do if it was your wife?''

''My wife?''

Connor was taken aback for a moment. His wife? He hadn't thought that far ahead—not in such detail, anyway. Sure, he'd decided he wanted a wife, a home, children of his own. He'd decided he wanted all those things that night in Kansas City when his whole life had changed. But until this moment, Connor hadn't considered everything that came with that decision.

His thoughts drifted upstairs to Elizabeth, whom he imagined to be naked at this very moment. He'd like to go up there, roll around in bed with her. But the outcome of that could land him in Freddie Brewster's place.

In that moment, Connor knew it would be all right. He wouldn't mind it at all. ''For better or worse'' in the wedding vows meant just that. Right now was the ''worse'' part, and there was nothing to do but buck up and go on. The ''better'' part would follow.

''Look, if Elizabeth says this is normal, then that's what it is. Elizabeth knows what she's talking about,'' Connor said.

''Well, I don't know…'' Freddie shook his head.

''Just sit with Betsy and hold her hand, or something,'' Connor said. ''Tell her you love her. Promise to buy her something. She'll come around. Look what she's been through. Just give her some time.''

Freddie thought for a moment, considering what Connor had said. ''Is that what you'd do?'' he finally asked.

''Yep. That's what I'd do,'' Connor told him.

''Okay. I'll give it a try.'' Freddie straightened his shoulders and disappeared into the surgery.

Connor walked out to the front porch and drew in breaths of morning air. The sun was bright, growing warm already. He stood there for a while, gazing out at the road, the town in the distance, the horses and carriages rolling past. Some of the townsfolk passing by called a welcome or waved. Connor waved back.

It was a nice feeling, waving to neighbors.

When he'd first heard about Elizabeth Hill, Connor had had just one thought in mind. Get to Sterling. Find her. Do what had to be done.

But now that he was here, things were different. Elizabeth was just as he'd imagined—better, really—but still, things had taken a turn he hadn't planned on.

Or maybe they hadn't, and he just didn't want to admit it.

Connor rubbed his palms against his eyes and drew in a big breath. Sure as hell, he'd be better off doing what had to be done here, and getting on with the rest of his plan.

But now, after all this, how could he ever bring himself to do it?

Chapter Sixteen

Garrett Whitmore showed up at Elizabeth's house just before they left for church, offering her a ride in his buggy. That didn't suit Connor. He didn't like Garrett. Didn't like watching Elizabeth ride off with the man.

Still, Connor did nothing more than stand at the window and watch the buggy pull away, Elizabeth in a deep purple dress and sassy little hat, sitting next to Garrett. What could Connor do, all things considered?

By the time he walked to church, the congregation was already moving inside. He greeted the people he knew, which was most of the folks in Sterling now, shook Reverend Brady's hand as he walked inside, and found a spot in the rear pew.

Elizabeth was already seated at the piano. Connor didn't see much of anything but her, managing only to acknowledge Heath Wheeler when he sat down beside him. He couldn't keep his eyes closed for the opening prayer, couldn't concentrate on the sermon. Connor figured the Lord would forgive him, just this once.

Afterward in the churchyard, Dixie Brady seemed quite taken with the new doctor in town. Tom Avery had been introduced by Reverend Brady during the service, and Dixie seemed anxious to make the young doctor feel welcome. Not so long ago she'd followed Connor around batting her eyelashes at him. He was glad she'd moved on to someone else.

Connor stood with a group of men talking about the weather and politics, but kept an eye on the church door. When Elizabeth finally appeared, he headed toward her. Anger sparked in his chest when Garrett Whitmore got to her first. Connor didn't stop, though.

But Sheriff Parker stepped in front of Connor as he crossed the churchyard. "I know about you, Wade," he said in a low voice.

Connor glared down at the sheriff, into eyes that were heavy with accusation and suspicion.

"Knew I'd seen your face somewhere," Parker said. "Found it on an old Wanted poster."

Connor's gut tightened. "I did my time."

"That don't mean spit to me." Parker nodded toward the townsfolk gathered nearby. "What do you think the good people of Sterling would say if they knew the truth about their so-called town hero?"

Connor didn't answer him.

"Think they'd run you out of town?" Parker proposed. "And Miss Hill along with you?"

Anger tightened Connor's jaw and his hand curled into a fist. "You leave Elizabeth out of this, you—"

"I'm keeping my eye on you, Wade. You so much as spit the wrong way in my town and you'll find yourself behind bars." A smirk pulled at his lips. "Then see what everybody says about Miss Hill."

Connor's stomach boiled as he watched Sheriff Parker amble away, and for the first time in a long time—a very long time—the drive to do bodily harm to someone nearly overcame Connor.

"Hey, Connor?"

He spun and saw Heath approach. Heath paused, seeing the look on Connor's face, and his smile disappeared. "Damn. Who put a burr under your saddle?"

Shaking the tension out of his shoulders, Connor tried to relax. "It's nothing," he said.

"Nothing?" Heath's brows drew together. "I wouldn't want you looking at me like that. Not after the way I saw you handle a gun at the bank shootout. What's troubling you?"

Connor pulled on the tight muscles at the back of his neck, tempted to tell Heath the truth. They were friends, after all, and Connor thought Heath would understand and not hold his past against him.

His past. Connor wasn't all that surprised that it had come back to haunt him. He knew he'd have to deal with what he'd done for the rest of his life. He didn't like it, but he was prepared for it.

What he wasn't prepared for was having Elizabeth dragged into the middle of it. He'd told her the truth and was glad he had. Still, he didn't want her to be hurt by what he'd done. And she would certainly be hurt, if the town found out and turned against her.

Connor blew out a heavy breath and turned to Heath. "Nothing's wrong. Just passing the time with the sheriff."

Heath glanced across the churchyard, then back to Connor. "Thought maybe Garrett Whitmore had your dander up."

Connor turned and saw Garrett escorting Elizabeth away from the church. He mumbled a curse.

"Most everybody's going over to her place," Heath said, "to see the new baby. The women brought food and things."

Connor noticed that nearly everyone was heading in the direction of Elizabeth's house. He didn't move, though. For a long moment Connor just stood there thinking.

Maybe he should leave Sterling. Leave now, before anyone else got hurt...before Elizabeth got hurt.

Connor glanced at Sheriff Parker heading toward town, then turned once again to see Elizabeth walking the other way on Garrett Whitmore's arm. Elizabeth. Beautiful Elizabeth. How the woman made his chest ache. How he wanted her.

He didn't deserve her. Connor knew that. But it didn't make him want her any less. Or make him hurt any less.

"You heading home?" Heath asked.

Connor's gaze homed in on Garrett as he tightened his grip on Elizabeth's arm.

"Damn right I am," Connor said, and started walking.

The house was full of people, laughter and chatter, making Elizabeth smile even as she scurried around the kitchen. The women were all gathered in the surgery visiting Betsy, taking turns passing the new baby around, relating their own childbirth stories. The men were strung out from the dining room to the parlor, talking about anything but babies.

"Gracious, I can't even remember the last time I had so many people here," Elizabeth said, taking a pan of hot biscuits from the oven.

At the sideboard, Connor sliced the ham Mrs. Rogers had brought over.

"Seems like it suits you," he said.

"Actually, it does." Elizabeth smiled. "Thank you so much for helping. I don't know what I'd do without you, Connor."

He'd come directly to the kitchen when he'd gotten home from church and found Elizabeth laying out all the food the townsfolk had brought with them. He'd no desire at all to be with the other men.

"The ladies deserve some time off," Connor said. "Besides, I don't think we could pry any of them away from that new baby."

"Such a blessing," Elizabeth said wistfully.

Heavy footsteps announced Garrett's entrance into the kitchen. He stopped short when he saw Connor. Connor straightened, holding the knife he'd sliced the ham with, returning Garrett's glower.

Elizabeth glanced back and forth between the two men and cleared her throat.

"Garrett, did you want something?" she asked.

Abruptly, he turned to her. "The new doctor is here, Elizabeth, and you need to get him in to see your father's medical equipment again," Garrett said. "You need to close that deal before he changes his mind."

Elizabeth's eyes widened. "Now? But that's hardly appropriate, Garrett. It's Sunday and this is a social gathering."

"The Lord says if the ox is in the ditch pull him out—even on Sunday," Garrett said.

"Betsy is in there recovering. I can hardly have a man traipsing through at a time like this."

"And that's another thing," Garrett said, moving closer, his frown deepening. "Why did you deliver that baby yourself? You should have sent for Dr. Avery."

Elizabeth didn't answer, stunned by his question. "I—I didn't even think of sending for him. I—"

"Exactly. You didn't think, Elizabeth," Garrett said. "What's Dr. Avery supposed to gather from that? The town doesn't need him, maybe? That he'll have no business here?"

Elizabeth touched her hand to her forehead. "I didn't mean to—"

"You'd better think about those things, Elizabeth.

The least you can do now is to invite Dr. Avery to examine that woman."

Her spine stiffened. "Betsy is perfectly healthy. There's no need."

Garrett frowned. "Do you want to be responsible for Sterling not having a doctor..."

Again?

The unspoken implication hung in the air. Elizabeth felt her cheeks flush.

"No," she whispered. "No, of course not."

Garrett gave her a brisk nod, then gazed around the kitchen. "Did you make your apple pies for today?"

Wearily, she wiped her hands on her apron. "I've been so busy with Betsy and the baby and—"

"You've got to think, Elizabeth," Garrett admonished. "You knew people would come over after church today to see that new baby. You've got to keep them interested in your pies if you want to sell them to the restaurants in town."

"Yes, I know that Garrett, but—"

"Better get this food out to the dining room," Garrett said. "You don't want people saying you're a bad hostess, on top of everything else."

"Maybe you'd like to give us a hand?" Connor's voice boomed from across the room. "Since you're so damn full of good ideas."

Garrett pointed his finger at Connor. "You'd better remember your place around here, Wade."

Connor jabbed the knife into the ham and crossed the kitchen. "Let me tell you—"

"Connor, don't," Elizabeth said.

She rushed forward, planting herself in front of him, forcing him to stop. He towered above her, glaring at Garrett over her head, his body tense and tight, heat wafting off of him.

Gracious, the last thing she needed was for a fight to break out in her kitchen—with a houseful of guests.

"Please," she whispered, her eyes silently pleading with him.

Connor didn't back off, but he didn't press forward, either. Elizabeth thought that was as good as she'd get from him.

She turned to Garrett. "I'll bring everything out in a few minutes."

He gave her a quick nod and started to leave, but turned back at the door. "I'll come to call on you tomorrow night, Elizabeth. Right after supper," he said, then disappeared.

Elizabeth should have heaved a sigh of relief that Garrett had left, that the threat of the two men coming to blows was over. But instead her body hummed with tension. She turned back to Connor and saw that he was still keyed up, too.

She gazed at him, his shoulders straight, his chest full and taut. Powerful. Intense. Capable, oh, so capable.

Desire rolled through her. Suddenly she wanted to throw herself against that chest of his, feel those strong arms around her. Elizabeth wanted that…and more.

Connor relaxed his stance then and backed up. Did he feel what she felt? Elizabeth wondered, and surprised herself by wishing that he did.

"If you think I'm going to apologize for what happened, you're wrong, Elizabeth," Connor said. "That man's got no business talking to you like that."

Elizabeth smiled, pleased for some reason she couldn't name. Gently, she patted his arm. They stood rooted to the kitchen floor, neither of them moving, neither wanting to move, both content with the moment.

She wondered if he'd kiss her. A brief second passed, during which she saw a spark in his eye, felt the jolt in her stomach. Connor must have changed his mind, she guessed, because he backed up a step. It was good that he had; Elizabeth wasn't sure she would have stopped him.

"That's probably Heath," Connor said, drying the last supper dish as a knock sounded at the back door. Things had been quiet since yesterday, when they'd had a houseful of guests after church services.

"I didn't know he was coming over tonight," Elizabeth said.

"We're working on the booths for Founders' Day."

Elizabeth wiped off her hands and opened the back door, surprised to see Gena on her doorstep alongside Heath. It must have showed in her face because Gena rushed ahead with an explanation.

"I wanted to see Betsy's baby again," she said, "and when Heath came by the store and said he was coming over, he was kind enough to ask me to come along, too."

Gena smiled up at Heath. He turned bright red.

Elizabeth waved them into the kitchen. "Freddie is here, but I think he'll appreciate a break."

"Betsy's still crying?" Gena asked.

"Spewing like a busted rain barrel," Connor said. He gave the women a quick smile. "Not that I blame her, of course."

Gena sighed longingly. "Still, it's worth it, having a baby."

Elizabeth and Gena left the kitchen, talking quietly. Heath's gaze stayed glued to Gena until she was out of sight.

"I could give her more babies than she'd know what to do with," he muttered.

Connor drew in a big breath, watching the last of Elizabeth's skirt disappear around the corner. Blood pumped through his veins a little hotter. Not so unusual around Elizabeth. For all the good it did him.

Connor exchanged a frustrated scowl with Heath and they both headed out to the barn. They spent about a half hour repairing the booths before Elizabeth and Gena appeared carrying a tray of lemonade and cookies.

"How's Betsy?" Heath asked, putting down his hammer.

"Still crying," Gena said. "But the baby is just precious."

"I've gotten so attached to the little fella I don't know what I'll do when they leave," Elizabeth said, serving the lemonade.

"Get a full night's sleep, maybe?" Connor asked.

"I don't even remember what that feels like," Elizabeth declared, and laughed gently.

"Maybe you could—" Heath gazed out the barn door, past Elizabeth. "Looks like you've got more company."

She turned and gasped softly as Garrett stepped into the barn; the look on his face made her feel guilty—about what, she didn't know.

He mumbled a greeting to the others and glared at Connor.

"Garrett, this is a surprise," Elizabeth said.

"I told you I was coming to call," he said. "I told you yesterday."

She remembered, then. He'd told her in the kitchen just after he and Connor had nearly come to blows. Somehow, she'd forgotten.

"Let's go, Elizabeth."

Garrett offered his arm. She hesitated, glancing quickly at Connor.

"Elizabeth," Garrett said, sharply enough to bring her attention back to him. "I've come to call on you. You're not planning to entertain in the barn, are you?"

"No," Elizabeth said. "Of course not."

Garrett took her arm and escorted her away from

the barn. He led her to the swing on the front porch, seated her, then made a show of removing his hat, unbuttoning his jacket, before sitting down beside her. To anyone who passed by, he looked settled and comfortable, as if he belonged there.

Garrett dived right in telling her about his day, everything he'd done, who he'd seen, what they'd said, what he'd said. Elizabeth listened, nodded politely, tried to be attentive. After all, how long had it been since a man had come to call on her? She couldn't even remember. Yet here he was, one of Sterling's most outstanding citizens, sitting on her front porch for all the town to see.

She should have been proud he'd come to call on her. Garrett was well thought of in town. Many a young woman would be pleased to have him on her front porch. He was respectable, a man of some wealth and power.

Not that such things meant much to Elizabeth. Her own family had had wealth and power at one point, but it hadn't lasted and hadn't kept her from suffering disappointment and heartache just like anyone less fortunate.

A little breeze stirred, bringing voices with it. Laughter, Elizabeth realized, from the barn. Gena, Heath and Connor drinking lemonade, working on the booths and laughing.

Elizabeth looked up at Garrett and told herself again how fortunate she was that he'd come to call on her.

Oh yes, so fortunate.

Chapter Seventeen

"**Y**ou're certainly making progress," Elizabeth called from the doorway of the upstairs bedroom.

Inside, Connor looked up from the board he was sawing. "It's coming along," he said, glancing around the room. "You'll have your boarders in here before you know it."

Elizabeth lingered in the doorway, wanting to go inside for a closer look. Technically, it was still a bedroom, though it hardly looked like one at the moment with the furniture gone and boards, nails and Connor's tools scattered about.

"I'm glad you talked me into dividing up these rooms," Elizabeth said.

"Looks like plenty of living space to me," Connor agreed.

"I don't supposed you've found anything behind the walls, have you?" she asked, twisting her fingers together.

Connor dragged his sleeve across his forehead,

wiping away sweat. "Like what? Some relative who disappeared suddenly?"

"No, of course not." Elizabeth's smile froze after a moment, and she struggled to hold it in place. "I was thinking maybe you'd come across the money Raymond embezzled."

Connor paused, then glanced around the room again. "You think this is where he hid it? In here?"

"I don't know," Elizabeth said, her gaze traveling the walls. "It could be anywhere."

Connor exhaled heavily. "Even if you found it and turned it in, Elizabeth, it wouldn't change anything," he said softly.

"I know. Really, I know that," she said. "I just thought that if by some miracle I found the money and gave it back…"

Connor crossed to her and tilted her chin up. She gazed at him with hopeful, sorrowful eyes that made his heart ache.

"It wouldn't make any difference," he said gently. "I wish it would. But what's done is done, Elizabeth. You can't go back and undo it, no matter how much you'd like to."

She managed a smile. "You're right. I know you're right."

Connor dropped his hand and forced himself to step away from her. It wasn't easy. In fact, it was getting harder and harder with each day that passed.

He wanted to tell her that. He wanted Elizabeth to know how he felt. He wanted the whole town, the whole world to know. There were so many things he wanted to tell her...but couldn't.

"I saw Heath in town this morning," Connor said, changing the subject. "He and Gena were together. He was carrying her packages and they had their heads together, talking."

Elizabeth nodded, seemingly relieved by the new topic of discussion. "I didn't think it was coincidence that Gena was over here three nights this week while you and Heath finished up the booths," she answered.

Garrett had showed up on Monday night but hadn't asked to call on Elizabeth again. So the next few nights when Heath and Gena had come over, the four of them had spent the evenings together in the barn working on the booths, then in the house for coffee, or on the front porch with lemonade.

Connor gestured around the room. "Am I making too much noise for Betsy and the baby?"

"No, she's fine. Says she likes it. Reminds her of home," Elizabeth said.

"Speaking of home, when is she going back to hers?"

Elizabeth shrugged. "In a while."

"I admit I don't know much about having babies," Connor said, "but seems to me she's been here a long time."

"I just want to be sure she's well rested."

"And you like having the baby here."

Elizabeth rolled her eyes. "Gracious, I can't get away with anything around you, can I?"

"I didn't say I blamed you," Connor said, smiling. "It's kind of nice having the little fella around."

"He's certainly found a place in my heart," Elizabeth admitted. "Supper's ready. Can you come down now?"

"For your cooking? You bet."

He followed her downstairs and washed up outside while she put their meal on the table; he'd long ago stopped eating alone in his room above the barn.

After they'd eaten, when they'd done the last of their chores for the day, Elizabeth slipped into the surgery for a final check on Betsy, and as had become her custom, she brought the baby out with her.

Connor sat on the front porch swing when she stepped outside, the sleeping baby wrapped tight in a soft blanket. She sat beside Connor in the dark and he got the swing to rocking as crickets chirped and birds sang their night songs.

They'd sat this way for days now, together, just the two of them and the baby. A peaceful way to end the day.

"You ladies got everything set for tomorrow?" Connor asked.

"We had our last meeting today," Elizabeth said, "and everything is as ready for Founders' Day as it's ever going to be. Did you and Heath get the booths delivered?"

"Delivered, set up and ready to go," Connor said. "That Abigail Rogers damn near talked my ear off, but it's done. I'm anxious to see what goes on tomorrow. I've never been to a Founders' Day festival before.''

She looked up at him. "You're kidding."

"Nope."

"Oh, that's right. Your mother was ill when you were growing up."

Connor gave her a little smile. "I was kind of hoping I could find me an experienced woman to show me around."

"Well, that depends on what kind of experience you're looking for," Elizabeth pointed out.

Connor stretched his arm along the back of the swing and leaned a little closer. "Well, actually—"

The baby wailed, stretching his little arms outward, sending Connor back to his half of the porch swing.

He scrubbed his hands over his face. "Are you *sure* it's not time to send Betsy and her baby home?"

Elizabeth bounced the baby gently in her arms, crooning softly to him until he quieted.

"I don't know when I'll ever again get to hold a baby this much," she said, gazing at the child. "The new doctor will take over now that he's in town, and, well, it's not likely I'll ever have one of my own."

Connor's blood began to pump harder as images filled his head. If she wanted a baby, he'd give her one—give everything he had, trying. And lately, he'd had a lot to give. Problem was, he didn't think she'd let him. And, really, he didn't deserve the opportunity.

"I'd better take him back inside," Elizabeth said, gathering the baby in her arms. "He might be hungry again."

That brought another vision into Connor's head, one that had little to do with a hungry baby but everything to do with breasts—Elizabeth's breasts.

At the doorway, she turned back toward Connor. "I really should let them go home, shouldn't I."

He rose, thinking how pretty she looked, holding the baby, trying so hard to be brave. It wasn't easy being brave by yourself. Still, she'd managed it for the last year or so since her father died and her brother left.

So much easier being brave and strong with another person at your side. Connor wished he could be that person. With all his heart, he wished it.

"If you want them to stay a couple of days longer," he said, "I guess it won't hurt anything."

Elizabeth favored him with a smile, then gave one to the baby. "Just a couple more days," she promised.

Betsy woke the next morning crying—crying this time because she wanted to go home.

"I—I just want to be in my own place, Miss Elizabeth," she said, sitting up in bed, sobbing into the handkerchief she'd about worn out. "With my own things, and—and my own husband, and—and my own things."

Freddie stood at the foot of the bed twisting his hat, looking a little pale, pleading with his eyes for Elizabeth to keep his wife awhile longer because he certainly didn't know what to do with her once he got her home.

"Betsy," Elizabeth said, "I just want to make sure you're strong enough to—"

"I want to go home!"

"Now, Betsy, darling," Freddie said, "if Miss Elizabeth says—"

"Freddie Brewster, if you don't take me home today, I'll just—"

"All right, honey pie, all right," Freddie said quickly. He turned to Elizabeth and shrugged helplessly.

With a deep sigh, Elizabeth nodded. She'd known Betsy was strong enough to go home a couple of days ago. Freddie would look after her and the baby, see to it she was taken care of. There was really no reason for her to stay.

Except...

Elizabeth walked to the cradle beside the bed, where the baby had managed to sleep through Betsy's crying and wailing. He was lying on his tummy with his legs tucked under him, his cap of red hair standing straight up and his fingers curled into tiny fists. A sleeping angel.

A deep ache settled in Elizabeth's chest. It bore down on her with such pain her breathing became labored.

She didn't understand what was happening to her.

She'd delivered babies before. Lots of them. And before her, her father had done the same. They'd stayed with their mothers in the surgery as far back as she could remember, and she'd sent them on their way with never a second thought.

So what was different now? Why was it so hard to let this baby go? Why, suddenly, did the fact that she would never have her own child hurt so badly?

And it did hurt. It hurt like nothing she'd ever felt before. Worse than when her mother died, and her father died, and her brother left. Worse, even, than the pain of the whole town talking about her.

Reaching down, Elizabeth rubbed her fingertip across the baby's soft knuckles. His little hand opened and clamped on to her.

A lump rose in Elizabeth's chest. She couldn't let him leave. She just couldn't.

Connor patted his stallion's neck as he led him into the corral, ready to brush him down. But he stopped when he saw Elizabeth walking toward him from the house. Connor dropped the brush. Something was wrong.

He didn't bother with the gate, just vaulted over the fence and hurried to her.

She stopped a few feet from him, her shoulders rigid, tears swimming in her eyes.

He waited, forcing himself to hold back, fighting against every instinct in his body to shout at her, demand to know what was wrong.

"What happened?" Connor asked after a moment, when he thought his chest would burst.

"She's—she's leaving. And taking the...baby."

Tears spilled onto Elizabeth's cheeks and she dissolved against his chest. Connor gathered her in his arms and held her tight against him.

She curled her fingers into his shirt and looked up at him. "I didn't expect to keep the baby here forever. I know he has to go home. But—but— Oh, Connor, I don't know what's wrong with me."

He held her and patted her shoulders, and leaned down to talk quietly against her ear.

"Who says something's wrong with you?" he asked. "Hell, Elizabeth, just because the whole town's saying you're too old to get married and have children doesn't make it so. You're a strong, healthy woman, and wanting to have children of your own is a normal part of life. Why wouldn't you want that?"

"I don't know, it's just..." She looked up at him, sniffed, then fell against his chest again. "Oh, Connor, I just don't know anything right now."

"Well, that's okay, too," he said, and wrapped his arms tighter around her.

Elizabeth clung to him, soaking up his strength and the comfort he gave so effortlessly. Her palms rode against the hard muscles of his chest. Her cheek rested on his wide shoulder. Never, never in her whole life had Elizabeth felt so secure.

And then it all came clear to her. In the blink of an eye, locked in the circle of Connor's arms, Elizabeth knew the reason she didn't want Betsy to leave, the reason she wanted the baby to stay and the reason she wanted a child of her own.

She'd fallen in love with Connor Wade.

She eased back a little and gazed up at him. His square chin, his crooked nose, those deep gray eyes. She loved them. She loved *him*.

But how could that be? She was too old for marrying—everybody said so. Besides, she'd never pursued having a husband, children, a family of her own. Oh, she'd imagined it occasionally, but she'd never *wanted* it. Not like she wanted it now.

The realization added another layer of confusion to her already muddled thoughts. What could she do? Blurt out how she felt? Ask if he shared her feelings? Gracious, no. She couldn't do either of those things. Not now, anyway. Not at this moment. Really, she couldn't do anything.

Except deal with the problem at hand.

Elizabeth backed away from Connor, sniffing. He passed her his handkerchief and she wiped her eyes and blew her nose.

"I have to let Betsy go," Elizabeth said. "It's the right thing to do."

"Sometimes the right thing is the hardest thing you can do."

Elizabeth gulped and fought back another round of tears. Connor was so smart in so many ways. He gave her strength she didn't know she had.

"How did I ever manage before you got here, Connor?" she whispered.

His expression hardened. "You're a strong woman, Elizabeth. You don't give yourself enough credit. I just hope one day you'll see that for yourself."

Elizabeth shook her head. "I don't feel very strong right now."

Connor grinned. "Well, that's the best part about having somebody else around. You can take turns holding each other up."

He tucked her arm through his and headed toward the house. "Between the two of us we'll get Betsy sent back home, maybe have another round of crying, then go to the Founders' Day celebration tonight and have a good time."

Elizabeth drew in a ragged breath. It made sense, like most everything else Connor said.

By the time they got to the house, Freddie had already gone home, fetched his wagon and come back, probably at a dead run. Elizabeth helped Betsy get dressed, then gathered the baby for the slow walk to the front of the house, while Connor and Freddie loaded the gifts the townsfolk had brought over.

Freddie assisted Betsy onto the wagon seat while Elizabeth reminded her what to do. "Get plenty of rest," she said. "And don't go up and down any steps. No heavy lifting, either."

"Don't worry, Miss Elizabeth, I'll take good care of her," Freddie said.

"I'll be at the Founders' Day celebration tonight

if you need anything," Elizabeth said. "Don't hesitate to come over if you have any problems."

"Yes, ma'am," Freddie said.

Elizabeth looked down at the baby in her arms, then sensed Connor beside her. With a big sigh, she gave the baby a final hug, then passed him to his father.

"Take good care of both of them," she said.

"I will," Freddie promised.

He passed the baby up to Betsy, then climbed into the wagon and jangled the reins. Connor guided Elizabeth onto the porch and stood beside her until the wagon pulled out of sight.

Several minutes passed while they both just stood there, staring down the empty road toward town. Without Connor near her, Elizabeth feared she'd fall to pieces again. She knew, too, that if she did, it would be all right with Connor. He'd understand.

Finally, he draped his arm around her shoulder and gave her a squeeze. "You handled that real well, Elizabeth," he said. "And just think, the hardest part of the day is over. Nothing can be worse than that."

Another wagon rumbled down the road and pulled to a stop in front of the house. Connor tensed and shifted in front of Elizabeth, sheltering her, as he saw Garrett seated atop the wagon alongside Dr. Avery.

"Good news, Elizabeth," Garrett called. "The doc's here to pick up your father's equipment."

Chapter Eighteen

How quickly everything was packed up. How quickly it was all gone.

Elizabeth stood off to the side as Dr. Avery and the two young men he'd brought with him packed up her father's surgery and loaded it onto the wagon.

The glass-fronted cabinets, the examination table, the medical supplies, the instruments, books, bandages, journals. Everything. Gone.

Just as quickly as when her father had died. In a moment, everything was different. Irrevocably different.

Elizabeth watched, unable to speak, hardly able to take it all in. Garrett bustled around the surgery, directing the loading of the equipment, cautioning the young men to be careful. Connor was there, too, standing behind her, his arms folded across his chest. He didn't offer to help, didn't say anything.

But what could be said at this point? That she was sentimental and wanted to keep her father's belongings for no good reason? That having his surgery intact was the same as still having him? That seeing it leave was like losing him all over again?

Elizabeth pressed her lips together and gulped hard as the last crate was carried out.

"Thank you, Miss Hill. I appreciate this," Dr. Avery said, his words seeming to echo in the empty room. He nodded politely and went out the door.

Garrett took a final look around the room and rubbed his hands together. "Well, I guess that's everything. Afternoon, Elizabeth."

"Not so fast," Connor said, stepping to the center of the room, stopping Garrett in his tracks. "What about her money?"

"I've got it right here," Garrett said, and patted his pocket. "But I'm holding on to it for safekeeping, until we can sit down and go over what you're to do with it, Elizabeth."

"She wants it now," Connor said, unable to keep the edge from his voice.

Garrett glared at Connor, then finally pulled a drawstring sack from his pocket. He opened it and counted out two half eagle gold pieces.

"For the boys who helped with the hauling," Garrett explained, and pocketed the two coins. He passed the sack to Elizabeth, then nodded briskly and left.

"Bastard..." Connor muttered.

Elizabeth glanced around the empty room, her sense of loss deepened by the weight of the drawstring sack in her hand. Still, as was so often the case, there was nothing she could do but go on.

"It's for the best," she said, straightening her shoulders. "Now the town has a doctor—a real doctor. He can practice medicine, care for everyone."

Elizabeth turned her gaze up to meet Connor's. Twin frown lines cut across his forehead, and she knew he didn't see things her way.

But he didn't say anything. Didn't disagree with her. Didn't do anything to make her feel worse than she already felt.

A small smile pulled at her lips. "Thank you."

He seemed to understand what she meant, because he just nodded and gave her the closest thing to a smile she'd seen on his face since Garrett had arrived. Elizabeth was grateful for that.

"Guess we'd better get things ready and head on down to the church," Connor said.

She went up to her room and Connor headed out to the barn. Elizabeth stood in her bedroom gazing at the sunny yellow dress she'd planned to wear today. She'd looked forward to the Founders' Day celebration for so long, had worked so hard to help organize it. But now...

Elizabeth pulled a black skirt and gray blouse from her armoire and put it on. It suited her, she decided, studying her reflection in the mirror. Old maid's clothing. For an old maid.

In the kitchen she loaded the apple pies she'd baked and the chicken she'd fried this morning into her basket, remembering Founders' Days of the past.

She'd worked on the organizing committee for years. Her father had always sponsored a booth. Likely as not, they'd run late each year trying to get to the celebration, a last-minute patient delaying them. Or they'd rushed home early when an emergency arose. Her brother, good sport that he was, usually volunteered for the dunking booth. Raymond could also be counted on to enter the pie and watermelon eating contests.

Elizabeth's hand stilled as she drew the checkered cloth over her basket. Nothing was the same this year. Her father was gone—dead. Her brother was in prison. She hadn't heard a word from him in all the months he'd been gone. He'd said he wouldn't write to her from prison and he'd kept his word. She didn't expect to hear from him until he turned up on her doorstep after his release—if he came here at all. Raymond may as well have been dead, too.

Memories pulled at Elizabeth, dragging her spirits lower. The vision of the empty surgery pressed upon her mind. Only yesterday it had been filled with her father's equipment—and life. Betsy and her new baby.

Tears threatened again, choking Elizabeth's throat and bearing down on her chest. Everything she'd held dear was gone. Everything.

A light knock sounded on the back door and Connor walked inside, not waiting for her to answer. Elizabeth sniffed and brushed away the tears standing in her eyes.

"We'd better go," she said, reaching for her bas-

ket. She stopped, though, seeing Connor still lingering beside the door, one hand behind him and an
odd expression on his face.

"What's wrong?" she asked.

He pushed the door closed and stepped nearer. "I
can't make up for the hurt you've had today, much
as I'd like to. But I got you something, Elizabeth,
and...well, right now just seemed like as good a
time as any to give it to you."

"You bought me something?"

He nodded and extended his hand, revealing a
package wrapped in brown paper, tied with waxed
string.

"What is it?" she asked.

He grinned and held it closer. "Open it and see."

Puzzled, Elizabeth took the package. She spent a
moment feeling the weight in her hands, shifting it,
listening for rattles. Finally, she untied the string and
pulled back the paper. A shawl lay inside. Pink, just
like the one ruined at the bank shoot-out. Just like
the one her father had given her.

"Oh, Connor..." Elizabeth lifted the shawl from
the paper and held it against her. "It's the same as
the one Papa gave me. The same—just the same."

She looked up at him, smiling. "How did you
know?"

"Gena helped me out," Connor admitted. "I told
her I wanted to get you another shawl, to make up
for the one you couldn't use anymore. She gave me
the particulars, helped me pick it out."

Connor walked closer. "I wanted it to be just perfect for you, Elizabeth."

"Oh, it is." Elizabeth rubbed the soft fabric against her cheek and smiled up at him. Then, on impulse, she rose on her toes and planted a kiss on his cheek. "Thank you, Connor. It's beautiful."

He smiled broadly, soaking up her happiness, the scent of her, the touch of her hand against his arm where she steadied herself.

"I'm glad you like it," Connor said, pleased with himself.

"I love it," Elizabeth insisted as she swung the shawl around her shoulders and tied it in front. She faced him, squaring her shoulders, tilting her chin at a saucy angle. "How do I look?"

Connor soaked in the sight of her standing before him, just for him. Lord, he could spend the rest of his life looking at her.

"Beautiful," he declared. "You look beautiful."

She turned to the little mirror that hung beside the stove, shifting to see as much of her reflection as she could. Then she leaned closer, tucked away a few strands of her silky hair and pinched her delicate cheeks.

Connor could have died right then, died a happy man, privileged to witness these few private moments with Elizabeth, the finest woman he'd laid eyes on in his life, thrilled that he'd made her happy.

She turned to him again, smiling. "Thank you, Connor. Thank you so much."

Elizabeth clutched his arm and rose on her toes

to kiss his cheek again, but Connor turned his head toward her. Her breath, hot and sweet, puffed against his mouth. She hung there for a moment, their lips inches apart, her hand tightening on his arm, and then finally, she kissed him.

Oh, so sweet a homecoming, Connor thought as he looped his arms around her and blended his mouth over hers. He kissed her deeply, hungrily, and Elizabeth kissed him back—just the same way. He slid his tongue inside her, and she welcomed him. She moaned. He groaned. Connor pressed closer, fitting his body against hers. His hardness against her softness. Her curves melting into his sharp angles.

He kissed her, glided his hand up her back to her neck, wanting more, unable to get enough. Realizing that, Connor came to his senses.

He pulled his lips from hers. "Elizabeth…"

"Yes?" She blinked up at him, her warm breath fanning his lips.

Holding her tight against him, Connor gulped. "We…we should probably go to the Founders' whatever-it-is."

"The…what?" she asked, her arms locked around his neck.

"That thing. At the church."

"Oh, yes. That." Elizabeth's grip on him eased slightly.

But Connor tightened his hold on her, pulling her fully against him. His body burned for her. It was about to take over where his brain left off.

"Of course," he murmured, and nuzzled his lips

against her throat, "there's always next year. The town will have it again next year, won't it?"

Elizabeth closed her eyes, sinking into the exquisite feel of his mouth on her flesh, helpless against it.

"Next year..." she whispered. "Oh, yes. Next year. Of course."

Her lips sought his and he accommodated her with a deep, hungry kiss.

"We'll just stay here," Elizabeth whispered, as he spread kisses across her jaw, down her throat. "Stay here and—"

Connor froze. Elizabeth froze. He lifted his mouth from her hot flesh. She eased back a fraction of an inch from the warmth of his body. They gazed into each other's eyes, realizing what they'd been doing—what they were about to do.

Demands of the body and the mind warred within Connor. He knew what he should say, what he should do, but it took a few minutes for his mouth to form the words.

"We should go," he finally said.

Elizabeth gazed up at him. "You're right. We should."

Still, neither of them moved. They remained locked together in each other's arms.

Finally, with a deep, anguished sigh, Connor took a full step away from her. "Let's go."

Elizabeth stepped away quickly. "Yes, we'd better."

Grabbing her market basket, Elizabeth headed for

the door, then stopped, Connor on her heels. She looked up at him, feeling the heat that radiated from him even though they no longer touched. For a long moment, they just stared at each other.

Finally, Connor ground his teeth together. "Let's go."

He gave her a little nudge and they left the house.

"Oh, look at you two. Why the long faces?" Gena called as they reached the churchyard.

Connor glanced down at Elizabeth. Neither had spoken since they'd left the house. Neither had to. The trip to the church had walked off enough of Connor's desire that he was fit to be seen in public. But inside, he still boiled.

"Nothing's wrong," Elizabeth said, chancing a glance at Connor. "We've been busy today."

"Busy *working*," Connor said quickly.

"Oh, yes, of course. Busy *working*," Elizabeth said, and dipped her gaze away from him.

Gena shook her head at the two of them, then took Elizabeth's arm. "Let's go put your food with the rest," she said, and the two women walked away.

Connor seethed, watching Elizabeth's bustle sway through the crowd. He wanted her. Wanted her so bad he hurt.

"Hey, Connor."

A big hand thudded on his back and Connor turned to find Heath beside him.

"For a while there I thought you wouldn't show up," Heath said.

"For a while, I thought I wouldn't, too," Connor muttered, savoring the last glimpse of Elizabeth.

"Come on," Heath said, and slapped his back again. "Let's see what's here this year."

Connor followed Heath across the churchyard, and still keeping one eye on Elizabeth, got a look at the first Founders' Day festival he'd ever seen.

Lanterns had been strung on wire between poles all around the perimeter of the churchyard, glowing now in the dusk. Circling the area were the booths Connor and Heath had repaired.

Most every business and civic organization in Sterling sponsored a booth and sold nearly everything imaginable. Fried chicken, slices of cake and pie, cookies, pickles and boiled eggs, honey biscuits, lemonade. Sock dolls, knitted scarfs, marbles, mittens.

In the center was a makeshift dance floor. Three men on guitar, fiddle and harmonica were already playing tunes.

Surely, everyone in Sterling was in attendance. Folks crowded together talking, children ran, couples danced, others sat on blankets eating, a few men threw horseshoes.

Connor walked alongside Heath, speaking to people he knew, nodding politely, while inside he was about to explode. He'd done the right thing back at Elizabeth's house, stopping before they went too far. And they could so easily have gone too far.

Heat snapped through his body, humming and bucking, bringing back the desire he'd struggled to keep under control. Connor forced away the thoughts that would do nothing but lead to trouble…or make him miserable the whole night.

"I had me a talk with Gena this afternoon," Heath said, as they walked. "I asked her if I could court her, serious-like."

Connor raised an eyebrow. "You got your nerve up all of a sudden."

"Yep, I did." Heath stopped and leaned a little closer. "I got to where I couldn't think straight for wanting her. Wanting her in bed, you know?"

Connor stifled a groan. "Yeah, I know."

"Me rolling around in bed with her. Every night. Making love until—"

Connor elbowed him in the ribs. "I got it!"

"Oh, yeah." Heath shook himself, getting back on track. "Of course, that's only part of it. I got to thinking about how nice it would be to come home to her every night. To look at her across the table every morning. To have somebody to build a life with. You know what I mean?"

Connor nodded slowly. He gazed across the churchyard, wishing he could spot Elizabeth. "Yeah, I know exactly what you mean."

"So," Heath said, "I finally got my nerve up and decided that I'd talk to her. She said she'd be proud to have me court her."

Connor looked at him. "Proud, huh?"

"Yep. Proud. That's what she said." Heath hitched up his trousers. "I think I'll go find Gena right now."

Watching his friend amble away, Connor's ardor cooled a little. Yes, Gena would be proud to have Heath court her. He was a good man. He ran a successful business, had a good-size nest egg put away, was well thought of in town. In fact, everybody in Sterling thought highly of him. Heath had a lot to offer a woman.

Would Elizabeth be equally proud to have Connor court her? he couldn't help but wonder.

He didn't have a successful business. Didn't have a long-term reputation in Sterling, just that quick flash from the bank shoot-out. Didn't have much to offer a woman. Especially a woman as fine as Elizabeth.

Connor stewed for a moment, angry at himself, angry at all the mistakes he'd made in his past. It would have been easy to blame others, others who reasonably had a hand in how things had turned out. But he didn't. He carried what he'd done on his own shoulders.

All he could do now was go forward as best he could.

With a quick intake of breath, Connor caught sight of Elizabeth on the other side of the dance floor beside the fried chicken booth. As usual, most of his problems disappeared at the sight of her.

She stood with Gena, talking the way women talk. Smiling, leaning close every so often, chattering so fast he often wondered how they knew what each other was saying.

But at this moment Connor knew Elizabeth was

talking about the new shawl he'd given her. He watched as she lovingly ran her hand down the pink fabric. Gena, no doubt, was relating her part in the purchasing of it. Elizabeth looked so happy that Connor beamed with pleasure. He'd put that smile on her face. He couldn't remember when anything meant so much to him.

He could have stood there all night looking at her, enjoying the way the shawl hung on her slim shoulders, eyeing the knot she'd tied in it at her breasts.

But Connor had never been much good at standing by watching things happen. He wanted to get closer, as close to Elizabeth as he could.

He mulled the situation over for a moment, then it occurred to him that he could ask Elizabeth to dance. Seemed easy enough, but he gave it a little more thought.

He wasn't much of a dancer, but that wasn't the real source of his dilemma. Once he got Elizabeth in his arms—dance floor or not—he could wind up embarrassing them both. In front of the whole town. And since Elizabeth was so all-fired worried about what people had to say, Lord knows what would happen after that. She'd probably have to leave town.

Connor watched her across the churchyard, watched her smile, the endearing way she tilted her head, the way she touched the back of her hair from time to time.

He had to have her.

Desire consumed him again. Town watching or not, Connor had to have Elizabeth in his arms.

Connor yanked his hat lower on his forehead and headed across the churchyard. But he stopped short when Garrett Whitmore appeared, took Elizabeth's hand and led her onto the dance floor.

Anger roiled through Connor's stomach. He charged across the churchyard.

Chapter Nineteen

Connor stopped at the edge of the dance floor. A group of men crowded in front of him and dancers whirled around in a circle.

Among them was Elizabeth and Garrett Whitmore. Anger churned inside Connor as he watched them sweep past. Whitmore held her a little too close, clasped her hand a little too firmly, eyed her like a wolf hunting its prey.

Curling his hand into a fist, Connor pushed his way through the few men in front of him. He'd pound that smug look off Whitmore's face. Then he'd claim Elizabeth for himself, take her in his arms and dance the night away with her.

Connor stopped at the edge of the dance floor, coming to his senses. Go out there and beat the stuffing out of Whitmore? In front of the whole town? Lay claim to Elizabeth? Oh yeah, she'd dance with him then.

He fumed, grumbled under his breath, huffed out

his anger. Connor became aware of all the townsfolk gathered around him. From the corner of his eye he caught sight of Sheriff Parker.

Drawing in a calming breath, Connor stayed where he was. He'd have his chance with Elizabeth as soon as the song ended.

Time dragged on, Elizabeth and Whitmore kept dancing, and Connor was contemplating doing away with the band when he noticed Jane Gunther and Boyd Sherman standing alone near the rear of the church, outside the circle of lantern light. As usual, they were arguing.

Gena had hinted that she didn't understand what her sister saw in Sherman, and Connor couldn't disagree with her. He didn't like the bastard, plain and simple.

As he watched, Sherman slapped Jane across the face. She reeled back, bumped into the church. Sherman grabbed her arm. Fury roiled inside Connor. He pushed through the crowd toward them.

He reached the couple just as Sherman drew back his hand again. Connor caught it, spun him around and slammed his fist into Sherman's face. The man staggered back. Jane screamed. Connor caught the front of Sherman's shirt, drove his fist into his stomach, then bashed him in the face again, sending him to the ground.

For a second, Jane stared down at Sherman, tears streaming down her face. Then she dropped to her knees beside him.

"Boyd...oh Boyd," she cried, and draped herself

across him. Jane looked up at Connor. "What have you done to him?"

A blow struck Connor from behind, sending him hard into the side of the church. He pushed away, but stopped at the sound of metal clicking at his ear—a hammer being pulled back.

Sheriff Parker's voice spoke from behind him. "Go ahead and move. Do it, Wade. Give me a reason to put a bullet in you."

Connor held up his hands. The sheriff jerked him around and slammed him against the wall. Jane was still crying, helping Boyd Sherman to his feet.

"You two get on out of here," Sheriff Parker said, waving them away.

Jane latched on to Sherman and they disappeared into the darkness behind the church.

Music drifted across the yard, along with chatter and laughter. The crowd kept to the festivities, unaware of what had just occurred.

"I told you what would happen if you caused any trouble in my town, Wade," Sheriff Parker said.

Connor gestured at the spot where Boyd Sherman had lain a moment ago. "He slapped her. Hit her in the face. I wasn't about to—"

"I didn't see nothing like that," Parker said. His eyes narrowed. "All I saw was you beating Sherman."

"Ask Jane Gunther," Connor said. But even as he spoke the words he doubted Jane would say anything against Boyd Sherman.

"I want you out of my town," Parker said, "by sundown tomorrow."

Connor tensed. He hadn't done anything wrong and the sheriff probably knew it. That didn't stop Parker from using it as an excuse to get what he wanted.

"I didn't break any law," Connor said.

"That's not the way I see it." Parker shook his head. "I don't want your kind in Sterling, Wade. You might have everybody else in town fooled, but you don't fool me. I know what you are." Parker leaned closer. "And unless you want the whole town to know, too, you'd better do like I say and move along."

Connor glared at him, holding his anger in check. A smug grin pulled at the sheriff's lips. "And unless you want the whole town to start talking about Miss Elizabeth Hill again. How she took you in, fed you, gave you work. What a fool she made of herself over you. How she trusted you. Oh, yeah, the good folks of Sterling will be talking about Elizabeth for a long time to come."

Anger seethed in Connor. His limbs shook with it. For an instant he was tempted to laugh in the sheriff's face, tell him he wasn't leaving Sterling and there wasn't a damn thing the sheriff could do about it. He hadn't broken any law. He'd done a decent, honorable thing coming to Jane Gunther's aid. The folks of Sterling would agree with him.

But they would also talk. Connor didn't doubt for a minute that Parker would spread the word of his crime, his arrest, his prison sentence. He could handle it. He'd handled it before.

Elizabeth, however, was another matter.

Connor's stomach ached at the prospect of him being the cause of her unhappiness, her humiliation. And surely that's what it would be when word got out. It would all fall back on Elizabeth.

He couldn't put her through that. He couldn't be responsible for heaping that embarrassment on her. Elizabeth was a private woman. She'd barely held up under the scorn of her father's death and her brother's embezzlement. Connor wouldn't let that happen to her—because of him.

"All right, Parker," Connor said in a low voice. "You'll get your way. I'll be leaving Sterling tomorrow."

The sheriff nodded slowly. "See that you do." He holstered his pistol and sauntered away.

For a long moment Connor stood at the side of the church. A short distance away the Founders' Day celebration was in full swing. Couples danced. People laughed, visited, chatted. Children played. The aroma of delicious food mingled with the music.

It was only a few yards away, but may as well have been on the other side of the world. The festivities, the people, the friends, the companionship, the feeling of belonging was all just out of Connor's reach.

His shoulders sagged. He slumped against the wall.

And Elizabeth, of course. She was beyond his reach, too. But, really, she always had been. Such a smart, refined woman. Connor's chest ached at the thought of never seeing her again.

He drew in a deep breath and righted himself. It hurt like hell, but he'd made the correct decision. The only decision he could make. No way would he put her through any embarrassment on account of him. He had to do as he'd told the sheriff. He had to leave Sterling.

Connor headed toward the dance floor, tempted for a moment to join the festivities. To have this one last night here among friends. A few moments with good, decent people who liked him, thought well of him. To revel in the joy of belonging, even if it was for only a short time.

But in the end, Connor turned the other way, away from the crowd. Better to make a clean break.

He paused for a moment, his gaze drawn to the dance floor. Elizabeth would have to be told, of course. He couldn't just leave without a word. It wouldn't be right, after all she'd done for him. He wanted to thank her.

Connor didn't move, though, didn't comb the gathering looking for her. He was being selfish and he knew it. He didn't want to thank her, not really. He wanted to see her again, one last time. Gaze into those blue eyes of hers, feast on her beauty, gather enough memories to last the rest of his life.

Someone bumped him from behind. Connor tensed, sure it was the sheriff again. Instead, Heath stepped in front of him. "Where you been?" he asked, frowning.

Connor didn't answer, didn't explain. He tensed, concerned by the look on Heath's face.

"What's wrong?" he asked.

"Elizabeth left awhile ago," Heath said, nodding toward the road.

"Left? Why? What happened? Was she sick?"

Heath shook his head. "She wouldn't say. Gena tried to talk to her but Elizabeth wouldn't open her mouth. I didn't like the looks of it."

"What do you mean?"

"Elizabeth left here with Garrett Whitmore."

Connor's lungs burned by the time he reached Elizabeth's place. He braced his hands against his knees, heaving from the run, then straightened and eyed the house.

No sign of Whitmore's buggy out front. The downstairs was dark; not one lantern burned in the parlor or dining room window. The place was quiet.

Already he'd imagined most everything that could have happened to Elizabeth at the Founders' Day celebration. She fell and hurt herself. She became ill. Someone hurt her feelings, embarrassed her, reminded her of her father or brother. Still, none of that seem worthy of Elizabeth departing so quickly, refusing to discuss it with Gena, and leaving with Garrett Whitmore, of all people.

Whitmore. Connor didn't trust that man. What if he'd told Elizabeth some lie to get her away from the church? More, uglier visions popped into Connor's head.

He headed down the side of the house. The kitchen was dark. He circled to the back of the house and stopped short.

Elizabeth's bedroom window glowed with lantern light.

Another dozen possibilities—all of them bad— burned in Connor's mind. He had to get to Elizabeth. He had to be sure she was all right.

Connor raced around the house to the kitchen door. Locked. He hoisted up the window he'd built in the little room Elizabeth tutored her students in, and climbed inside.

He banged his shin, crashed into the table and felt his way along in the dark until he'd crossed the kitchen. In the hallway, faint light shone from upstairs.

"Elizabeth!"

Connor pounded up the stairs. He strode toward the back of the house, following the lantern light that beamed from her bedroom.

"Elizabeth!"

He stopped short. Elizabeth stepped into the doorway of her bedroom.

"Gracious, Connor, what's wrong?" she asked, frowning and clutching her hand to her chest.

He didn't say anything. Couldn't. Connor was so damn glad to see her, to know that she was safe, he couldn't speak.

And she had on her nightclothes.

Elizabeth was swathed in her pale yellow robe. Her thick brown hair hung loose around her shoulders.

"Connor?" she asked, taking a step closer. "What is it? What's wrong?"

"I was worried about you," he said. "You disappeared. Heath said you left with Whitmore."

"Oh, yes…Garrett." Elizabeth drew in a deep breath, her lips curling down distastefully.

Connor's hand clenched into a fist. He gaze swept her nightclothes. "Did he—did he hurt you?"

"No," Elizabeth said. "Garrett didn't hurt me."

"Then what the hell is going on?" Connor demanded.

"Garrett asked me to marry him."

Chapter Twenty

"Garrett asked me to marry him."

Elizabeth spoke the words again, probably because Connor could do nothing more than stare at her.

"He—what?" Connor finally asked.

"He proposed marriage," Elizabeth said, and pushed her hair back off her shoulder. "I guess that's what you'd call it."

Connor took a step closer. "You want to explain that?"

Elizabeth glanced down at her fingers. "Oh, he said it nicely enough, I suppose. Garrett reminded me of my age, and that I was only the third prettiest woman in town. He pointed out that I wasn't likely to get another marriage proposal from anyone here in Sterling, or the entire state of Texas, for that matter."

"He said that?"

"He did." Elizabeth looked up at him. "He said he'd marry me."

Connor hesitated, reluctant to ask the next logical question. "What did you tell him?"

Elizabeth's lips pinched together and she drew herself up straighter. "I told him to go to hell."

Connor's eyes widened; he was sure he hadn't heard her correctly. "You told him what?"

Elizabeth gave her chin a little jerk. "You heard me."

A big smile broke over Connor's face. "Well... damn."

"I did it. I said it." Elizabeth nodded emphatically. "'You can just go to hell, Garrett Whitmore' is what I said. And I said it loud, too. Right to his face. Just—"

She gasped and covered her mouth with her fingers. "Oh, dear. You don't think I'll burn in everlasting damnation for saying that, do you?"

Connor did his best to hold his smile in check. "I'm sure the Lord will forgive you, just this once."

"Oh, good." Elizabeth took in a deep breath, then reached out and touched Connor's arm. "You were so right, Connor. About everything. Hearing Garrett say those things to me made me realize that I'm not old at all. And I don't have to settle for a marriage to someone who considers me a consolation prize."

Elizabeth stepped a little closer and went on. "And do you know what else? It's really not my fault that the town didn't have a doctor after my father died. And it's not my fault that my brother embezzled money from the bank."

"That's for sure, Elizabeth," Connor said, grinning.

She straightened her shoulders. "And—and if the town doesn't like me for who I am, well…well, they can all go to hell, too!"

Connor could have thrown his arms around her, hugged her tight. "Good for you, Elizabeth. I always said you were a strong woman."

She glanced down, then at him again. "Maybe so. But having you here caused me to realize it. You've made such a difference in my life, Connor. A wonderful difference. I don't know what I would have done without you."

Connor studied her for a moment, his heart aching anew. "I'm leaving Sterling."

She gasped softly. "You're what?"

"Tomorrow," Connor said.

"But—but I don't understand. What about your plan to have a business and a home? I thought you liked it here. I thought you liked…"

"I have to leave, Elizabeth," Connor said. "Sheriff Parker found out about my prison record. He's going to tell the town. I don't care for myself, but it will set everybody to talking. Talking about you. I don't want to be responsible for that, for causing you so much hurt."

Elizabeth shook her head. "I don't care what they say."

"Yes, you do."

"I used to, but not anymore," Elizabeth insisted. "If the townspeople can't see you for who you *are*,

Connor, not who you *were,* then what difference does it make what they say?''

A hint of a grin pulled at Connor's lips. ''You're starting to sound like me.''

''Well, you're right,'' Elizabeth told him. ''And so am I. You can't leave because of this.''

He shook his head. ''I won't put you through that.''

''But I don't care what people say. Not now. Not anymore.''

Connor studied her in the faint light that flowed from her room. He'd never seen that determined look on her face before, that stubborn jut to her chin. He'd never heard such conviction in her voice.

''You really mean that?'' he asked.

''Yes, I do.'' Elizabeth released a deep cleansing sigh. ''Goodness, I feel so much lighter. Like a burden's been lifted.''

''Carrying a lot of guilt around with you can be a heavy load.'' Connor glanced downward. ''Believe me, I know.''

Elizabeth drew nearer and stopped in front of him. ''So you're not leaving?''

He gazed at her for a moment. ''It would be better if I did. But...''

''But what?'' Elizabeth touched her palm to his face.

Connor almost moaned aloud with delight at the feel of her soft hand against his cheek. His eyelids closed.

"Connor?" she asked gently. "Are you leaving?"

He breathed deeply, drawing in Elizabeth's scent. "Well, now, honestly, you're making it a little difficult for me to think straight."

"Oh..." Elizabeth withdrew her hand.

Connor's eyes popped open and he caught her wrist. He grinned. "I never said I especially wanted to think straight at this moment."

Elizabeth smiled. "Then what do you want?"

The grin fell from Connor's face. Desire that had simmered in him all evening pumped harder. He pulled her closer until her body touched his.

"You know what I want," he told her.

Connor expected her to blush, back away, slap his face. But Elizabeth did none of those things. He saw the fire that burned inside him reflected in her eyes.

"Yes, I know what you want," Elizabeth said softly gazing up at him. "But we shouldn't."

"You don't want to?" he asked.

"Yes, I want to, but—" She blushed and looked away.

Connor leaned around her, catching her gaze. "But what?"

"It's not right," she said. "It's a sin. We're not married."

"Then let's get married."

Stunned, Elizabeth blinked up at him. Had she heard him right? Connor had proposed? He wanted her to marry him?

"You heard me right," Connor said. "Let's get married."

Elizabeth's eyes widened as she stared up at him. Connor wanted her to marry him? She was supposed to be the last bride in Texas, and here she'd had two marriage proposals on the same night.

"You really want to marry me?" Elizabeth asked.

Connor sighed deeply. "Oh, Elizabeth, I've wanted to marry you since—"

"Since the bank shoot-out?"

"Since before that."

She frowned. "Before that? But—"

Connor waved away her words. "I want you to marry me, Elizabeth. You'd make me the proudest man alive if you'd honor me with your hand in marriage."

He took both her hands and pulled them to his lips kissing them softly.

"Will you, Elizabeth? Will you marry me?" he asked.

When Garrett Whitmore had said those words to her earlier in the evening, she'd cringed. Now, hearing Connor say them, her heart soared.

"Oh, yes, Connor. Yes, I'll marry you," she said.

A big grin spread over his face as he moaned, then kissed her.

Connor's lips took hers in a deep kiss as his arms encircled her. His first instinct was to sweep her into his arms and carry her into the bedroom. His body demanded it. His brain—what little of it was still functioning—declared it a good idea.

But instead Connor held back. He didn't want to rush her. She'd agreed to marry him—yes, marry him! He'd have her forever.

He kissed her and she responded, parting her lips as she'd done before, welcoming him. Their private, exquisite duel went on until Elizabeth curled her hands around his neck.

Quickly, Connor pulled loose the sash of her robe and worked the buttons open. He slid his hand inside, settling his palm on the curve on her hip. Soft, pliant flesh radiated through the fabric of her nightgown. He groaned with pleasure.

Sliding the other hand inside, Connor encircled her waist, marveling at her delicate frame. His fingers burned with the feel of her. He deepened their kiss and raised one hand to cup her breast.

Elizabeth shivered but didn't pull away. Instead, she pressed closer. Awkwardly, Connor opened the buttons of her nightgown and pushed his fingers inside. His knees weakened at the feel of her soft breasts. She mewled as his thumb circled her nipple, making it taut, hot with wanting.

Elizabeth's head spun with the strange new desires that pulsed through her. She'd never felt these things before, but here, now, with Connor, she knew they were right. She knew she wanted them.

Her fingers found their way to his shirt and opened the buttons, then slid inside. His chest was rock hard. His hair crinkled against her fingertips. When she pressed deeper, he groaned aloud and shuddered.

His lips kissed a hot line across her jaw into the hollow of her throat. Elizabeth tipped her head back as he dipped his lips lower, lower, then gasped as his mouth covered her breast.

Connor pushed her robe off her shoulders and slid her gown down her arms. He stepped back to look at her, her beautiful body glowing in the lantern light. Oh, he'd imagined she'd be this beautiful. He'd lain awake nights wondering what she looked like. Now he knew. And knowing wasn't enough.

He swept her up and carried her into the bedroom. The coverlet was already turned down, revealing pristine white linens embroidered with tiny pink rosebuds. Connor held Elizabeth in his arms at the bedside as he gazed into her face, sealing this moment in his memory forever.

Carefully he laid her on the bed, then turned down the lantern's flame and sat on the edge of the bed beside her. Her skin glowed pink in the dim light. Her dark hair spread across the pillows. He'd never seen a more beautiful sight in his life.

Elizabeth took his hand, lacing her fingers through his. "I love you," she whispered.

Connor closed his eyes, savoring those words, this moment. Then he looked down at her. "You're sure? About…this?"

She'd never been more sure of anything in her life. "Yes, very sure."

Connor didn't waste another second. He pulled off his clothes, fighting with sleeves he hadn't bothered to unbutton, tossing off his boots, hopping on one foot to yank his off trousers, heaving his socks and long johns over his shoulder. Then, naked, he climbed into bed beside Elizabeth.

Immediately she rolled into the circle of his arms, and their bodies melded, heat sealing them together.

Connor acquainted himself with her, cupping her breasts, teasing the nipples until she moaned, tasting them with his tongue. His hand slid down over her hips to her thighs, settling between them. She gasped, and he groaned aloud.

Elizabeth returned the favor, touching his chest, teasing his tiny nipples. She pressed her hand against the hard muscles of his belly, then ventured lower. When she touched him, he breathed her name through clenched teeth.

He couldn't wait any longer. Connor settled himself between her thighs, touching her intimately. He kissed her, stroked her hair, her face, her breasts as he claimed her.

Elizabeth's body tingled as he moved within her. Slowly, gently at first until she'd accepted him. Then her hips answered him, moving with him, against him, for him. Tension built inside her, growing and growing. Her head spun. Higher she climbed, the sensations more demanding. Elizabeth clung to Connor, holding him, answering him, loving him, until great waves of pleasure broke through her. She held him tighter as she drifted downward.

Connor buried his face against her neck as he pushed himself into her one final time. He gritted his teeth, then moaned helplessly in release. His body shuddered, spent, in her arms.

"Is that what it will always be like?" Elizabeth asked.

Connor smiled down at her curled in his arms, lying against his chest. He'd fallen asleep, then awakened a short while ago. He hadn't realized Elizabeth had awakened, too.

"Well," Connor said, not sure if her question meant that she'd liked their lovemaking or not, "after we've practiced some it will get better."

"Better?" Elizabeth turned her head to look up at him. "Is that possible?"

His chest swelled a little. "Yeah, I think we can do better."

She smiled, and his heart melted. "Really? How?"

"There're a few other things we can do," he said.

"Tell me."

"Actually," Connor said, "some things are better demonstrated than explained.

"Will you show me now?"

"Now?"

Faint color blushed her cheeks. "Yes, now. Can you do that?"

A big grin broke over Connor's face. "You bet I can," he said, and took her in his arms again.

Morning sunlight streaming through the window woke Connor. He squinted against it, cursed under his breath, but finally opened his eyes.

And he was glad that he had. Elizabeth lay beside him, still in his arms, where she'd slept all night. She looked more beautiful than ever.

Connor settled back on the pillow. He'd never imagined he'd sleep in such a sturdy house, on pink rosebud linens. Never imagined he'd wake with Elizabeth Hill in the bed with him.

Well, he'd imagined it, Connor reminded himself. At times, she had been the only thing that had kept him going. And now that he was here, now that he had her, he didn't want to lose her. Not Elizabeth. He couldn't bear the thought of being without her now.

"Good morning," she whispered.

He looked down as Elizabeth's eyes fluttered open, and to his immense pleasure, she smiled at him.

"And a very good morning it is," Connor declared.

Elizabeth glanced at the window, gauging the sunlight beaming in on them. "Gracious, we slept late. Good thing church services are starting later today."

Connor rolled her onto her back and propped himself up on his elbow above her. "Are you anxious to leave?"

Elizabeth ran her hand across his wide shoulders and down his chest, combing her fingers through the thick hair.

"No, not at all," she said, smiling the smile lovers share.

Connor's heart thundered in his chest. "Then how about if we get some breakfast and come back up here to discuss wedding plans."

"Wedding plans?"

"Sure," he said, then frowned. "You still want to marry me, don't you?"

"Of course I want to marry you," she told him, still toying with the hair on his chest. "Especially now that I've discovered a whole new reason to keep you around."

Connor growled playfully and nibbled at her neck before he rolled out of bed. Elizabeth rose, and his insides warmed at the sight of her struggling to conceal herself with the quilt. After what they'd spent the night doing, Elizabeth wanted to hide behind the covers.

"I'll go down and heat up the stove," Connor said, pulling on his long johns and trousers. He'd give Elizabeth her privacy—for now.

He caught a glimpse of pale white bosom before he gathered the rest of his clothes and left the bedroom.

In the kitchen, Connor stoked the fire, put on some coffee and finished dressing. A few minutes later, Elizabeth walked in.

She wore a simple day dress, no corset, no bustle. His heart warmed at the knowledge that all those curves filling out the dress belonged to Elizabeth.

She'd drawn her hair back and caught it in a ribbon; it cascaded down her back.

Desire stirred in Connor again. At this rate, they wouldn't get any breakfast cooked—and they sure as hell wouldn't make it to church on time.

"I'm starving this morning," Elizabeth said, crossing to the stove.

Connor followed, unable to keep any distance from her. She looked back over her shoulder and saw him, then turned. They fell against each other, kissing.

Elizabeth hadn't known she could be so happy. Last night in Connor's arms had been heaven. And the best part of it all was that it would go on forever. Connor wanted to marry her. She certainly wanted to marry him.

Elizabeth laid her head against his chest, feeling the strength in his arms, the steady pounding of his heart. For a moment she considered that at this very moment Connor's child might be growing inside her. Elizabeth smiled and rose on her toes to kiss him again.

A knock at the back door interrupted them. Elizabeth tried to ease away but Connor held her firmly against him.

"Leave it," he whispered. "If we're really quiet, maybe whoever it is will go away."

"Connor," she admonished lightly. "It might be important. A patient, maybe."

He heaved a heavy sigh and stepped away from

her reluctantly. She gave him a sassy little smile and opened the door.

A strangled scream escaped her lips and she stumbled back into the kitchen. A man stepped inside.

Elizabeth pressed her hand to her mouth as her heart pounded in her chest. Tears sprang to her eyes. She could hardly believe what she saw.

"Raymond!"

Her brother stood in the middle of the kitchen floor. Shocked by the sight of him, Elizabeth could only stare.

He was thin, so painfully thin that the suit he wore hung loosely on him. His skin was pasty white, and his dark hair lay unkempt against his collar.

"Oh, Raymond." Elizabeth rushed toward her brother, tears pooling in her eyes. "I didn't know— I had no idea. Why didn't you tell me you were coming home?"

He eased away from her, uncomfortable with their closeness. "I got paroled early. I wanted to surprise—"

Raymond did a double take as he spotted Connor standing across the room. Deep frown lines cut across his forehead and he squared off at Connor.

"What the hell is he doing here?" Raymond asked.

A little blush reddened Elizabeth's face. Was it so obvious what had gone on last night? The early morning hour, the two of them alone in the house, her dress, her hair down, the intimacy?

Elizabeth straightened her shoulders. "Raymond, I'd like you to meet—"

"Connor Wade," Raymond snarled. "Yeah, I know who the hell he is."

Elizabeth glanced back and forth between the two men. For the first time she noticed Connor hadn't moved since her brother had entered the kitchen. He stood still, hardly even breathing, it seemed.

"What I want to know," Raymond said, "is what the hell he's doing here."

Elizabeth touched her hand to her brow. "Raymond, I—I don't understand. How do you know Connor?"

The two men glared at each other. Elizabeth glanced from one to the other, but neither spoke.

"Raymond—" she began again.

"He was in prison!" Raymond shouted, turning to Elizabeth.

She relaxed a little, glad she already knew, glad Connor had told her about his past. "Yes, I know that. He told me all about it."

"Did he tell you he was in prison with *me?* That we were cell mates?"

A knot jerked in Elizabeth's stomach. She turned to Connor. She thought she saw him flinch, but he didn't say anything.

"No," Elizabeth whispered. "No, he didn't mention it. But—"

Raymond turned on Connor. "What the hell are you doing here? Are you—"

He stopped then, understanding hardening his

drawn features. Raymond took a step closer to Connor. "You bastard. You dirty bastard. You came here looking for my money!"

"Raymond, no!" Elizabeth stepped between the two men. "It's not like that. You don't understand."

"I understand plenty," Raymond growled, pointing at Connor. "We were cell mates. I told him about the money I stole, about how I'd hidden it here."

"No," Elizabeth insisted. "Connor wouldn't do something like that."

"Then why is he here?" Raymond asked, his gaze impaling her. "Why? Tell me why? Of all the states, all the towns, all the places he could have gone, what's he doing here? In Sterling, in this house?"

"Because..." Elizabeth's breath left her. She turned to Connor. Why wouldn't he speak? Why hadn't he said anything? Where was his denial?

"Connor?" she asked.

"I didn't come here to find your stolen money," Connor said.

"Like hell." Raymond uttered a bitter laugh. "So if you didn't come here for the money, why did you come?"

Again Elizabeth waited. Waited for the logical explanation that would clear up the whole matter. Waited for Connor to state the reason and put a stop to her brother's accusations.

She turned to Connor. His gaze met and held hers. The strong, forthright countenance she'd always seen on Connor's face crumbled. His shoulders sagged. His chest heaved with heavy breaths.

Elizabeth's heart raced. "Connor?"

"Elizabeth…" He spoke the word in a plea. He reached out to her, then let his hand fall uselessly to his side.

Connor shook his head slowly. "Elizabeth…I…"

Chapter Twenty-One

"Don't bother with another lie, Wade," Raymond demanded. "I know why you're here."

"Raymond, stop!" Elizabeth's heart thundered in her chest. "Connor is not after your stolen money. He came to Sterling to make a new life. He's planning to start a business here. Raise a family. Right now he's renovating this house for me. He volunteered to help me—he isn't even being paid."

Again Raymond's gaze impaled her. "That's mighty damn convenient, don't you think? Him having the run of the house? Was it your idea or his?"

"It was—" Elizabeth's breath caught.

"Well?" Raymond demanded.

The day Connor had come to the house flashed in her mind. He'd shown up unexpectedly. He'd volunteered his services. He refused to accept any payment. It had been Connor's idea to renovate the upstairs.

"Connor suggested it," Elizabeth began, "but—"

"But you didn't question any of it? You didn't wonder why he was here offering that *kindness?*"

"I…" Elizabeth stopped, stunned, too stunned to speak. She whirled to Connor. "Tell him, Connor."

"Admit it, Wade," Raymond said, approaching Connor. "You took up with my sister to get at that money, didn't you. Didn't you!"

"No!" Elizabeth said. "It's not like that, Raymond. You don't understand."

He turned on her. "Do you think a man like him would really be interested in a spinster like you, Elizabeth? Do you? He's been using you. Using you to get to the money I hid."

The breath went whooshing out of Elizabeth as she turned to Connor. Why wouldn't he say anything? Why didn't he answer her brother? Why hadn't he denied these accusations?

"Connor?" she asked, venturing closer. "Connor, tell him the truth. Tell him why you're here."

He looked at her for a long moment as if he bore the weight of the world on his shoulders, then finally spoke. "I told you, I didn't come here to find that money."

"Like hell." Raymond grunted bitterly. "What other reason could there be?"

Elizabeth twisted her fingers together as suspicion gnawed in her stomach. "Why did you come here, Connor? To Sterling, of all places? If it wasn't for the money, what was the reason? Why did you come?"

Connor winced and looked away. He shook his

head wearily, then turned to Elizabeth once more. "I should have told you the truth, Elizabeth," Connor said. "I should have told you when I first got here."

She pressed her fingers to her lips, afraid to hear him say anything else. Bits of her world seemed to be crumbling around her.

Was he about to admit to the deception Raymond accused him of? Would he say everything that had happened between the two of them over the past weeks had been a lie? A sham? A farce?

"Just tell me the truth, Connor," Elizabeth said. "I want to know the truth, whatever it is."

A long moment dragged by. Connor gripped the back of the kitchen chair, seemingly unable to hold himself upright under the weight of what he was about to say. He gulped and drew in a breath.

"All right. I'll tell you the truth, Elizabeth," he said. "I came here looking for you."

"You came to Sterling looking for me?" she asked, stunned. "Me?"

Miserably, Connor nodded. "Your brother talked about you all the time in prison. I came here because of you."

"But why?" she asked. "For what possible reason?"

"To get the money," Raymond said.

"No!" Connor said. "The money had nothing to do with it. Nothing!"

He turned to Elizabeth. "I came here... I came to Sterling to find you because..."

He pushed his hand through his hair and squeezed his eyes shut as if gathering his strength. Finally, he looked at her again.

"I came to Sterling, Elizabeth, because I wanted you to teach me to...read and write."

She just stared at him. *"What?"*

He winced, then looked away. "I—I can't...read or write, Elizabeth."

"You expect her to believe a lie like that?" Raymond demanded.

"Your brother told me you tutored kids here in town. I came to ask you to teach me, too." Connor cast his gaze downward, unable to look at Elizabeth. "It's the truth. I'm not proud of it, but it's the truth."

"Don't listen to him, Elizabeth," Raymond said. "He's been using you. All he cares about is the money. He's an outlaw, for God's sake. Why do you think he was in prison?"

"He told me why," Elizabeth said, barely able to force the words out. "He robbed a train."

"Robbed a train? Hell, he robbed dozens of trains," Raymond declared.

Elizabeth gasped. "No..."

"Trains, banks, everything. You name it and Connor Wade's robbed it," Raymond said. "He's been an outlaw all his life."

Elizabeth turned to Connor, waiting again for his denial. Finally, he lifted his gaze to her, but still he didn't speak.

"Connor," she whispered. "I don't understand."

"I didn't come here to hurt you, Elizabeth," Connor said softly. "I'd never do that."

"You shut up!" Raymond shouted. "And leave my sister the hell alone!"

"Keep out of this!" Connor shouted back. "This doesn't concern you. It's between Elizabeth and me."

"If you think I'm going to—"

"I don't give a damn—"

"Stop it! Stop it, both of you!" Elizabeth pressed her palms against her ears, trying to block out their shouts, wishing she could block out all that had happened this morning.

It was too much. She couldn't stand another minute of this. She couldn't.

"Just leave!" she said. "Both of you!"

Connor ventured a step closer. "Elizabeth, if you'll just let me explain—"

She faced him, tears threatening. "You lied to me, Connor. You lied about your past, about your reason for coming to Sterling. You deceived me about knowing my brother."

"Please, Elizabeth," he said, and reached for her. "Just listen—"

Elizabeth pushed him away. "What *else* did you lie about?"

Connor froze, hurt and anguish twisting his face. "Elizabeth..."

She whirled away, unable to look at him any longer. "Leave."

"Yeah," Raymond said. "Get out of here."

"You, too!" Elizabeth said, flinging her hand toward her brother.

He frowned. "This is my home. I just got out of prison. You can't—"

"It's not your home anymore! It's mine! I'm the one who's cleaned it, repaired it, taken care of it since you got yourself sent to prison!" Elizabeth clenched her fists at her sides. "Leave. Stay at the hotel, sleep in the barn. I don't care where you go. But leave me alone until I can sort all of this out!"

Raymond grumbled, threw Connor a sour look, then headed toward the back door. He didn't leave, though, but glared at Connor instead.

Connor took another step toward Elizabeth. "If you'll just let me explain—"

She turned away, fighting back the tears pooling in her eyes. "Just go. Please."

The heat of Connor's gaze burned into the side of her face, but Elizabeth refused to acknowledge him. Finally, he moved away. She kept her back to them both until she heard the door close.

Elizabeth turned then, her gaze sweeping the empty, silent room. She collapsed into a chair and cried.

The knocking on Elizabeth's front door persisted, but she ignored it. Upstairs in her room, lying in bed clutching a damp handkerchief, she didn't care who'd come to call. She didn't want to see anyone or talk to anyone.

For a second it occurred to her that it might be

her brother banging away on the door. Perhaps, even after she'd banished him from the house, he'd returned to make sure she was all right.

As if she could ever be all right again.

Fresh tears trickled down Elizabeth's face. She sniffed and wiped her eyes with her handkerchief, then gulped, looking at the big square of cloth clutched in her hand.

It was Connor's handkerchief. The one he'd lent her at the water trough behind the church that Sunday the town had honored him for stopping the bank robbery. She'd plucked it out of her drawer just now, not realizing it was his.

Elizabeth closed her eyes, remembering that day. How handsome he'd looked. How he'd made her laugh right there in the churchyard.

She sniffed the fabric. Even after laundering it, the handkerchief still smelled like Connor.

Another wave of tears poured down her cheeks.

Connor. Oh, Connor. How was it possible to love a man—and hate him at the same time?

Did she hate him? The thought caused Elizabeth to sit up on the bed. Yes, she decided, she most certainly did hate him.

Did she love him? Her shoulders sagged. Yes, oh, yes. She definitely loved him.

The knocking at her front door turned into pounding. Elizabeth glared out her open doorway into the hall. Was Connor at her door, demanding to be let inside? Did that man have the gall, the nerve, to come back to her house after she'd insisted he leave?

Yes, he probably did.

"Oh!"

Elizabeth hopped off the bed and strode downstairs, the ache in her chest dropping to form a hard knot in her stomach. How dare Connor come back? How dare he pound on her door, making a spectacle in front of everyone passing by? After she'd specifically instructed him to leave her alone? Oh, that man!

She marched across the foyer, her mind formulating the verbal thrashing she'd inflict on Connor Wade, and yanked the door open.

Gena Blake stood on the porch.

Elizabeth burst into tears again.

"Oh, gracious, Elizabeth," Gena crooned, wrapping an arm around her waist, leading her into the house again. She closed the front door. "When you didn't show up at church this morning, I knew something wasn't right. What is it, Elizabeth? What's wrong?"

"Oh, everything. Just everything," Elizabeth declared, sobbing into her handkerchief. She didn't know where to start, how to begin to explain what had happened.

"Tell me what happened," Gena said.

"All right." Elizabeth hiccuped, trying to stem the flood of tears. "It started last night when Garrett asked me to marry him."

Gena's eyes widened. "Garrett asked you to marry him?"

"Yes," Elizabeth said, nodding. "And so did Connor."

"*Two* men asked you to marry them last night?" Gena exclaimed. She rolled her eyes. "Gracious, no wonder you're a mess. Come along."

Gena guided her into the kitchen, sat her at the table, then put on a fresh pot of coffee. Elizabeth sniffled, glad her friend had come over. She needed someone to talk to.

When the coffee was ready, Gena poured a cup for each of them and sat down beside Elizabeth.

"While you were out gathering marriage proposals like daisies in a field," Gena said, "another couple broke up."

At first Elizabeth didn't respond, embarrassed that she'd been so absorbed in her own problems she hadn't thought of much of anything else.

"Who called off their wedding?" she asked.

"Jane and Boyd," Gena said, sipping her coffee.

Elizabeth shook her head. "I can't say I'm sorry. What happened?"

Gena explained briefly what had happened at the Founders' Day festival last night. When she related Connor's part in it, Elizabeth started to tear up again. "Connor did that? He helped Jane?" she asked.

"Of course," Gena said. "You know he would."

Elizabeth nodded. Yes, of course she knew Connor would do just that.

"Jane finally came to her senses after Boyd hit her," Gena explained. "She realized she'd been making excuses for him all along. She broke off their engagement."

"Good," Elizabeth said. "It's for the best."

"All right now," Gena said, setting her coffee cup aside. "Tell me what happened with you."

Though she wasn't sure Connor would appreciate her discussing his personal business with anyone, Elizabeth told Gena about his past—what she knew of it, at least. His prison sentence, his life as an outlaw, her brother's suspicion that he'd come to Sterling just to get at the money hidden in the house.

But instead of giving her an opinion, Gena simply asked, "What do you think Connor is capable of? Do you honestly believe he would do such a thing?"

Elizabeth fumbled with her coffee cup, staring into the cold grounds swimming at the bottom of it. In her mind she played out all the times she and Connor had spent together, the things Connor had done for her, the things he'd said since he'd come into her life.

He'd never tried to harm her.

He'd tried to make life easier for her.

He'd stood up for her.

He'd made her laugh.

He'd encouraged her, pushed her in ways she'd resisted, but in the end she'd felt better for what he'd done.

He'd helped her, made her feel good about herself, told her she was pretty, smart and capable.

Elizabeth thought of all the days they'd spent together. And of the nights—last night in particular. Connor, so gentle, so loving. She hadn't imagined a night with a man could be so wonderful.

But how could he have deceived her so?

And how—how—could she still love him?

"I don't know what to think," Elizabeth said, touching her hand to her forehead. Her heart ached, her stomach hurt and her head pounded. "Or what to do. I'm so confused, so hurt. All I know is that I don't want to see Connor yet. Or my brother, either, for that matter."

Gena patted her hand. "That's probably a good idea. Give yourself some time to think things through."

Rising from the table, Gena said, "Heath is coming over for supper tonight. Why don't you come over, too?"

Despite all her own inner turmoil, Elizabeth managed a small smile. "Heath is coming over? What's going on with you two? Will your mother be planning *your* wedding instead of Jane's?"

Gena tilted her head. "We'll see."

Elizabeth sent her friend on her way, declining the supper invitation. She just wasn't up to it. She simply wanted to be left alone.

Standing in the foyer, listening to the quiet house, Elizabeth couldn't help but think that just yesterday she'd had two marriage proposals.

And today, she was alone again.

* * *

Morning sunlight streaming in through the bedroom window woke Elizabeth. She shielded her eyes from its brightness, realizing she'd slept late.

Small wonder, since she'd tossed and turned most of the night.

From downstairs she heard someone banging on her door again. Listlessly, Elizabeth rose. A memory stabbed her heart; just yesterday morning she'd awakened in this bed with Connor.

She splashed water on her face, dressed and twisted her hair into a knot atop her head, hoping that if she dawdled long enough whoever was rapping on her front door would go away. She didn't want to face anyone, talk to anyone. Surely, word had spread through town that Raymond was back. Gossip about Connor had followed on its heels, probably.

Elizabeth paused at the washstand, catching her reflection in the mirror. She didn't care if they talked about her. She just didn't want to discuss the situation.

In the mirror, Elizabeth saw herself smile, just a little. No, she honestly didn't care if the whole town talked about her.

Her smile faded. Connor had convinced her of that.

During one of her many sleepless hours last night, Elizabeth had become convinced of something else: Connor hadn't come to Sterling to use her, or trick her, nor to attempt to recover her brother's stolen money. He might have lied about other things, but

Connor couldn't have done what Raymond accused him of doing. She had no proof, except what her heart told her.

But for Elizabeth, that was good enough.

Knocking sounded again from downstairs, rousing Elizabeth from her thoughts.

"Good gracious," she huffed.

Apparently whoever was down there hadn't gotten her not-so-subtle hint that she didn't want to be disturbed right now.

Elizabeth clomped down the stairs, only to realize the knocking came from the back door. Maybe Gena had come to check on her, she thought, heading for the rear of the house. Elizabeth actually smiled a bit, thinking of her friend.

That smile dropped from her lips as she pulled open the back door.

Connor stood on her porch.

Grim, his face drawn in taut lines, he pointed his finger at her.

"You owe me," he said in a low voice.

She stared, not sure what he meant.

"You owe me," Connor said again. "From the day of the bank shoot-out. You owe me. Remember?"

"Well, yes, I remember what you said, but—"

"I've decided what I want," Connor told her. "And I'm here to collect it."

Chapter Twenty-Two

Elizabeth's mouth flew open. "Of all the nerve! After what happened yesterday, after what you did, you have the gall to come here today and—"

Connor pushed past her into the kitchen, then spun toward her, not a trace of good humor or kindness in his face.

"You owe me," he told her again in a low, guttural voice.

Pushing her chin out, Elizabeth glared up at him. Her first instinct was to tell Connor Wade exactly what she thought of him, then toss him out of the house.

But instead, her heart melted a little at the sight of him. Connor looked tired and haggard. He didn't seem to stand quite as straight as he had yesterday. His shoulders weren't nearly as square.

It was his pride, she realized, and for the first time it occurred to her how he must have felt humiliated, having to admit to her that he couldn't read or write.

Surely that would be a difficult thing for a grown man to reveal to anyone.

How it must have hurt him to admit it to her. Here, in this house crammed with books, where she tutored children, where she read medical journals, where she'd admitted having once aspired to becoming a doctor herself.

Elizabeth's heart ached for him. She wanted to throw her arms around him and tell him it was all right.

She wanted to, but didn't.

"Very well, I owe you," she said. "What do you want?"

A flash of heat snapped between them. Visions of two nights ago upstairs in her room exploded in her head. From the quick intake of Connor's breath, Elizabeth knew he was thinking the same.

Elizabeth looked away, breaking their connection. "What do you want—within reason?"

"I want you to teach me to read and write."

Her gaze swung back to him. Connor looked at her, unflinching, pushing past the embarrassment that brought light color to his cheeks.

What had it cost his pride to come to her now, after all that had gone on between them, and ask this of her? Leaving himself vulnerable, opening himself up to what surely he considered his most grave shortcoming? To admit this gross inadequacy to her, of all people...

Elizabeth nodded, her heart aching. "All right. I'll teach you. Come back tomorrow and—"

"Now."

She gulped, her emotions ragged. Tomorrow would be better for her, after she'd had a chance to compose herself. Right now, she could hardly think straight.

But still she couldn't deny him. He'd come to her at great personal expense. And she did owe him.

"Very well. Let's go into the schoolroom."

Elizabeth led the way into the little room off the kitchen and sat down. Connor took the chair across from her.

"Can you read or write at all?" she asked gently.

"My name," he said. "I can write my name. And a few other letters."

She lifted a tablet and pencil from the nearby shelf and passed it to him. "Write down all the letters you know. That will give us a place to start."

Connor took the pencil and bent over the tablet. Elizabeth selected a book from the shelf and opened it, not wanting to make him feel pressured to rush by her watching him.

She couldn't focus on the page before her, though. Surreptitiously, she watched him over the top of the book.

His big hand dwarfed the pencil. He gripped it tightly in his long fingers. Lips pressed together, he worked slowly, diligently, carefully forming the letters.

When he finished, Connor wiped his forehead with the back of his hand, gave the paper one final glance, then passed the tablet to Elizabeth.

She took it and looked at the few letters he'd managed to write. Tears sprang to her eyes, clouding the three words he'd written: *I love you.*

Elizabeth gave a ragged sob, then plastered her fingers across her mouth and looked across the table at Connor.

"Did I spell it right?" he asked, looking worried.

She gulped. "I guess that depends on what you were trying to say."

"I was trying to say the same thing I've been trying to tell you since I got here, Elizabeth. I love you."

"Oh, Connor..." Tears rolled from her eyes once more.

"I know I don't deserve you, Elizabeth. A man like me never deserves a woman as fine as you," he said. "But if you'll just hear me out, just let me explain."

How could she refuse? After the humiliation he'd suffered, after his confession of love, how could she tell him she didn't care?

Because she *did* care. With all her heart she cared.

"I'll listen," Elizabeth said, wiping away her tears. "But you'll have to tell me everything. No more lies. No secrets."

"No," Connor agreed, "no more lies, no more secrets. Ever."

He paused for a moment, as if collecting his thoughts, then pushed his fingers through his hair and looked across the table at her.

"I lied to you when I told you that story about my pa dying, and about my ma being sick and me taking care of her," Connor said. "Truth is, I don't have any idea who my pa is. My mama, she never knew, either. He was just another...customer. She had no want or need for me, drunk half the time, *working* the rest of the time. I ate what I could find, or what people tossed away. I wore what hand-me-downs came my way.''

''Oh, Connor, that's terrible,'' Elizabeth said. ''What an awful way for you to grow up. Didn't anyone in town try to help you?''

''Yes, they tried, but...'' Connor shook his head. ''I couldn't stand the looks of pity on their faces, like I wasn't as good as everybody else. The whispering, the finger-pointing. Handouts, castoffs. So I started stealing what I needed. It may not have been right, but it was a damn sight better than having everybody looking down on me.''

''So you never went to school,'' Elizabeth said.

''I went some, but it was always the same. Me, ragged and dirty. The other boys talking about my ma. So, soon as I could, I left,'' Connor said. ''I got hooked up with a bad bunch. I was already pretty good at stealing things. Everything just got bigger—trains, banks.''

''You never tried to get a real job, an honest job?'' Elizabeth asked.

''Oh, yeah, sure, I tried,'' Connor said. ''But with no education, all I could do was shovel up after horses, break my back mining, work sun-to-sun at a lumber camp. All so that at the end of the week the boss could cheat me out of part of my pay.''

''You must have gotten caught, finally,'' Elizabeth said. ''You went to prison.''

Connor drew in a deep breath and nodded. "Yep. That's where I met your brother. We were in the same cell."

"Prison can have a great effect on a man, I'd imagine," Elizabeth said. "Is that what changed you, what made you want to start over, make an honest life for yourself?"

Connor uttered a bitter laugh. "Yeah, you'd think that, wouldn't you. But the truth is, Elizabeth, when I was let out of prison I went back to the same way of life. I didn't know any other way to live."

"But I don't understand, Connor. How did you end up here?"

"Kansas City," Connor said. "Late one night I was looking over the bank building when the sheriff came up behind me in the alley. He knew who I was, suspected what I was doing. He drew his gun. I drew mine."

Elizabeth gasped. "You—you didn't..."

"Shoot that lawman?" Connor pressed his lips together and shook his head. "It was the damnedest thing, Elizabeth, the damnedest thing. The sheriff's gun misfired. Mine jammed. Neither gun went off."

"Oh, my goodness," Elizabeth said. "It's almost like it was a—"

"A miracle?" Connor nodded slowly. "Well, honest to heaven, that's how I looked at it. The sheriff and I just stood there for a long time looking at each other across that dark alley. Finally, he moved on. So did I.

"But, Elizabeth, I knew my life had changed. Yes, I know guns misfire and jam all the time. But this was different. I knew that was my chance to do something with my life, to make something of myself.''

Elizabeth smiled. ''I'm glad, Connor. I'm very glad.''

''That's why I decided to come here to Sterling.'' He reached across the table and covered her hand with his. ''To you, Elizabeth.''

''So I could teach you to read and write?'' she asked.

''Yes, but it was more than that,'' Connor said. ''Your brother used to read every one of your letters out loud to me, over and over again. Through those letters I got to know you better than I'd known anyone in my life. I used to lie awake at night, Elizabeth, and think about you. I used to imagine what you looked like, how you wore your hair, what you smelled like. I...I started to fall in love with you.''

''Oh, Connor...'' She tightened her grip on his hand.

''When I got here to Sterling and met you, I saw that you were prettier than I'd imagined. I saw what a fine, upstanding lady you are.'' Connor shook his head. ''I should have told you the truth right from the start, Elizabeth. I came over here that first morning to do just that. But after I saw this respectable house you live in, my pride wouldn't let me tell you. Instead, I offered to renovate your place just so I could be close to you, hoping that sooner or later I'd get up the nerve to tell you the truth, ask for your help.''

Connor rose from the table and pulled Elizabeth

up with him, taking both her hands in his. He nodded toward the tablet lying on the table. ''But I
meant it when I said I love you. I do love you, with
all my heart. I want to marry you, Elizabeth, if
you'll have me. Will you?''

She watched his face closely, saw the fear, the
hope, the anxiety there. When he'd asked her to
marry him the night of the Founders' Day festival,
she'd said yes so easily. There'd not been one question in her mind, one reason to hesitate.

And now, even after hearing all he'd told her,
there was still no reason to hesitate.

Elizabeth smiled. ''Connor, I—''

''I know I'm not smart, not like you, Elizabeth.
But I'm willing to learn.''

She shook her head. ''There's all sorts of intelli-
gence, Connor. Look at the work you did here on
the house, the barn, the festival booths. And you
were much smarter than me when it came to dealing
with the people here in Sterling.''

''I just wanted you to be happy,'' Connor said.

''You made me happy,'' she whispered.

''Wait,'' he said, frowning slightly. ''Before we
go any further, there's something else you have to
know.''

''What is it?'' she asked, feeling a little concerned
now.

''If you agree to marry me you have to know
we'll be leaving Sterling.''

''Leaving Sterling? But why?'' she asked.

''Because I'm taking you back east so you can
enroll in one of those medical schools,'' Connor

said. "You're going to become a doctor, Elizabeth. A real doctor."

"What?"

"It's what you've always wanted to do, and you're good at it," Connor said. "There are lots of folks out there who need a doctor."

"Connor, those schools cost a great deal of money."

"I have money."

She looked at him. "Stolen money."

"It was the only trade I had, Elizabeth, and I was good at it," Connor said. "Besides, how could I give that money back now? Where would I even start? Isn't it better that it's used for something good, something that will help a lot of folks?"

"Still, Connor, it's stolen money," she insisted.

"All right, fine. We'll give it to the church, if you want," Connor said. "But you're still going to medical school. Then we're going out west somewhere. To California, maybe. There's lots of little places out there that are just begging for a doctor. And when we get settled I'm starting a business of some kind because I'll know how to read and write by then. We're building us a big house and filling it up with kids."

Elizabeth smiled up at him. "Sounds like you've got this all thought out."

He gave her a brisk nod. "Told you I had a plan."

"I didn't think I figured so prominently in it."

"Well, you do." Connor paused. "If you want to, that is."

It sounded wonderful. Too wonderful to believe.

Marriage to Connor. Moving back east. Going to medical school—something she'd always dreamed of.

Wonderful, but a little scary, too.

Connor slid his arms around her and pulled her closer. "I know what you're thinking," he said softly against her ear. "It's a big change for you. But even though you feel better about how the townsfolk treat you, there's still no life for you here. Come with me, Elizabeth. Marry me. I'll take care of you. We'll take care of each other. I love you."

Elizabeth smiled up at him, knowing in her heart there was only one answer. "I love you, too, Connor. And yes, I'll marry you."

He pulled her hard against him and smothered her lips with his. She kissed him back, never more sure in her life that she'd made the right choice.

Connor lifted his head after a long moment. "We've got some plans to make."

"Yes, we do," Elizabeth said. "Let's get started over breakfast. I'm starving. How about you?"

He grinned as he followed her swaying hips into the kitchen. "You could say I'm having a craving."

She stopped suddenly. "But what about this house?"

"Once you've taken the keepsakes you want, we'll turn it over to Raymond." A mischievous grin pulled at his lips. "After we tell the sheriff the bank money is hidden in here somewhere."

Elizabeth nodded thoughtfully. "I'd say that's an excellent start to our plan."

"Well, since we're talking about this plan of

ours," Connor said, "how about if we get started on you teaching me to read and write?"

"Now?" she asked, looking back over her shoulder from the stove.

"Yeah, sure," Connor said. "Just a few basics, like how to spell things."

Elizabeth bent over and pulled the frying pan from the cupboard. "All right. What would you like me to teach you to spell?"

Connor pulled his brows together in concentration. "How do you spell *bedroom?*"

"B-e-d-r-o-o-m."

"How do you spell *naked?*"

She raised an eyebrow at him. *"N-a-k-e-d."*

Connor moved closer and settled his hands on her hips.

"How do you spell *tonight?*" he asked.

Elizabeth rose on her tiptoes until her mouth hovered near his.

"N-o-w."

*   *   *   *   *

Take a trip to the Old West with four handsome heroes from Harlequin Historicals.

ON SALE JANUARY 2001

MAGGIE'S BEAU
by **Carolyn Davidson**

Beau Jackson, former soldier/rancher

and

BRIDE ON THE RUN
by **Elizabeth Lane**

Malachi Stone, ferry owner

ON SALE FEBRUARY 2001

SWEET ANNIE
by **Cheryl St.John**

Luke Carpenter, horseman

and

THE RANGER'S BRIDE
by **Laurie Grant**

Rede Smith, Texas Ranger

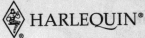
HARLEQUIN®

makes any time special—online...

your romantic life

●—Romance 101

♥ Guides to romance, dating and flirting.

●—Dr. Romance

♥ Get romance advice and tips from
our expert, Dr. Romance.

●—Recipes for Romance

♥ How to plan romantic meals for you
and your sweetie.

●—Daily Love Dose

♥ Tips on how to keep the romance
alive every day.

●—Tales from the Heart

♥ Discuss romantic dilemmas with other
members in our Tales from the Heart
message board.

Each month
you can find three
enchanting new stories from
the leader of inspirational romance—

♥ _Love Inspired_®

More than heartwarming tales of inspirational
romance, these original stories celebrate the
triumph over life's trials and tribulations
with an editorial integrity you can trust.

Featuring new releases each month by the
world's most respected authors, Love Inspired
is the name you count on most for value,
convenience and above all else, integrity.

Available at fine retailers near you.

Steeple
Hill™

Tyler Brides

It happened one weekend...

Quinn and Molly Spencer are delighted to accept three
bookings for their newly opened B&B, Breakfast Inn Bed,
located in America's favorite hometown, Tyler, Wisconsin.

But Gina Santori is anything but thrilled to discover her
best friend has tricked her into sharing a room with
the man who broke her heart eight years ago....

And Delia Mayhew can hardly believe that she's
gotten herself locked in the Breakfast Inn Bed
basement with the sexiest man in America.

Then there's Rebecca Salter. She's turned up at the
Inn in her wedding gown. Minus her groom.

*Come home to Tyler for three delightful novellas
by three of your favorite authors: Kristine Rolofson,
Heather MacAllister and Jacqueline Diamond.*

HARLEQUIN®
Makes any time special™

Fall in love with the timeless
charm of the British Isles
in Harlequin Historicals

ON SALE JANUARY 2001
SUMMER'S BRIDE
by **Catherine Archer**
(England, 15th century)
and
THE SEA NYMPH
by **Ruth Langan**
(England, 17th century)

ON SALE FEBRUARY 2001
KNAVE OF HEARTS
by **Shari Anton**
(England, 12th century)
and
ICE MAIDEN
by **Debra Lee Brown**
(Scotland, 13th century)

HARLEQUIN®
Makes any time special ™

JUDITH STACY

Judith Stacy decided to take up writing because all the daydreaming she was doing interfered with her driving. Putting those thoughts on paper has led to the publication of eleven historical novels and safer highways.

Judith is married to her high school sweetheart and has two daughters. They live in Southern California.

HHBIO541